A PIECE OF
MALICE

*A Modern Mystery with a
Shakespearean Twist*

E. P. Marwick

It may be you think me an impostor. Then think you right: I am not what I am. Nothing that is so is so

WILLIAM SHAKESPEARE

CONTENTS

Title Page

Copyright

Epigraph

Preface

Monday, June 15. Day.   1

Monday, June 15. EvenIng.   63

Tuesday, June 16. Day.   91

Tuesday, June 16. Evening.   122

Wednesday, June 17. Day.   147

Wednesday, June 17. Evening.   186

Thursday, June 18. Day.   224

Thursday, June 18. Evening.   267

Friday, June 19. Morning.   285

Friday, June 19. Evening.   345

Saturday, June 20. Morning.   353

Epilogue   377

Acknowledgement   385

The Jake Benatsky Trilogy   387

P REFACE

When I was sixteen, I began to keep a journal of my daily life. Just a page or two per day, mostly filled with the trifles and traumas of my teenage existence. Though that period of my life has long passed (thank goodness), the habit has stayed with me. I can't say why, exactly. I suppose I've always had the feeling that I might want to revisit my life someday – or at least certain portions of it. In moments of whimsy, I've even imagined that my children – should I have any – might develop some curiosity.

Not that there is much to be curious about, to be perfectly frank. Since university, my time has been mostly consumed with the mundane task of introducing sullen high-school students to the unwelcome classics of English literature. The only high point is the summer, which not only brings a break from the students but also a chance to act in a local Shakespearean festival. I love the acting. In fact, my whole cocooned existence – including the teaching – has suited me well enough. But none of it would be of any particular interest to anyone, perhaps not even to my future self, were it not for an extraordinary sequence of events that took place during one tumultuous week five years ago.

These events are poorly known today, although they made quite a splash at the time. They concluded in such a way as to eliminate any on-going interest from either the press or the public – or perhaps it would be more correct to say that forces colluded to bring about that end. In fairness, it was probably some combination of the two.

This does not mean that they were trivial or evanescent – anything but. Life in that brief expanse of time took on an intensity, a pace, that was beyond my imagining, and its effects were, for me at least, quite transformative. Now that the dust is well and truly settled, I've decided that the story of that incredible week needs to be written out in full. What follows, therefore, is that story, as best as I can piece it together.

This piecing-together took place in several stages. The speed and volume of events meant that I was only able to put down the most cursory of notes as they were unfolding. In the days and weeks that followed, I found myself with an unexpected amount of free time, so I returned to those hurried jottings to flesh them out. As one might imagine, the tricky part was re-creating the conversations, but I was aided in this task by voice recordings I'd taken using my mobile phone. I was also aided, for reasons which will become clear, by my professional familiarity with Shakespeare.

For this final version, I've added some amplifying material to make things clearer and more complete, but I kept the account in the style of my journal, that is to say, without foreknowledge of what was to transpire or what it all meant. None of my thoughts or feelings has been redacted, though many of them turned out to have been off-base, if not totally mistaken. I have been as honest in this as I can be, though this was not always easy when the subject is murder.

E.M.

*M*ONDAY, JUNE 15. DAY.

I 've never recorded a day like this. In fact, I've never experienced a day like this in my entire life. Nor did I ever expect to. Nothing in my relatively humdrum existence could possibly have prepared me for what was to come.

This is not to say that I wasn't expecting it to be a big day, as these things go. It was the first day of rehearsals for *Othello*, this summer's main production in our local Shakespearean festival. Unlike several of the bard's plays – which, quite frankly, aren't terribly good – this one is a genuine masterpiece. The part I'd been given isn't big, but I was undeniably excited to have even a modest role in bringing to life a work of this calibre. Or at least I was when I left in the morning – by midday, I wasn't even sure the production would go ahead. Life, it appeared, had overtaken art. Desdemona really was dead.

I'd better start at the beginning. There's always a certain excitement in the air on the first day of rehearsals, since every theatrical production is a gamble and much depends on the overall vision of the play that the director will deliver. I chose to savour the quiet before the storm, so to speak, with a double latte and an apricot croissant at Ingrid's, a local coffee house. As I did so, I reflected on my life.

Shakespearean tragedy tends to bring that on. It deals with lives which seem rather ideal – a talented military commander (Othello), a powerful aristocrat (Macbeth), a monarch entering a comfortable retirement (Lear), the heir to a throne (Hamlet) or to a prominent family's fortunes (both Romeo and Juliet) – but which spiral out of control to their ultimate demise. My life wasn't in a death spiral by any stretch, but neither was it clear that it was going anywhere at all. The fact that the two principal female characters in *Othello*, of which I was playing one, are both murdered through little or no fault of their own probably didn't help my mood.

I was aware of the irony of brooding on such matters when everyone around me was beaming with the optimism that only a glorious late-spring morning can bring. It was perhaps the distance I felt from the rest of the world that drew my attention, as I stared distractedly through the window, to a peculiar man crossing the street. It wasn't that he was peculiar-looking – pretty ordinary, I'd say: tallish, quite slender, with sandy hair and dark brown eyes (rather intense ones at that). Nor was it the way he was dressed, which was perhaps a little formal for the artsy, slightly down-at-the-heels neighbourhood we were in, but not conspicuously so. It was the way he was walking. It is typical in this neighbourhood, which surrounds the farmers' market, for people to meander across the streets without paying much attention to vehicles; it's basically a pedestrian-first, let-the-cars-beware area. But this man took it a degree further: he was oblivious to everything. Vehicles, pedestrians, stacks of boxes, trash cans, animals – nothing appeared to attract his notice. It was as though he were on a mission, a mission from which no distractions could be permitted. In a way, his self-absorption gave him a kind of fascination. I decided to follow him; I was pretty sure I knew where he was going.

That destination was the Festival itself. We arrived, separated by a span of perhaps fifteen or twenty paces, at the stage entrance some twenty minutes later. It was manned by Stan Burns, an occasional actor and general dogsbody for the Festival. Stan's a burly man who lives well within his skin, as they say, and is always fast with a quip, especially if a Shakespearean phrase or two can be worked into it. It's hard not to like him; his good humour is infectious.

As the man approached, Stan declared with his usual bonhomie: "'Tis he: O brave Iago, honest and just."

"You know me well; I am he," the man replied.

"You are welcome, sir."

"I thank you for that. How is't with you?"

"Why, very well." Stan turned and gestured towards the corridor leading to the dressing area. "The door is open, sir, there lies your way."

3

The man thanked Stan and moved on without further comment. By the time Stan had turned back, I was at the entrance. My arrival instantly provoked more lines from the play: "Yes, 'tis Emilia! How do you, my good lady?"

Though I was fairly confident that Stan had prepared these lines in advance, I took it as a challenge of sorts and struggled for a response in kind. All I could think of was, "Excellent well! I thank you, sir."

It wasn't much of a response, really. I would have preferred a more elaborate answer, perhaps something suited to two people meeting the morning after a rather boisterous and well-lubricated party, but it was the best I could do on the spot. I really should remember to prepare a few opening lines for Stan, since he's usually in these productions and always up for some Shakespearean banter. I guess I don't because Stan's just Stan: there's no implicit threat or challenge behind his quips; you can take them or leave them.

It's a good sign when he's in a production because it means there'll be someone who can be counted on to lighten the atmosphere when it starts to get too heavy – as it invariably does. He's also an excellent fount of information. "Say, Stan, what's that guy's name?"

"The guy who just went in? That's Jake Benatsky. He arrived Saturday from London. He's going to be our villain."

"Oh right, our Iago. I think I saw him at the party

last night but didn't get a chance to talk to him. Do you know anything about him?"

"Nothing at all. You must awhile be patient. Pray you, come in."

These, too, are quotations from the play. I was all the more impressed, since he probably couldn't have anticipated needing them. "And what about you?" I replied. "You must be in the play – I hope you have a decent part this time."

"I'm to be Brabantio, the father of poor Desdemona," he responded. "Alas, 'I have no great devotion to the deed'."

"Why not?"

"It's a small part. Well, I expect that. But it's not a very interesting one, either. Basically, all I do is bemoan the fact that my daughter has run off and married Othello without my permission. You've got Emilia, which gives you something to sink your teeth into." A grin swept across his face. "Even though you're Iago's dupe, as well as being his wife."

"Yes, it's definitely like winning second prize in a beauty contest," I replied. "Still, it's a heck of a play. I'm glad to be back."

"You'd better go on in, Emma. We'll be starting shortly."

I proceeded to the back stage area, where most of the other performers were milling about. I knew almost all of them from previous productions, and at the party last night we'd had a good chance to catch up. The first person I greeted was Kendrick Page. He's a tall, rather good-looking black man who'd been awarded the role of Othello, the Moor. Why black men are almost always cast in this role has long puzzled me, since the Moors were originally from north Africa and probably looked like Arabs. But that's the way it is and, in any case, Kendrick is a talented actor, fully deserving of the part. He seemed quite excited to be here and with good reason: this is his first leading role and, with the exceptions of Hamlet and Lear (maybe Macbeth), it's the juiciest in all of Shakespeare.

On the far side of the room, I spotted Michael Calthorpe, who would be playing the part of Cassio. In the play, Cassio is a bit of a wastrel – to use a lovely old word – occupying a senior military post acquired through connections rather than competence, and carrying on in a casual way with Bianca, a tart. He's the one Othello suspects of having an affair with his wife, Desdemona. Michael's rather dreamy looks make it easy to picture him in that role. He was chatting with Oliver Allen, who would play Roderigo, the one who really is after Desdemona.

After nodding to Ollie, I turned my attention to Jake Benatsky, our villain. He was occupying another remote corner of the room, not speaking with anyone and still looking rather lost in himself. I recalled that the same had been true at the party. Of course, he'd just arrived from London and didn't know anyone, yet I had the sense that there was more to this than just shyness or jet-lag.

I thought about going over and introducing my-self, but the nine o'clock starting-time was almost upon us and I could feel the tension in the room mounting. It may seem odd that the first read-through of the play should generate any tension at all, but most of us knew from experience that it often gives an initial impression of the chemistry that may, or may not, develop. Perhaps this tension showed more on me than the others, for Stan and Ollie quickly sought to relieve it with their usual brand of jokiness. Approaching from my left side, Stan coyly pointed out that in this play I get killed, but without the benefit of having any love scenes be-forehand. In other words, death without sex. If I had won the role of Desdemona, Oliver helpfully added from my other flank, I would at least have got a kiss.

Unfortunately, their stratagem – if that's what it was – served only to get me thinking, once more, about why I hadn't got that role. It certainly wasn't for lack of experience. I'm a regular here, as much as anyone merits that distinction in this free-floating business. In fact, I've played the female lead on more than one occasion. The real problem, though no one would admit it, is my age. In most contexts, thirty-three is not considered old or even middle-aged, but the theatre is a cruel mistress. In the play, Des-demona is young, beautiful and virginal – none of which I can claim. If she'd been a more experienced and nuanced character, a Cleopatra, for example, I would have had a legitimate shot (though, truth be told, the beauty thing might still have sunk me). But Desdemona is a naïve innocent, and all her lines convey that quality – which leads inextricably to her murder. I couldn't pull that off, not anymore, so I had to step aside for a younger actress. Not exactly the first time that's happened in the theatre, but a first for me.

When our director, Walt Whitmore, broke the news, I took it in good grace – what choice did I have? – but it made me wonder. In the future, what roles could I hope to get? If they do King Lear next year, as has been suggested, I probably wouldn't get the role of Cordelia. It's a great role. True, Cordelia doesn't get kissed either, at least not on stage, but she has a lot more on the ball than the naïve Desdemona (not to mention the rather pathetic Emilia, my current role). Yet, chances are I'd be stuck playing one of the evil sisters – shallow, vain creatures without a single saving grace and few good lines to boot. I suppose there's always Lady Macbeth to look forward to. She's just as evil, but at least she has some wonderful speeches. And of course a mad scene. Audiences love that.

My rescue ultimately came a few minutes later when Eddie Haskell, the stage manager, summoned us onto the main stage, where a table large enough to accommodate the entire cast had been set up. My relief wasn't total, however, for I quickly noticed that our leading lady, Mandy Bennett, hadn't yet arrived. This was exceedingly strange behaviour for someone who'd just got her first major break, and it clearly annoyed Walt, who was taking a big chance on her. It didn't take long for him to decide to begin without her. Perhaps he sensed a power play on her part.

"Okay, listen up everyone. Let's . . . ."

A few people, mainly crew members, looked his way, but his words failed to penetrate the buzz of conversation that flourished among the cast – driven, no doubt, by the general aura of excitement and anticipation. This gave occasion for Ollie to display his Shakespearean chops:

"Arise, arise;
Awake the snorting citizens with the bell . . .
Arise, I say!"

Stan did arise, but it was to the implicit challenge in Ollie's words, rather than their content. Addressing the rest of us, he asked, "Are his wits safe? Is he not light of brain?"

There were a few snickers in the group, since some think Ollie really does have a screw loose. Nonetheless, the pause afforded Walt the opportunity he needed to assert control over the gathering and launch into his opening remarks. I got out my phone and set it to 'record'; I wanted to be able to review his comments later as I worked on my part. Fortunately, what he had to say was reasonably coherent. In fact, it was a relief to hear that he hadn't given in to the temptation few directors can resist nowadays to impose some radical new take on the play. When he started to explain that he wanted the audience to feel intensely the tragic loss of Desdemona, however, the producer suddenly interjected: "Where the hell is she?" Then Stan jumped in with, "Yes, where is 'the divine Desdemona'?"

That set it all off. Ollie immediately came back with, "Perhaps she's 'making the beast with two backs'." He chuckled at this, as did several of the others (actors being children at heart).

Stan, who plays Desdemona's father, naturally felt obliged to defend her honour. "Thou art a villain," he proclaimed magisterially.

This gave Ollie the cue he'd undoubtedly been hoping for:

"Your daughter, if you have not given her leave,
I say again, hath made a gross revolt;
Tying her duty, beauty, wit and fortunes
In an extravagant and wheeling stranger
Of here and every where."

Stan, true to form, refused to yield the day without a further sally, and happily for him, the play provided a good one:

"It is too true an evil: gone she is;
And what's to come of my despised time
Is nought but bitterness."

An exaggerated display of sorrow followed. Then, to round it off, he asked Kendrick: "O thou foul thief, where hast thou stow'd my daughter?"

I was enjoying the exchange, as were several of the others. It's always fun to see these old farts going at it, and their repartee was doing an excellent job of easing the tension around the table. But Walt clearly was not in a mood to be amused. I could well appreciate why. It's hard to get far in a rehearsal without the female lead, and she was now a good thirty minutes late. She wasn't answering her phone, either. I can't say I knew Mandy well, but I was one of the few who had a car, so I volunteered to go to her place and see what I could find out. It was a long shot, but at this point, Walt had little option but to agree.

This is where things started to get bizarre. As I was getting ready to go, Jake abruptly rose to his feet and announced to the table: "I will leave you now to your gossip-like humour." Then, turning to me, he declared pleasantly but firmly, "I'll go along with you."

I wouldn't have minded some company, but I was uneasy; I didn't know this guy at all. "No, it's all right," I replied. "Why don't you just stay here and work on the play; I won't be long."

But he was having none of it. "Nay, come, let's go together. I'll keep you company."

He's a strange bird, I thought, but there really is something about his manner that – I don't know – draws one in. I confess I felt quite curious about him. Besides, what could go wrong? – everyone knows who I'd be with. So I decided to yield to his suggestion, but with one precaution. As I sat down behind the steering wheel, I pretended to check my messages and then laid my phone on the center console. I'd put the voice recorder on again, just in case.

I had no idea what to expect from this man, but the last thing of all was criticism of my driving. We had scarcely started up before he started in: "Why, one that rode to's execution could never go so slow."

"I beg your pardon?"

"The affair cries haste, and speed must answer it."

What an asshole! I thought, as a flash of anger swept over me. But I suppressed it, opting instead to try to divert the conversation. "What do you think has happened to Mandy? Do you think those jokers, Stan and Ollie, could be right? About the beast-with-two-backs thing, I mean."

"I know not if't be true," he replied. "I'll see before I doubt. But I fear."

"You're afraid we'll find her in bed with someone? Really?"

"That's not my fear."

"Then what is?"

"Why I should fear I know not, but yet I feel I fear." After a slight pause, he added, "What, in your own part, can you say to this?"

I recognized what he was doing, of course. It was a continuation of what Stan and Ollie had been doing: the game of competitive quotations. I had to admit that he was better at it. The lines were less artificial, they fit the flow of the conversation more aptly, and they were delivered with much greater naturalness. But it was the same old bullshit. Or rather it wasn't, not exactly. This was the English version, the one that's wheeled out and put on display in the presence of colonials. In this version, English actors feel a compulsion to prove that no one knows Shakespeare, or can do Shakespeare, quite as well as they can. Maybe that's true (I am, after all, a colonial), but I was in no mood to let the challenge pass.

"It is merely a lust of the blood and a permission of the will," I declared. "Well, happiness to their sheets!"

His reaction was unexpected. "Why do you speak so startingly and rash? We have reason to cool our raging motions, our carnal stings, our unbitted lusts."

Was he serious? Or were these just the lines that had sprung most quickly to his mind, since they, too, were from the play? I decided to pursue it, see where it would lead. "Unbitted lusts?" I said. "Amen to that, sweet powers!"

"What do you mean by that?" His tone was now softer, almost pleading. "O gentle lady, do not put me to't."

He'd backed off. I hadn't expected it, but it gave me the advantage and I knew exactly how to exploit it. "Prithee, bear some charity to my wit," I answered. "Do not think it so unwholesome. What sense had I of her stol'n hours of lust? If ever I did dream of such

13

a matter!" I exclaimed, just to gild the lily. It's not for nothing that I'd studied this play to death.

But again, his response nonplussed me. All he said was, "I am glad of it." Was this a surrender in the game, or was he really pleased that I had protested my 'wholesomeness'? If so, why? Could he be interested in me?

We rode the rest of the way in silence. It gradually dawned on me that what bothered me about our exchange was not the possibility that he was attracted to me. It was the possibility that he wasn't playing a game.

❊ ❊ ❊

Mandy's apartment building is a three-storey walk-up about fifteen minutes' drive from the Festival grounds. Jake chose to remain in the car while I walked to the entrance to buzz her unit. There was no response. Phoning her again produced the same result. Figuring that she might be already at the theatre or on her way, I checked back with Eddie. No one there had heard a peep from her.

This all seemed most odd; the only explanation I could come up with was that she might have been overcome by an acute attack of nerves. Or drugs, though I didn't think she was that type. Yet how could it be nerves? I'd competed with her for the role of Desdemona and I knew how badly she wanted it;

could she really have let nerves get in her way? It's true that they are often an issue in this business, especially for relatively inexperienced performers, but it didn't seem likely that they could have played such an overpowering role when the task at hand, an initial read-through, made relatively little demand on one's abilities. I was beginning to feel the disquiet that Jake had expressed in the car. I buzzed the manager's unit.

Fortunately (or so I thought), the building manager, a man named Lapierre, agreed to meet me in the lobby. My impression when he arrived a couple of minutes later was that he had the trim, close-cropped look of an ex-military man. Perhaps influenced by his look, I explained the situation as succinctly as I could.

At first, he claimed that there was really nothing he could do without the tenant's permission. I might have left it at that, but Jake, who had joined us by that point, wasn't having it. Ultimately, I think it was his somewhat theatrical bombast – "Fear not, man, but yield me up the keys!" – plus the mesmerizing intensity of his gaze that won the manager over. He reluctantly agreed that the circumstances did perhaps warrant a look, but he wasn't going to let us go alone – a decision he would soon have cause to regret.

We followed him to Mandy's second-storey apartment, where, after knocking loudly and calling out her name, he proceeded to unlock the door with his passkey. The door opened onto a short hallway, with a galley kitchen on the left, a hall closet on the right, and the main living/dining area straight ahead. At first, everything seemed perfectly normal – just an empty apartment, like any other. Then Jake reached the living room.

"This is a sorry sight," he murmured quietly, his head bent downwards. Mr. Lapierre leaned forward to peer over him, but said nothing.

I felt my anxiety rising. "What is it, Jake? Is she there?"

"She is."

"On the floor? Is she strung out or something?"

"Much worse. She's dead."

These words drove a shock through me. My feet felt welded to the hallway floor. I was glad that the two men were blocking my view; I didn't want to see what they were seeing. The only response I could manage was, "Are you sure?"

"I know when one is dead, and when one lives," he replied. "She's dead as earth."

Mr. Lapierre appeared to be as stunned as I was, but at least he had the gumption to pull out his phone and dial 911. I remained affixed to the floor. After a few moments, Jake provided a further piece of disturbing information: "This is a piece of malice," he muttered.

"What do you mean, a piece of malice? Are you saying she was *murdered*?"

"Most sure she was. It was a piteous deed; the saddest spectacle that e'er I view'd."

For some reason that doesn't bear thinking about, this comment released my feet and allowed me to advance cautiously into the living-room. I paused when her body came into full view. It was, indeed, a sad spectacle. She was lying in the middle of the floor, her clothing intact but disheveled and her hair in total disarray. That plus the splaying of her arms and legs suggested that she'd been violently thrashing about; her last moments must have been spent in sheer agony. Looking more closely, I noticed that several of her fingernails were broken. Her fingers had bled as well, though only slightly. The only other sign of physical damage was a ring of bruising bracketing the white scarf that was tightly knotted around her neck. Much as I hate stating the obvious, I couldn't help it. "She's been strangled."

"Most probable that so she died," Jake concurred. He was now squatting beside the body, studying it intently. I was about to tell him not to touch anything, but it was clear that he was already incorporating that precaution.

Suddenly, I felt a wave of nausea sweeping over me. I staggered back to the safer realm of the hallway, where I braced myself against the wall and took several deep breaths.

That was enough to break Jake's focus. He pivoted towards me. "You look not well. For your own sake, depart the chamber; leave us here alone."

"The authorities are on their way," added Mr. Lapierre solicitously. "There's no need for you to be here. Maybe you should wait outside in the corridor."

"I'll be all right," I replied. I wasn't at all sure it was the truth, but I was determined not to retreat any further.

"I'm going to wait out there – you sure you won't join me?"

"I'll be there in a moment."

To divert myself, I began a slow visual scan of the living-room. Although cushions had been scattered and a coffee table overturned, I was struck by how untouched everything else seemed. Obvious targets for burglars, such as her laptop computer or mobile phone, were in plain sight. Nothing suggested that the desk drawers had been ransacked, as far as I could tell.

I took another deep breath and edged down a short hallway to the bedroom. I was a little fearful of what I might find, but I needn't have been. There wasn't a drawer or closet door left open, nor an item out of place. Either the killer had been very careful, or the room hadn't been touched. The same seemed true of the adjacent bathroom.

Passing back into the entry hall, I noticed that the front door frame seemed undamaged. The chain lock for the door hadn't even been forced. What other points of entry were there? My eyes strayed immediately to the far end of the living-room, where a sliding door provided access to a small balcony. I couldn't see if the door was latched, so I carefully skirted around Jake and the body (my eyes rigidly averted) to reach it. The latch was firmly in place. The only other possible point of entry was the bedroom window. I wended my way back to check. It, too, was locked from the inside. The lock wasn't terribly strong, but I could see no signs that it had been forced or jimmied. I returned to the entry hall, where Jake rose to join me.

"How goes it now?"

"I'm fine. Well, more or less. I was just looking around. It's bizarre."

"Why? What do you see?"

"It's what I didn't see. There are no signs of anyone breaking in or anything having been taken. Whatever this was, it wasn't a burglary gone wrong. She must have let the guy in. Or else he had a key."

He hesitated for a moment. "Is it a man, think you?"

"I do. Why? You're not so sure about it?"

He shook his head. "Nay, I am sure it is."

"Another thing. She's still wearing the clothes she had on at the party last night, so it must have happened before she had a chance to turn in. I seem to recall that she left the party quite early – around ten or so – which would make it ten-thirty at the earliest by the time she got here. If she let some guy in after that, she must have known him quite well."

"Yes, I agree. Here's much to do with hate, but more with love."

Strange as it might seem, I knew precisely what he meant. "But what I don't get is, why kill her?"

"Alas, who knows? But I can tell you one thing: that death's unnatural that kills for loving."

It felt more than unnatural; the whole scenario made no sense. If they were involved, he'd have known that she had a big rehearsal in the morning; it was no night to try to get together with her. And if they'd split up, why would she let him in? Why not secure the chain lock, just in case?

I glanced furtively at the body, which was no longer totally obscured from view. It was a foolish move, achieving nothing but the release of another wave of revulsion. "Someone has to pay for this," I muttered.

"Be sure of it," Jake replied as he angled me away from the living-room with a gentle nudge. "For murder, though it have no tongue, will speak."

My immediate thought was, 'yes, that must be so', but I knew that it was a hollow reaction: a wish rather than a belief. In truth, I had no idea at all whether there was any evidence here (or anywhere else) that would point to the killer; lots of murders never 'speak' at all. Did Jake know any better? I couldn't help feeling that his comment had been nothing more than bravado.

Within a very few minutes, several sirens announced the arrival of the police. It was a welcome development. I wanted the professionals to take over and let me go back to my normal life (as if that were still possible). Mr. Lapierre went straight away to the building entrance to let them in, and before I knew it, the head detective – for so he seemed by his take-charge manner – was rushing into the apartment. He was a short, thickly-built man, sporting an ample belly, precious little hair on top, and a complexion that pleaded too much alcohol. He surveyed the room quickly, then honed in on us. "Who are you?"

I jumped in to introduce ourselves and explain the reason for our presence in the apartment. 'Explained' may be too generous a term; it just blurted out, driven, no doubt, by my concern about the impression Jake might make if I gave him a chance to speak. But my efforts were of no avail as he immediately asked, "What's your name, sir?"

A brief flash of anger crossed the detective's face, but he quickly composed himself. "I'm Lieutenant Knutsen, Homicide."

"I'll have some proof."

"What?"

"Give me the ocular proof."

Knutsen stared at him for a good two seconds before realizing what was being asked of him. He reached into the breast pocket of his overly-tight jacket, pulled out his identification and flashed it to us both, declaring "I'm in charge here." He then asked Jake if the account I'd given was correct.

"It's true, good Lieutenant."

I quickly interjected, "Jake says she was murdered for love."

Again, this just blurted out. I'm not sure why; I guess I sensed the mounting tension between the two men. But it didn't help. Knutsen turned on Jake and asked quite aggressively, "What do you know about it?"

"Nothing, or if – I know not what."

That seemed to appease the Lieutenant a little, which is strange when you think of it, because it ought to have been precisely what he didn't want hear from any witness. After all, isn't information, rather than silence, the grist of detection? I began to wonder whether being in charge is more important to this officer than solving the case.

As if reading my thoughts, Knutsen declared, "I want to get to the bottom of this . . ."

"And so do I too, Lieutenant," Jake replied.

". . . and I expect you to stay out of my way."

"That will I do, as well as I can."

"As well as you can? What do you mean by that?"

That perked up the ears of all of his crime-scene crew. I gathered that challenging the boss was not something that happened every day. "Shall I tell you?" Jake coyly asked.

Knutsen paused for a moment. I'm sure he was tempted to push the issue, but discretion overtook his baser instinct. "Not now," he replied. "We've got a lot to do here. I want you out of this apartment. Go stand in the corridor; I'll talk to you later."

We stationed ourselves just outside the entrance to the apartment. That was at Jake's insistence; he wanted to be as close as possible to hear the muted comments of the scene-of-crime officers, who were now beginning their grim duties. Unfortunately for him, very little was audible from that distance. It didn't take long for his impatience to get the better of him.

"Let's have no more of this; let's to our affairs. Will you go with me?"

"Jake, we can't just leave."

He looked at me with intense, unreadable eyes. "I have no power upon you." The eyes then softened a bit. "Prithee, go with me."

I don't normally like being told what to do by any man, but I again found it strangely difficult to resist his request. Perhaps, in this instance, it was that one man was urging me to disobey what another man had ordered me to do. Or perhaps I'm just making excuses. We didn't make it very far down the corridor, however, before the Lieutenant intervened. "Wait a minute!" he shouted from the door frame, "Where do you think you're going?"

Again the seas looked to become rough. I stepped back towards Knutsen and tried to explain: "Lieutenant, we've got to get back to the theatre. We've got to tell the others; they're waiting to hear from us."

He was having none of it. "You're not going anywhere, either of you. Just stand right here and wait for me." He noticed the phone in my hand. "And don't use that thing."

Little did he suspect that I was already using it, though not to contact anyone. I'd forgotten to turn the recorder off.

As we stood in the corridor watching the slow and methodical efforts of the police crew, my mind drifted to the man who was standing beside me. I'm not sure why he should have been drawing my thoughts, given that I was standing not fifteen feet from a dead body, the body of a person I'd known. Maybe it was just a sensible division of labour: several people were looking into the mystery in the apartment, but only I was concerned with the mystery standing next to me. My mystery man sensed my attention.

"Why look you so upon me?" he asked.

"There's something we need to clear up."

"What matter have you against me?"

There was an edge in his voice as he spoke these words. Was he agitated because of the murder, or merely because he'd been relegated to the periphery by the alpha male on the scene? Or was it perhaps that he knew what was coming from me?

"Jake, I know that you're not from around here; maybe things are different where you grew up . . . ."

"Presume not that I am the thing I was."

"Well, I hope not, but the point is, you've been acting – how shall I put it? – a little strangely. You *seem* . . . ."

"What seem I that I am not?" he cut in indignantly as I struggled to find the right term. "I know not what you mean by that."

"You don't? How do you think you appear to other people?"

"What know I how the world may deem of me?" he bristled.

"Jake, I'm an English teacher and I've done a lot of Shakespeare, both on stage and in the classroom. So it hasn't escaped me that every single thing you've said so far is a quotation from his work. And, unlike Ollie and Stan's little performance, it's not just *Othello*. Your quotations are from several of the plays, as far as I can tell. That's just weird."

"Call it what you will," he declared. "I am not in the roll of common men."

"Come on, Jake. It's all very amusing for a while. Very clever, in fact. I don't know how you can pull out these lines so quickly. I'm impressed, really I am. But this is serious. It's not a game anymore."

E. P. MARWICK

"Madam, you do me wrong. By the very fangs of malice I swear, I am not that I play."

"By the fangs of malice! For God's sake, Jake, get real. There's been a murder!"

I paused for a moment; it was something he had just said. "So you admit that you've been playing a part? Is that it?"

His reply was laden with sarcasm. "It may be you think me an impostor. Then think you right: I am not what I am. Nothing that is so is so."

That's about as cryptic as it gets, I thought. Whatever he meant by those comments, he was clearly not willing to admit that he'd been playing the quotation game all along. Maybe it was just that he didn't like being cornered by me, called to account like some naughty little school-boy. But I couldn't dismiss the thought that he may be more deeply disturbed than I'd even begun to imagine.

These thoughts, had they been allowed to fester, might have really sunk my spirits – if spirits can go any lower, mere minutes after finding a murdered corpse – but they were soon interrupted by the sound of footsteps running towards us. We turned toward its source just in time to avoid being struck by a short, rather thin gray-haired man who brushed past us and stumbled into the apartment. Fortunately, his view was partially covered by Lieutenant Knutsen, still bent over the body and engrossed in examining it.

"I'm Henry Bennett, Amanda's father," the man declared, panting heavily. "What happened here? Is she going to be all right?" He then staggered anew when he caught a glimpse of the gruesome sight.

Knutsen stood up, but as he hesitated to respond, Jake stepped towards the man. "I'll tell you, sir, in private, if you please to give me hearing."

Mr. Bennett glanced briefly at Jake, but returned his eyes immediately to the spectacle on the living-room floor. Another officer stood up to block his view.

"Turn this way, Henry, and regard them not," Jake said. Without waiting, he placed his hands on Mr. Bennett's arms and began to steer the poor man into the corridor. I could see Knutsen turning back to the body, clearly relieved that someone else was taking on that task. Apparently not a people person, our Lieutenant.

Mr. Bennett looked from Jake to me. "Who are you?" he asked.

"I'm Emma Marwick," I replied, "and this is Jake Benatsky. We're in the play with her."

"Is she . . . ?"

"Good sir," Jake replied in a beautifully gentle, almost lilting voice, "let not your ears despise my tongue for ever, which shall possess them with the heaviest sound that ever yet they heard."

Mr. Bennett sucked in a sudden breath, which

caught in his throat, producing a indescribable squeal. I, too, felt a shudder pass through me.

"My heart is sorry for your daughter's death," Jake continued. "Death lies on her like an untimely frost upon the sweetest flower of all the field."

The comment was touchingly rendered and it had its desired effect: it froze any further attempt by Mr. Bennett to look past us at the horrid sight beyond. I think he instinctively understood that it was better to focus on the image conjured up by Jake's, or rather Shakespeare's, words. He began to sob quietly, almost as if he felt that it would be bad manners to make too open a display of grief. In truth, I'm not sure I could have managed it. Finally, he asked, "How?"

"Alas, sir, it is apparent foul play," Jake replied.

"What do you mean?"

As cool as he had been to this point, Jake, too, started to look wobbly. I jumped in: "I sorry, Mr. Bennett. We're not sure yet, but it looks like she was strangled with a scarf."

"Did she suffer a lot?" he inquired, a muted tone of desperation in his voice.

"I don't know, sir. We didn't notice any other signs of violence, so perhaps it was very quick."

Mr. Bennett now began to convulse repeatedly. My attempt to alleviate his pain probably had no effect other than to focus his mind once more on what had been done to his daughter. We gave him a few moments. When he spoke at last, his voice was no louder than a whisper. "Who could have done this to my beautiful girl?"

Men have this wonderful way of displacing emotions with practicalities, even if, as in this instance, what was to follow seemed anything but practical. Jake's comment hit exactly the right note: "I cannot tell, but this I am assured: truth will come to light; murder cannot be hid long. In the end, truth will out."

It was the same thing he'd said to me. Whether accurate or not – I still had my doubts, especially since meeting Lieutenant Knutsen – it succeeded in keeping Mr. Bennett's attention diverted from the wretched sight just a few feet away. "You seem to know something about this sort of thing," he said. "You're not with the police, are you? Are you some kind of private investigator?"

"Why ask you?" Jake replied. His tone was neutral, but underneath it I could detect a slight hint of anticipation.

Mr. Bennett hesitated for a moment, then took in another deep breath and said, "Look, the only way I'm going to be able to cope with this is by focusing on finding the murderer. My wife passed away several years ago. Mandy was at a delicate age at the time and she took it very hard, as you can imagine."

"So I can, sir."

"She left home as soon as she could," he continued, "and I don't know much about her life anymore. Well, there's a lot that a daughter wouldn't tell her father, isn't there? It's only natural, I suppose. But I can't help feeling I've let her down somehow, and I don't want to let her down anymore. Can you help?"

If Jake felt any emotion at this heart-felt plea, it didn't show in his face. "What would you have me do?" he asked.

"I want you to look into this for me."

It's one thing to divert Mr. Bennett's attention, but this was becoming crazy. I again felt obliged to point out the obvious. "Look, Mr. Bennett, we're both very sorry for your loss. I knew your daughter a bit, but I probably know even less than you about her private life. Jake had scarcely met her. We're just fellow performers, not private detectives."

Mr. Bennett was undeterred. "I get that," he said resignedly. "But he seems like a decent guy, and so do you. And you both know the theatre crowd, the people she liked to hang around with. You may be able to find out things that the police can't. Besides, I don't really trust the police to do a thorough job."

"Why not?"

He shrugged. "This won't be a priority for them; Mandy wasn't important enough for that. It's just another case that's been added to their workload."

There might have been something to what he said, but my gut feeling was still against his request – and it wasn't because I'd just been called a 'decent guy'. I couldn't see that it made any sense for us to get involved. We would have no authority to question anyone, or to gather evidence, or even to find out what the police knew; all we could do is get in their way. Besides, if we did beat the odds and make some headway, how do we know we wouldn't be putting ourselves at risk? This was a murder, after all. Everything pointed to this being a job best left to the professionals.

Everything except Jake; he showed not the slightest hesitation. "I will do this, if I can bring it to any opportunity," he declared. "'Tis a burden which I am proud to bear."

Mr. Bennett seemed to brighten up on hearing these words. "Do you really promise you'll help?"

"In the due reverence of a sacred vow, I here engage my words. As much as I can do, I will effect."

"Thank you so much, sir," Mr. Bennett said. He gripped Jake's fore-arm with his right hand. His entire demeanour signalled relief that he'd been offered a straw to clutch. "I'll pay anything you ask. Let me give you an advance right now."

He pulled out his wallet, but Jake's hand quickly shot out to stop him going any further. "I cannot with conscience take it. My duty then shall pay me for my pains."

"Are you sure?"

"This life is nobler than attending for a cheque," Jake assured him.

"I thank you. It means a lot to me. My number's on this card. Please call me as soon as you learn something. Anything."

With these words, the sobbing and shaking resumed. It was more uncontrolled this time; reality was beginning to sink in for him. Jake sensed it, too. "We'll leave you for this time: go in and rest," he said. "We'll not be long away." He shook Mr. Bennett's hand again as a police officer, showing some sense at last, approached to lead him away.

I was starting to feel a little relieved about Jake. The promise he'd made to Mr. Bennett had seemed astounding at first, but on reflection I could see that it was actually rather innocuous. What could he do, really? Try to keep tabs on what the police were doing? That might be worthwhile, if only to ease Mr. Bennett's burden. Knutsen, given his evident discomfort in dealing with the aggrieved, might even appreciate it. In exchange, Jake might provide the police with some background information about the theatrical world, or even find out a thing or two from the other performers that they hadn't been willing to report directly to the police. I couldn't see a lot of risk in that; it might even turn up something useful to the investigation.

It wasn't only that possibility that reassured me. Jake's 'peculiarity', which had seemed so embarrassing, even provocative, when we were talking to Lieutenant Knutsen, had actually proved remarkably effective in soothing Mr. Bennett. True, a cynic might describe his words as the oral equivalent of a high-end sympathy card, but for Mr. Bennett, they had worked. They couldn't take the pain away – that would hit over and over, very frequently and probably, at times, even harder than now – but I couldn't think of any other approach that would have done better. In this instance, at least, I was forced to rethink my impression of this curious man.

No sooner had Mr. Bennett been led away than Jake again became keen to leave. As he put it, nodding toward Lieutenant Knutsen, "Patience is for poltroons, such as he." He stepped into the apartment again, causing the poltroon in question to look up from his position beside the body. He seemed astonished, but before he could put words to his puzzlement, Jake grandly declared: "I take my leave of you. I am sure you have your hands full all in this so sudden business."

"Now, just a second, you can't . . . ."

"I'll be gone, sir, and not trouble you."

I decided to follow suit. If Jake could bluff his way out, then why couldn't I? "I'm going, too," I announced. "We'll be at the theatre. We've got to tell the others."

Knutsen thought about this for a moment. "Okay, go ahead and let them know what happened, but keep everyone there so that we can interview them all. We'll be there as soon as we can." Then he had a further thought. He stood up and approached us. "Oh, and one thing more: don't mention *how* she was killed to anyone. You got that? Say nothing about her being strangled."

Jake nodded his consent and turned to me: "Come, let's be gone. The swifter speed the better."

Was that another shot at my driving? If so, I was determined that he wasn't going to get the car keys. I may have felt some grudging admiration for the man, but I certainly didn't trust him. Not where speed was the issue, at any rate.

He was already half way down the corridor when the Lieutenant caught up to me and grabbed my sleeve. This time his demeanour was more subdued. "What's with that guy, anyway? Is he nuts?"

"No, he's just an actor," I replied. Bizarrely, that seemed to satisfy him and he returned to his dismal work.

✽ ✽ ✽

No sooner had we reached the car than Jake's hand shot out impatiently for the keys. I refused to yield them. "Jake, about the driving. This is my car and . . . ."

"Nay, stay not to expostulate; make speed."

"I know I'm not a fast driver. I probably don't drive as fast as you . . . ."

"Well, I will do't."

"The thing is, Jake, I'm worried you'll drive too

fast. It's not safe."

"Madam, I go with all convenient speed. It were impossible I should speed amiss."

I yielded; I didn't think I could have endured his carping, however poetically phrased, if I hadn't. Besides, letting him drive allowed me some time to think. It was a welcome pause; so much had happened.

The first thing my mind turned to was the unlikelihood, not to mention the irony, of an actress who was about to play Desdemona being strangled to death. The circumstances were very different – in the play, Desdemona is strangled in the final scene and everyone knows who did it – but it felt spooky, nonetheless. For once, Jake was on the same page. "If this were played upon a stage now," he observed, "I could condemn it as an improbable fiction."

Yet it had happened. I realized that it wasn't the improbability of it that bothered me, or even the grim irony. Nor was it even the basic reality that a young woman – a talented, beautiful woman with her whole life in front of her – had lost that life, although that was certainly horrendous. What bothered me particularly was the manner of it. If it had been a traffic accident or even a drug overdose, I would have felt – strangely – better. As it was, I was left with an overwhelming sense of unease. I had to understand what Jake had in mind.

"Jake, why did you promise Mr. Bennett that you'd get involved? Was it just to make him feel better?"

"Wherefore do I this?" he replied, apparently puzzled that I should even ask. "The bravery of his grief did put me into a towering passion."

I mulled this over as we proceeded to the theatre. It had been very difficult to look at Mr. Bennett's anguished face and not feel the urge to do something. And, to be frank, Lieutenant Knutsen didn't exactly inspire a lot of confidence. Jake obviously shared that impression. But it's one thing to want to do something and another to bring it off successfully. Apart from talking with the other performers and periodically pestering the police for information, I had no idea how to proceed. Did Jake?

"What will you do?" I asked bluntly.

"Search, seek, and know how this foul murder comes."

That sounded disturbingly much like running a parallel investigation. "Don't you think you should leave that to the police? It's their job, after all. Maybe you should just liaise with them on Mr. Bennett's behalf?"

"Must there no more be done?" he snapped back. He then paused to composed himself a little. "Hear me with patience. I would do the man what honour I can."

"Honour? What's honour got to do with it?"

He looked at me as if my objection were totally unfathomable. "Shall I be tempted to infringe my vow in the same time 'tis made?" he asked indignantly. "I will not."

"Okay, I get it: you gave your word. But what do you know about these things? You can't solve a murder with beautiful quotations."

"Indeed, no, for in such business, action is eloquence."

"Spoken like a true super-hero," I retorted, "and about as sensible as one of those comic-book plots." The remark passed him by completely. I decided to dispense with flippancy and adopt a tone equally as stern as his own. "You go to do you know not what."

"I know it," he admitted reluctantly.

I was a little embarrassed to have thrown in a line from Shakespeare. Perhaps it was the heat of the moment, or just the cumulative effect of conversing with him. But the line was apposite, and he hadn't batted an eye. In fact, he'd shown a little humility, which I liked better than all the gung-ho macho stuff. We drove the rest of the way without a further word, lost in our separate thoughts.

With our arrival back at the main stage, we found ourselves thrust once more into the realm of Shakespearean banter. Stan launched the initial salvo: "Ah, here they come and without the object of their quest. Apparently, 'love's quick pants in Desdemona's arms' aren't so quick, after all!"

Ollie, of course, was eager to respond:

"Sir, would she give you so much of her lips

As of her tongue she oft bestows on me,
You'll have enough."

The response didn't make a lot of sense, given that Stan plays Desdemona's father in the play, but I don't think that's what stopped him from replying. Instead, I think it was simple curiosity. He turned to us and said, "Tell me, where is the 'impudent strumpet'? Has she 'shuffled off this mortal coil'?"

Stan could not have known how disastrous his choice of expression was. Both Jake and I were stunned for a moment; we must have looked like deer caught in the headlights. Finally, Jake exhaled deeply, stepped forward and addressed the whole troupe. "Before we proceed any further," he declared, "hear me speak." Such was the solemnity in his voice that conversations quickly died out and heads pivoted to face him. "I should report that which I saw, but know not how to do it. If you have tears, prepare to shed them now. God rest her soul, she's dead."

These words cast everyone else into the role of headlit deer. It was obvious what they were thinking. Surely, he's just jerking our chains? This is taking the game too far. Unless . . . .

Jake sensed the unease that had enveloped the room. "Little joy have I to breathe this news," he added, "yet what I say is true."

There followed some uncomfortable shuffling of limbs and a few incomprehensible mutterings. Stan must have felt the most embarrassed, or perhaps the most abused. "O well done," he responded, his voice dripping with sarcasm.

The tension by this point was palpable. The cast and crew probably didn't know how to take Jake, but most of them knew me; I had to intervene. I stepped forward and said, "Unfortunately, what Jake's saying isn't a joke."

There was an audible sucking in of air as several of the others began to grasp that we weren't kidding. But Stan – God help him! – couldn't let it go. I'm sure that at some level the reality must have begun to sink in, but it was intolerable to him; he had been so fond of Mandy. So he continued with the game: "Come, mistress, you must tell's another tale."

Perhaps it was the use of another line from *Othello* that jogged Jake. In any case, he intervened again: "Pardon me for bringing these ill news. I say she's dead; I'll swear't. I am sorry I should force you to believe that which I would to God I had not seen."

It may have been the gravity of his tone of voice that convinced Walt, our director, that he meant every word. The shock was etched across his face as he spoke: "You're serious, aren't you?"

"Hear me more plainly," Jake responded. "Honest plain words best pierce the ear of grief. For certain she is dead, and by strange manner."

"What are you saying?" Walt asked.

"She died by foul play," he confirmed.

This comment stunned Stan back to life, but he

still couldn't let go: "What do you mean? Was it 'murder most foul'? Heh, heh."

Jake's response was succinct: "In the direst degree."

Again, Walt cut straight to the point. "How?" he asked.

"How should she be murder'd? I cannot rightly say."

I knew I'd better explain. "The police have ordered us not to say anything about it. They'll be here soon. We've been asked to tell you that no one is to leave."

"Oh my God," Stan gasped. He had at last assimilated the cruel reality. I knew that in the future, he would always be embarrassed about how he'd reacted to the news, especially in front of the whole cast and crew, but for now his focus was not on himself. "Can you at least tell us whether it was . . . very violent? I mean, did she suffer a lot?" His throat was so tight that the last few words barely eked their way out.

Some of the others added their support to this request. They needed to know more about what had happened. I'm not sure why that is about people: how can more details make the pain any less difficult to bear? Be that as it may, Jake seemed to sense what they needed. "Alack, my fellows, what should I say to you? Mine eyes did sicken at the sight, and could not endure a further view."

It was, again, touchingly put, and I'm sure many

of them were so seduced by the sentiment that they failed to notice that he was still quoting Shakespeare. And that he hadn't answered the question. He does have a knack with these things, I had to admit. But it was still disturbing.

At this point, another disturbing thing happened: someone left from the far side of the stage. A few moments later, I could hear the faint report of a distant door slamming. Whoever it was had left the theatre entirely.

Jake had picked up on it, too. "But this is something odd," he whispered. "Emilia, come. I would speak a word with you."

He took my arm and guided me over to the nearest corner, well away from the others. "Did you see who that was?" I asked.

"That's he that was Othello."

"Kendrick?"

"I cannot think it, that he would steal away so guilty-like."

It seemed odd to me as well. "It must be because he's upset. I suppose some people just need to be alone at times like this."

It wasn't just Kendrick's sudden disappearance that bothered me. Why, I wondered, had Jake used the term 'guilty-like'? It crossed my mind that perhaps he's so seriously deluded as to be incapable of separating reality from fiction. Othello kills Desdemona in the play, therefore the real-life murderer must be Othello. I couldn't let that pass. "You said 'guilty-like'. Do you actually think he could be the murderer? Why? Just because he's playing Othello?"

"Do you think I am so far deceived in him?" he replied. "There was no such stuff in my thoughts."

I certainly hoped so, but I was still far from satisfied concerning his capacity to undertake serious detective work. "But what *is* in your thoughts?" I asked. "I still don't understand why you think you can do something about this business. You don't have any experience in criminal investigations, do you?"

"True, madam, none at all."

"Then why are you getting involved?"

"What I can do can do no hurt to try."

"That makes no bloody sense!" I exclaimed. "Well, okay, it does," I admitted after a moment's reflection, "but what you're doing doesn't." Another thing I'd noticed about him was that he was still calling everyone in the cast by their character's name; the possibility that he can't distinguish between reality and fiction was still on my mind. "Jake, is it because you're playing Iago and you think you've got to clear your name?"

"What, have you lost your wits?"

Just so long as you haven't, my strange friend. "Okay then, what?"

"I am bound by oath, and therefore pardon me."

"That's really not good enough," I insisted. "You

say that getting involved can't hurt, but that may not be true. This is murder, after all. Your efforts to meddle in the investigation could end up being disastrous."

"Our doubts are traitors, and make us lose the good we oft might win by fearing to attempt," he gravely replied.

I was beginning to realize, albeit grudgingly, how much can be obfuscated with appropriate quotations from Shakespeare. Pull them out of context and they can mean a lot of things, or nothing at all. I was also starting to grasp something else: this man could be profoundly annoying. I decided to take another approach.

"Tell me, Jake, what do you expect me to do while you run around playing the amateur sleuth?"

"I am most fortunate, thus accidentally to encounter you," he replied. "Prithee, be my present partner in this business. It is a business of some heat."

"What?"

"Will you help? I do desire it."

His request stunned me momentarily. Then I realized that Mr. Bennett may have intended for both of us to look into the murder. I couldn't deny the idea made some sense: I'm the one who actually knows most of the cast and crew, as well as the local theatre scene in general. In fact, unlike Jake, I knew the victim, although not terribly well. Could I possibly refuse this request to help?

"All right, I'll do it."

"I knew it would be your answer."

"Hold on; there's got to be some ground rules."

"Name them. You shall have anything."

"First, will you promise not to do anything illegal?"

"Willingly. I am not partial to infringe our laws."

"Do you really mean that?"

"I promise you. I'll be no breaker of the law."

"Second, will you promise that you won't just run all over the place, trampling on the evidence and getting in the way of the authorities."

"I must be patient; there is no fettering of authority."

"And you won't lie to me or deceive me? I won't be your pawn in this business."

"Though I am not naturally honest, I am so sometimes by chance."

"That's not good enough."

He exhaled deeply, as if in exasperation at my refusal to take a joke. "I will tell truth, by grace itself I swear. Is that all?"

"No, it isn't." Humorless or not, I wanted more assurance that I wasn't going to be played for a dupe. "You'll keep me informed; you won't hold information back from me?"

"Truth loves open dealing," he declared.

"And you won't do anything that I don't agree with?"

"I shall in all my best obey you, madam. Let us swear our resolution." He held out his hand.

"Okay, then," I replied, "you have my word – provided you keep yours. I'm not convinced we can achieve much, but I suppose we can try." I offered my hand and we shook on it.

"I thank you," he said. "I am not of many words, but I thank you."

We were interrupted at this point by a commotion in the corridor leading to the main stage, which signalled the arrival of Lieutenant Knutsen and his contingent. As soon as they entered the stage, they could see by the expressions on our faces that we all knew the news. Knutsen introduced himself and announced that they were going to interview each of us individually. What they particularly needed to know is what we were doing last evening.

Hearing this, Jake immediately asked: "Within the volume of which time?"

A puzzled expression rippled across the Lieutenant's well-worn face. "What?"

I came to the rescue. I could see that, if for nothing else, I could at least be useful for interpreting. "He means, Lieutenant, what is the time frame you're looking at?"

Knutsen thought about this for a second or two,

then announced that they were interested in the period up till one a.m. last night. He couldn't be more precise at the moment.

"How . . . did it happen?" Stan asked shakily. "Can't you tell us something, for God's sake?" He was clearly still haunted by the spectre of pain having been inflicted on Mandy.

If Knutsen felt any sympathy for the man's plight, he was not showing any signs of it. All he said was, "We'll have to wait for the autopsy."

Jake quickly responded, "I would most gladly know the issue of it."

Knutsen was again taken aback. "What?" Then he paused for a moment; the penny was finally dropping. "Wait a moment, why did you say that? I told you to stay out of this. If you're getting any ideas of interfering . . . ."

Before the Lieutenant could finish his no-doubt-stern admonition, Ollie interjected: "If that's the time frame, Lieutenant, you have to realize that it lets all of us off the hook. We had a pre-production party last night at Walt's house. He's our director." Ollie nodded towards Walt, who nodded back. "Mandy left early, but the rest of us stayed till quite late – till at least one, I think."

That comment immediately roused Michael, our Cassio. "No, that's not quite true," he said. "Most of us were there till late, but Kendrick left shortly after Mandy did."

"Which one of you is Kendrick?"

Everyone looked around. "He's not here," Michael replied. "He must have left."

"Was he here when the death was announced?"

"I think so, yes."

Knutsen frowned. "I want the rest of you to move over by that wall. My officers and I will interview each of you. Once you've been interviewed, you'll be free to leave. Not before that. It shouldn't take long."

As the police herded the group toward the designated area, Jake quickly worked his way to the back of the crowd and started to head for the far exit. I'd expected as much. Whatever his virtues may be, patience didn't seem to be one of them. I quickly caught up to him and grabbed his arm.

"What are you doing? You can't leave now."

"I cannot, nor I will not, hold me still."

"Jake, they've told us to wait," I pleaded. "You promised to be patient."

"Who can be patient in such extremes? Come, let's make haste."

"Make haste where? Where do you think you're going?"

"Where should Othello go?"

I, too, was more than a little curious about Kendrick's sudden disappearance, but I was determined to keep the reins on Jake. Apart from translation, it was becoming clear that another of my contributions to this business – perhaps the most important one – would be to hold him back.

"Well," I replied, "he's probably just gone home. At least, that would be the obvious place to look. But we can't go there now; we've got to be interviewed first."

"What's that to us? At this time most easy 'tis to do't."

"Perhaps, but 'easy' doesn't mean 'wise'. We need to respect the police's procedures and that means being interviewed when they ask. Or in this case, demand."

"But small to greater matters must give way," he countered.

Being interviewed was evidently not a priority for him, and I could understand why: we were both at the party all evening and really that's all there was to say. But he had given me an opening: I recognized the quotation and knew the response: "Not if the small come first."

He showed not the slightest appreciation for my sally. "I would not be delay'd," he insisted. "This weighty business will not brook delay. You shall have time to wrangle in when you have nothing else to do."

Dammit, a triple. He'd out-quoted me again. It seemed that this quotation game, if that's what it was, was not one I could win. But I held the trump card: "If you leave now, you're really going to annoy Knutsen. That's not going to do much for our ability to conduct an investigation. We need the police on our side."

He contemplated this for a moment. "O, very well. I will give him some relief, if it be but for that. I wait upon his pleasure."

I had at least won the common-sense game. For now.

❋ ❋ ❋

The interview process held us longer than Lieutenant Knutsen had suggested, in large measure because Jake and I weren't interviewed until near the end. Jake was beside himself with frustration.

"You realize what this is," I said to him. "This is Knutsen showing us how obstructive he can be if we get on his wrong side. In fact, we probably shouldn't go to Kendrick's place till after his people have . . . ."

"Nay, before them, if we can," he cut in.

"Why? Are you afraid they may warn him off talking to us?"

"I am, indeed."

It wouldn't have surprised me, either, to be honest. I tracked Eddie down and persuaded him to give us Kendrick's address. With that in hand, we set off. Jake insisted on doing the driving, of course, and I let him. I figured it would be better to get in and out before the police got there than to be caught mid-interview by them.

Kendrick's place proved to be a small bungalow in the distant southeastern reaches of the city. Twenty-five years ago, it would have been an affordable home for an average wage-earner, but that hadn't been true for some time. Either he was sharing the house with friends, or he was still living with his parents. I suspected the latter even before the door was opened by a slightly stooped woman of ripe middle age.

"Yes, can I help you?"

"I hope so," I replied. "This is Jake and I'm Emma. We're in the play with Kendrick. Are you his mother?"

"Yes, that's right. I'm Gracie."

"Hi, Gracie. Is Kendrick here, by any chance?"

"No, he isn't. He should be at the rehearsal right now." She paused for a moment. "Are you all right?"

The latter comment was directed at Jake, who did indeed look a little peaky. "Yes, madam," he responded. "Though it be honest, it is never good to bring bad news."

"Bad news!" she exclaimed. "Has there been an accident or something?"

"I would it were no worse."

"Oh dear, this sounds serious."

Before either of us could say anything to mollify her, she turned towards the staircase and shouted for George, whom I took to be her husband. I could hear footsteps above us, which stopped abruptly when the phone rang. He shouted down that he'd get it.

Turning back to us, Gracie swung the door further open. "Well, you'd better come in."

She led us into the living-room and motioned us to be seated. As Jake eased himself into a plushly-upholstered armchair, he launched into full sympathy-card mode: "I am sorry, madam, for the news I bring is heavy in my tongue."

"Would you like something to drink? Perhaps some tea?"

I don't think she meant this as a humorous comeback, but I had to struggle to keep a straight face. Maybe the shock was making me giddy. Fortunately, Jake showed no such difficulty. "Madam, not now, but I thank you."

"Are you sure I can't get you something?"

"I am very ill at ease, unfit for mine own purposes; that is all."

Kendrick's father entered the room just then. He was a heavy-set man, with not much hair on top but very thick eyebrows that shaded kind, sincere eyes. He approached Jake, stuck out his hand, and in a surprisingly soft voice, said, "I'm George. George Page. How do you do?"

"I am not so well as I should be," Jake replied as he rose to grip Mr. Page's hand. It was a large and powerful hand, but fortunately he had the foresight – not shared by all men, alas – to ease up when it was my turn to shake it.

George motioned for Jake to sit down again. "That call was from the police, asking if Kendrick was here. I gather you have some news for us?"

"There is no composition in these news that gives them credit," Jake responded. "I am sorry you must hear."

With this remark, I could see that anxiety was starting to overwhelm their puzzlement, so I quickly intervened. "Unfortunately, there has been a death."

"Oh my God!" Gracie exclaimed. George immediately asked: "Whose?"

"Her name was Mandy Bennett," I replied. "She was going to play Othello's wife, Desdemona. She was found dead in her apartment this morning."

After a few moments of awkward silence, George gravely asked, "Was she murdered?"

The question seemed to pique Jake. "Why ask you this?" he responded with a sharpness that surprised me. "What do you know of it?"

If the Pages took offence at Jake's tone, they showed no sign of it. "We haven't heard anything about this, have we, Gracie?" George replied. "When did it happen?"

I replied simply, "It was last night, sometime after she left the party."

"Kendrick must be very upset," Gracie observed. "She is, or was, a very good-looking girl, or so he says. I think he was a little sweet on her."

Jake's next comment also surprised me, but for its content rather than its tone. "I knew of this before," he said, "but, to speak truth, this present grief had wiped it from my mind."

It took me a moment to realize what he meant. He didn't mean that Mandy was attractive – that was obvious to everyone – but rather that he knew Kendrick had had his eye on her. But how could he have known that? He didn't really know any of the cast. Then I realized he must have noticed something at the party. Apparently, he's not as oblivious to his surroundings as he seems.

These musings were interrupted by George's next question. "How was she killed?"

God, do all men's minds follow exactly the same track? "I'm afraid we can't say as yet," I said, "but we've got to talk to Kendrick as soon as possible. You don't have any idea where he is, do you?"

"You think our boy did it?" George retorted. "If you do, you're way off-base. We weren't awake when he got in last night – your cast party must have gone late – but this morning, he was just busting to get started on the new play. He wouldn't have been like that if he'd just killed his leading lady, now would he?"

"No, no, Mr. . . . George. It's just that . . . ."

"Let me tell you something," he continued. "There aren't that many parts for black men in this town and this is a big one. In fact, he says there's nothing else in Shakespeare like it. He wouldn't blow an opportunity like that for anything, believe me."

"No, of course not," I replied. "It's just that he left the theatre early this afternoon and we . . . the police didn't get a chance to interview him. We wanted to let him know."

That seemed to appease George enough for him to sit back and allow his wife to take over. Or perhaps it was that he'd just realized that his son's big break may now be finished.

"I'm afraid we can't help you," Gracie said. "We haven't seen or heard from him since he left for the rehearsal this morning."

"You have no idea where he might be now? Perhaps at a girlfriend's?"

"He doesn't have anyone special right now. George?"

"He's probably gone to some bar. He'll be devastated."

I didn't doubt it. "We should get going now. If you hear from him, will you have him contact us right away? It's very important."

They assured us they would as we headed for the door. At the porch, Jake turned to them and, with funereal gravity, shook their hands again. "I thank you for your pains," he said.

With that, he headed briskly for the car. I delayed a moment to write my mobile number on a scrap of paper. As I did so, George asked in a very gentle voice,

"Why was he talking like that?"

It was a question I wished I could answer. But I couldn't, so I improvised. "He's English."

They both stared blankly at me.

"I think he went to a boarding school."

"Oh?" Gracie said.

"From a very young age."

"I see," said George after another awkward pause.

I doubt he did. Leaving them both looking slightly puzzled, I scurried to the car, where Jake had again occupied the driver's seat. He looked impatient and with good reason: the police would be there soon and we needed to move on. But where?

Naturally, he had an answer. "Two things are to be done," he declared as we pulled from the curb.

"What's the first – return to the scene of the crime?"

He smiled grimly. "Ay, that's the first thing that we have to do."

My suggestion had been facetious, but I'd nailed it in one. Perhaps, I thought, I have a knack for these things.

❊ ❊ ❊

We arrived at Mandy's building around half past two, after a brief pit-stop for lunch (at my insistence). We found Mr. Lapierre intensely engaged in mowing the front lawn. He seemed a little cautious about talking to us at first, but soon relented. Perhaps he'd heard Mr. Bennett asking us to look into Mandy's death, or simply was pleased to have someone to talk it over with. It wouldn't have been easy to go back to his normal routine after this morning's events.

I wasn't sure how the questioning should proceed, so I decided to begin with a general question: "Mr. Lapierre, what can you tell us about Mandy?"

"Not much, really," he replied. "Very good looking, as you know. But nice. Always polite. I had no problems with her, none at all."

"Do you know where she worked when she wasn't acting?" I wasn't going out on a limb here; in this town, almost all actors have day jobs (unless they have someone willing to support them).

"Yes, she was a waitress, or whatever, at a nightclub. The Brown Pelican. That's all I know."

There was a subtle change to his demeanour as he said this, a slight edginess that hadn't been there. Jake picked up on it immediately: "I pray you, sir, deliver with more openness your answers." His manner made it sound like a good deal more than merely a polite request.

Mr. Lapierre was becoming genuinely agitated now. "Listen," he said, "I don't want no trouble and I don't stick my nose in nobody else's business. Besides, I told the police everything."

I began to fear that if we pushed harder, we'd get nothing further from him. "Jake, he's had a shock."

He must have realized it, too, because he shifted course noticeably. "I know this act shows horrible and grim," he said. "Let me but move one question: had she no lover? Tell us something of him."

"There was someone, now that you mention it. An older man, very well-dressed – you know, in a suit. He comes – came – around now and then, usually at night. I never really got much of a look at him."

"Do you know his name?" I asked.

"No. Sorry."

"Well, would you recognize him if you saw him again?"

"Yeah, maybe. I'm not sure."

"What about last night? Did he come then?"

Mr. Lapierre hesitated, as if scanning his memory. "No, . . . I don't think so." He brightened up a little. "But someone came. It was late."

"Can you be a little more precise about the time?"

"Let's see. It must have been eleven-forty or so. I usually go to bed around eleven, but I'd stayed up to see the end of a movie. It lasted till about eleven-thirty."

"Please, Mr. Lapierre, tell us exactly what happened."

"Sure." He seemed on more comfortable ground

now. "I was just getting into bed when I heard a car door slam. It was quite loud. I walked over to the window to see who would be arriving at that time of night. It was a young man. He walked up to the front door and rang a buzzer."

"How do you know he pressed a buzzer? You can't see the building entrance from your bedroom, can you?"

"No, but my apartment is right next to the entrance, so I can hear the sound through my bedroom wall. Fortunately, we don't get many people arriving in the middle of the night. That's how I knew it was Mandy he wanted to see; the other residents are quite elderly and not very lively at that hour."

"Did you get a good look at this man?"

"Not really. He was fairly tall, slender, quite good-looking, I'd say. I'm not sure I could recognize him again, though, if that's what you mean."

"But you're sure it wasn't the man Mandy had been seeing?"

"Yes, very sure. This man was quite a lot younger. I've never seen him before. Besides, the older man has his own keys; he wouldn't have needed to buzz."

"Do you know what time he left?"

"I think so. I was still trying to get to sleep when I heard a car drive off about fifteen minutes later. It must have been him."

"One last question: did you mention this to the police?"

"Yeah, I did." Unfortunately, bringing up the police brought everything back, causing him to begin to lose his grip again. "God, I can't believe this is happening. She was such a nice girl. A real gem, you know what I mean?"

He was almost in tears. It was clear that we wouldn't get much more out of him. Jake took the only feasible course: "I thank you for your pains and courtesy. I am much bound to you."

Then Mr. Lapierre surprised us. "Are you really going to look into this?" he asked.

"What we can do, we'll do," Jake replied.

"I hope so. I don't trust the police to do it properly."

Jake leapt on this comment: "How mean you, sir?"

Mr. Lapierre's face went rigid. "Just be careful, that's all."

"Ay, so we will."

That seemed to appease him, somewhat anyway, and we made our good-byes.

As we were heading to the car, Jake observed, "This honest creature doubtless sees and knows more, much more, than he unfolds."

I could only agree. Mr. Lapierre was frightened. We might have to go back to him, but we would need to discover a good deal more first. He might confirm things when they're put to him, but I doubted that he would open any new doors.

We drove back to the theatre in silence, only to find that it, too, was silent; the entire cast and most of the crew had left. Doubtless, the powers that be – the director, producer and Festival board – were considering what to do next. One of the crew members said that tomorrow's rehearsal was still on, but that that might change. We'd be notified.

It was difficult to know what to think of this news. I was torn between desire for the play to go on, the better to forget what had occurred today, and guilt for the callous selfishness of that wish. Then something occurred to me. "Jake, you said earlier that there are two things to be done."

"I do remember it."

"I think I can guess the other one: find out where Mandy worked and go there. That's our next stop, isn't it?"

"Well guessed," he replied with a smile.

"There's no point doing it now, but I think we should try early tonight. Otherwise, the police will get there first, which might make it difficult for us to get information out of anyone. Perhaps we should count on showing up at the nightclub around, say, eight o'clock?"

"That time best fits the work we have in hand," he agreed. "Will you walk with me about the town, and then go to my inn and dine with me?"

Under other circumstances, I might have taken this as a come-on, but I knew better: it wasn't the moment for that kind of thing. Nevertheless, I'd had enough; I needed to be alone for a bit. "Thanks, but no. I need some time to collect myself. Let's just meet there at eight."

"Very well. Farewell till then." He started to head off.

"Don't you want a drive back?"

"I do not. I'll see you soon."

I decided to leave him to his own devices. It was clear that he, too, was keen to be on his own.

As soon as I got home, I pulled out my laptop computer. I wanted to write up as much of the day's events as possible for the journal. Enough had occurred so far today to equal a month's worth of normal entries and I didn't want to omit a thing. If ever I were to feel the desire to re-visit my past, I thought, it would probably be because of today.

✳ ✳ ✳

It was about five o'clock when I finished. What I'd managed to put down was rather rough – just points, really – but I knew I could always flesh it out later on, when things slowed down. The important thing was just to record the key developments in sequence while they were crystal clear in my mind. I also downloaded the voice recordings; these covered, I must confess, virtually every conversation that had occurred. Nothing seemed too trivial to record. Surely when this was over, I reflected, I'll find that many of them can safely be ignored, but for now they would remain on my laptop. I then placed the phone in the recharger to ready it for the evening's activities.

With these duties taken care of, I took a long, hot bath, demolished a frozen dinner, and put my feet up. There was more to come to-night – much more, I was sure of it.

MONDAY, JUNE 15. EVENING.

I arrived at the Brown Pelican just after eight. My immediate impression on entering was that the décor and atmosphere were a little on the garish side. It felt like the kind of place where you didn't really want to touch anything. Lots of men were there already, many of them quite boozy and boisterous, but almost no women – customers, that is. There was no shortage of cocktail waitresses – you couldn't call them 'servers' – wearing tight, skimpy black dresses that didn't leave a lot to the imagination. They seemed very touchable.

Within a few moments, my eyes settled on Jake. He was installed at the bar, distractedly fondling a drink. I turned on my voice recorder and walked over to him. "It looks like you've started without me," I observed.

"I have drunk but one cup tonight." His response was belied by the empty glasses beside him; he'd obviously been there for a while.

"Let's find a table," I said. Glancing around, I spotted an empty bar table around the far corner of the bar and hastened to it. He meandered slowly behind, drink in hand.

"How do you now?" he asked, as he hoisted himself a little unsteadily onto a stool.

"I'm all right, I guess. Still a little agitated. I'm not sure it's all sunk in. How about you?"

"I am able to endure much."

I looked around the room. "This place isn't exactly the nicest place I've been in."

"To speak truth, epicurism and lust make it more like a tavern or a brothel than a grac'd palace."

The comparison seemed a little extreme, but I knew what he meant. His next comments, however, made me genuinely concerned about how much he'd imbibed. Pointing towards a rather dishy waitress of around thirty who was coyly stooping – knees discreetly bent, back straight – to distribute drinks to group of already well-lubricated businessmen, he asked, "Is not my hostess of the tavern a most sweet wench?"

"She's quite attractive," I replied neutrally. In fact, she was a good deal more than that; she was taller and leaner than me, with dark hair carefully arranged in a French braid and perfectly arched black eyebrows surmounting deep green eyes of surprising lustre and sparkle. "Okay, she's very attractive," I admitted.

"And, I'll warrant her, full of game. Her wanton spirits look out at every joint and motive of her body. If ladies be but young and fair, they have the gift to know it."

"Jake, that's a bit . . . ."

"O look! She gives the leer of invitation. Shall I entreat a word?"

He didn't wait for an answer. And, to be fair, the waitress he was focusing on was working her hips like a slightly stoned fashion model and flashing the emerald high-beams to everyone within range. As soon as the beams fell upon Jake again, he gave the signal. She didn't need to be summoned twice.

"Hi, I'm Helen." She smiled demurely and placed a couple of paper coasters in front of us. "What can I do you for?"

It was a tired old line, but – who knows? – perhaps it still worked here; the clientele didn't exactly look sophisticated. Given Jake's comments, I figured we might get further with her if I did the talking.

"I'd like a glass of white wine – Chardonnay, if you have it." Giving her my best girlfriend-to-girl-friend smile, I added, as casually as I could: "Tell me, Helen, how do things work around here? With the waitresses, I mean? They seem exceptionally . . . friendly."

She was taken aback, but only for a second. She's probably used to inappropriate comments and, as these things go, mine hadn't been all that bad. Still, her eyes narrowed a little (intensifying the beams) and her voice tightened: "Oh yeah, we're a friendly bunch."

Jake wasn't buying it. "These women are shrewd tempters with their tongues."

"Most of the girls are quite talkative, that's true," she replied, choosing to go with the more benign interpretation of his comment. "It makes for a better atmosphere."

"So the management doesn't mind?"

"It's encouraged here. Most of our clientele are men. They like to get to know the waitresses."

"And the waitresses?"

"Set them down for sluttish spoils of opportunity and daughters of the game," Jake answered for her.

I cringed. However true it might be – and I wasn't at all sure there was much truth in it – I had no doubt how she would take it. If it had been me, I'd have been struggling with an urge to belt him one.

"What the h. . . ?!" she exclaimed.

Fortunately, she was called away to another table. I'm sure she would have jumped at any excuse to leave. Jake seemed to harbour a lot of hostility, even prejudice, against her and the other women who worked there. His next comment only served to reinforce that impression. "This woman's an easy glove; she goes off and on at pleasure."

I had to take him to task. Men, in my opinion, are inclined to judge women too severely too quickly, and I don't like it. "Jake, that was really uncalled for. Why are you being so hard on her?"

"On my honour," he replied nonchalantly, "she

was charged with nothing but what was true and very full of proof."

"Nonsense! You basically called her a prostitute and you have no proof whatever. Besides, why charge her with anything at all? You're forgetting that we need her help."

"So should I give consent to flatter sin?" He bristled with indignation – false or not, I couldn't tell. "She's a bed-swerver, even as bad as those that vulgars give bold'st titles."

"A bed-swerver?!! Give me a break!"

"O, most true," he insisted, "she is a strumpet."

As he uttered this ever-so-charming epithet, I noticed out of the corner of my eye that Helen was almost upon us again. "Careful – she's coming," I whispered.

Unfortunately, my warning came too late. "What did he call me?" she asked briskly as she plonked a glass of wine in front of me.

He replied calmly, "Are you not a strumpet?"

She looked at me. I shrugged and translated: "He means a slut."

She was livid. "I am not a slut – or anything like it!"

"What, not a whore?" he replied, as if he were simply trying to clarify an obscure point of fact. "Now, pretty one, how long have you been at this trade?"

"What?! Now you're calling me a whore?!" It looked as if she were about to hyperventilate. I think it was the only thing that kept her in place.

"Jake, for God's sake!" I exclaimed.

"What is that wrong whereof you both complain?" he answered coolly. "First let me know, and then I'll answer you."

Unsurprisingly, this attempt to sound like the voice of reason failed miserably. Helen, having recovered her wind and a fair bit of her composure, replied in a measured, almost steely, voice: "Listen, buddy, I don't think I'll talk to you anymore. If you have any more orders, you can place them at the bar."

"Please, Helen," I pleaded to absolutely no avail. Neither of them was listening to me; I'd vanished from their radar.

Jake showed not even the slightest concern that our source had just decided to clam up. In fact, her exasperation only seemed to feed his calmness. "What's the matter, lady?" he repeated. "Why, stay, and hear me speak," he added as she turned toward another table. "I have put you out: but to your protestation, let me hear what you profess."

She stopped abruptly and turned back. "Why should I profess anything? As far as I'm concerned, you can get out of here right now."

Again, he was unphased: "I will not, till I please. I have a little yet to say."

"Whatever it is, I'm not interested. The door's that way."

"No, madam, no; I may not leave it so. You shall hear me."

It did not seem to occur to him that he had absolutely no power to force her to hear anything. There was probably a bouncer around somewhere who'd be summoned any moment now. I wouldn't have minded giving him a bounce or two myself. I played the only card we had left: "Listen, Helen, we're here about Mandy. We're wondering if you could . . . ?"

The mention of Mandy riveted her attention. "What? You want to ask me questions about Mandy? I don't believe it. Why the fuck should I tell you anything about her?"

"Come on your ways," Jake wheedled. "Open your mouth; here is that which will give language to you, cat. She is dead. Tell her, Emilia." He leaned back to drain his glass.

Yeah, thanks Jake, that was real smooth. My mind was too jumbled to respond at first, but I knew I had to do it. "It's true, Helen. It might have been broken to you more delicately" – I glanced at Jake, whose face was totally blank – "but I'm sorry to say it is true. She's been murdered."

These words hit her like a ton of bricks; there's no better way to describe it. Her breathing seized up and her face flushed. Tears welled in her eyes. I wasn't sure she was going to be able to remain on her feet, so I pulled a stool over and motioned for her to sit on it. Usually that's discouraged in these places, but she didn't hesitate. With her elbows on the table and her hands covering her face, she began to sob quietly.

We needed to take a step back. "We should introduce ourselves, Helen. This is Jake and I'm Emma. We're in the play with her – you know, at the Shakespearean festival. She didn't show up this morning for rehearsal, so we were sent to fetch her. We went to her apartment building and persuaded the manager to let us in." Helen looked up slowly. "We found her body on the living-room floor. I don't know what to say. I'm so sorry."

She buried her face again and resumed her weeping. It was worse now. Jake was as sympathetic as ever: "O, now you weep, and I perceive you feel the dint of pity."

Helen seemed not to have noticed the sarcasm in his voice. She was struggling desperately to control, or at least contain, her emotions so as not to attract attention, and for a while it didn't look like a battle she had much hope of winning. Slowly, however, her breathing became less strained. Lifting her face from her hands once more, she dabbed the corners of her eyes with a napkin and began to speak softly: "She was supposed to be here tonight. It's unusual for her to miss a shift; she always calls in if she can't make it. I've been so worried about her."

With this, she started to break down again. I gave her another few moments, then I reached across to place a hand on her shoulder. Jake surprised me by doing the same to her other shoulder.

"What, still in tears?" he prodded, much more gently this time. "No more of this, Helena; go to, no more; lest it be rather thought you affect a sorrow than have it."

I was just about to translate when, still looking down, she replied, "Believe me, I have it. Mandy was the closest thing to a friend I have – had – in this town, certainly around here." She waved her hand around to indicate the club, then paused to blow her nose and wipe her eyes again. Those tasks accomplished, she looked up at us with large, tear-ringed eyes and asked: "Tell me how . . . it was done."

"We would do so, but we are prevented," Jake replied, shrugging slightly to indicate that it wasn't our fault that we couldn't give details.

Unfortunately, his gesture failed utterly; she was livid again. "Fucking hell! You're just going to tell me she's dead, but nothing else? Well, you can go fuck yourselves."

"Helen," I pleaded, "we really need to talk with you."

"That's not going to happen. No fucking way! If I do any talking, it will be to the police and nobody else."

She would have stomped off – who could blame her? – were it not for the firm grip that Jake maintained on her shoulder. "Do not play in wench-like words with that which is so serious," he said, bringing his face close to hers and staring intensely into her eyes. Her high-beams had dimmed, but his were on full strength. "Show those things you found about her, those secret things. This being done, let the law go whistle." So much, I thought, for the promise to stay within the bounds of legality.

"Why should I?" she retorted. "Are you a private investigator or something?"

"I do not say I am one," he replied, "but I have a hand."

"You 'have a hand'? What the fuck does that mean?"

I stepped in again. "What he means, Helen, is that Mandy's father asked Jake and me to look into it."

She looked at me incredulously. "Why?"

"I think he wasn't that confident of the police."

"Can't blame him," she muttered.

What did she mean? Was she just expressing a sense of caution, perhaps a skepticism of the authorities in general, or was there something more specific behind that remark? "Also," I continued, "he thought that since we knew her – or I did – and we move in the same theatrical circles, we might be able to discover things that the police miss."

"Well, I suppose that's possible," she allowed. "There's certainly a lot going on here that no one knows about – or if they do, they're not saying anything about it."

Another provocative comment. Jake had registered it as well. "I prithee, tell me what you meant by that," he asked, his tone now much more subdued.

Is there something about a 'prithee' that women cannot resist? It had worked on me (as the preceding pages testify) and it was having the same effect on her. She sighed heavily, took a sip from the glass of water on her tray, and began. "Listen, it's not the way you think. No one's obliged to do anything with the customers. It's not like that. But that doesn't mean it's just an ordinary club. The owner of this place is Brian Chiang. He's a big property developer; he's also a good friend of Winfred Gates, the city counsellor. Gates is as powerful as they come in this town, believe me. Nothing gets built without his say-so."

"I know who you mean," I said. "He's a big patron of the arts as well. In fact, he was at a party our cast had last night, although I think he was there for just a few minutes. Doesn't he chair the board that controls zoning and building permits for the city?"

She nodded. "I think that's what gives him the leverage. That and his connections to big money. It means the rest of the City Council don't dare stand in his way. Even the mayor won't stand up to him. That's what people say, anyway."

"I have heard of such," Jake said. "Our whole city is much bound to him."

"So are a lot of the girls who pass through here." She leaned a little closer. It felt as if it were all going to come out now, and so it was. "These guys – they're both loaded. Big bucks. And they like to play. If you catch their eye, they take you out, splash some money around. Many of the girls really go for that – the limousines, the high-end restaurants, the exclusive clubs. And especially the parties with important people – big shots, high rollers, even celebrities. Who's going to say 'no' to that? Of course, the girls understand that there are expectations, and most of them are okay with that . . . most of the time, anyway."

"What about Mandy?" I asked. "She was very beautiful. She must have drawn a lot of interest."

"It would be every man's thought," Jake observed. Thank you, Jake. Good to know we can always count on you for the male perspective.

"Oh, she drew a lot of attention, all right," she replied, "but her situation was different. You see, she was involved with Mr. Gates himself, and that protected her, more or less. At least from the other patrons."

"So they were an item?"

"I guess you could call it that."

A thought suddenly came to me. "Did he ever visit Mandy at her apartment?"

"Oh, sure. He'd pick her up there when they were going out. Lots of times."

Then he must be the regular visitor Mr. Lapierre mentioned, I realized, the one he couldn't – or as now seemed more probable, wouldn't – identify. I glanced at Jake, who indicated with a slight tightening of his lips that he'd reached the same conclusion.

"To be fair, Mr. Gates did a lot for her," she went on. "It wasn't just wining, dining and partying. He got her this job and he was also promoting her acting career."

Promoting her acting career? Did that mean he got her the Desdemona role? It would certainly explain a lot. Her rise in the local theatrical scene had been exceptionally rapid. I'd put it down to her talent – which was undeniable – and her youth and looks (also undeniable), but perhaps it was Gates's pull that had really got her over the top. The Festival depended not just on the good will of the city but also on its subsidies, I knew, and Gates controlled the city's arts subsidies program. His opinion could count for a lot.

The idea that Mandy might have slept her way into the Desdemona part was a comforting one – though rather perversely so, now that I think about it – but I didn't dwell on it at the time. Instead, it made me wonder about Mandy herself. Had she just been using Gates to get ahead? I wouldn't have thought so, but – who knows? – my impression of her may have been entirely mistaken. I decided to ask.

"Tell me, Helen, what did Mandy think of him, really? Was she with him just because of his money or his influence? Or could she have been genuinely involved with him? Even in love with him?"

"In love with him? No, I don't think so. Actually, I'm sure she wasn't. Mind you, he can be a lot of fun, even charming at times. Confidence is attractive, after all, and he has plenty of it. He also knows how to show a girl a good time. But she knew it wasn't for real; he has too much of a roving eye. Also, he's a lot older than her and probably married."

"You don't know?"

"I don't know and she didn't want to ask. All she really wanted was to get out of here as soon as she could. So would I, if I had any brains."

Jake had become very pensive as she was giving this account. When he spoke at last, his manner was almost confessional. "I prithee, lady, give me your pardon; I've done you wrong. The thorny point of bare distress hath ta'en from me the show of smooth civility." He placed his hand over hers.

"Yeah, thanks," she said. "Listen, I've got to get back to work."

"Are you going to be all right?" I asked.

"I don't know, to tell you the truth." She suddenly looked lost, even desperate. "I don't want to talk, or even think, about it right now. I just want to work."

Jake nodded and released her hand. "I can but thank you. We will speak further."

"Okay, whatever," she replied. "But do me a favour: don't tell anybody that I talked to you about this. It's not just my job that's at stake. Mr. Gates is a danger-ous man. You don't know him like we do."

"Do not you fear," he reassured her. "Upon mine honour, I will stand betwixt you and danger." He apparently has a thing for damsels in distress.

This damsel's eyes were now dry, though still edged in red. She returned his intense stare for the first time. "That's really not possible," she said. "You don't know what you're talking about. Please . . . don't say anything to anybody."

"Good, very good; let it be concealed awhile," he agreed. "I'll not speak a word."

"You promise?"

"'Tis in my memory lock'd, and you yourself shall keep the key of it."

I don't think she was entirely happy with this poetic response to what was clearly a serious concern. All she said was, "I've got to go," and quickly disappeared into the sea of increasingly rowdy patrons.

Jake leaned over to me. "I cannot choose but pity her. Believe me, she has had much wrong. There is more owing her than is paid; and more shall be paid her than she'll demand."

"You've certainly changed your tune."

"She is indeed more than I took her for. Much more."

As soon as I could find a different waitress in the vicinity (I didn't want to bother Helen again), I ordered another drink. We sat silently waiting for it to be delivered. My mind was anything but quiet, however. It was churning, struggling to make sense of what had just taken place. It was Jake's behaviour that obsessed me the most. He had begun by insulting and demeaning Helen, then had totally switched around and treated her as a victim, a woman trapped in a place that was beneath her. The ending was understandable, but why the brutal beginning? It had almost blown to bits our attempt to get information from her.

Perhaps, I wondered, he's one of those men who can only conceive of women as either tarts or madonnas, exceptional only in his ability to switch from one perspective to the other at the drop of a hat. And perhaps his sense of honour or honesty, his lack of patience, is so great that he really can't contain himself, even when it threatens a mission he has so solemnly sworn to undertake. These possibilities lend credibility, I was forced to admit, to my fear that he really is insane. For the most part, this fear had been displaced by the pace and tenor of events, but it couldn't be dismissed. Not entirely, at any rate.

Yet there was a second possibility, I soon realized. Perhaps there may have been some method in his madness, to put it in Shakespearean terms. The more I thought about it, the more likely it seemed that what we'd learned from Helen – in the end – was more than we ever would have got by questioning her calmly and respectfully. Had this been his strategy all along – to shake her up first, then reel her in with sympathy? And if so, what does it say about him? Is this whole Shakespeare thing, including the sudden outbursts of anger and indignation, just an elaborate ploy, a device he uses to achieve his ends? Who is he really?

These disquieting thoughts were interrupted by the sudden appearance of Kendrick Page, our missing colleague. He headed straight towards the far end of the bar. Although not in Jake's line of sight, he cottoned on to it immediately: "What sneaking fellow comes yonder?" He swivelled his stool to see better. "He's shrewdly vexed at something: look, he has spied us. Come, therefore, let's about it speedily."

He strode quickly across the room to occupy the barstool to Kendrick's left, while I followed suit by slipping onto the perch to his right. Our target had probably chosen that spot with the idea of avoiding company, but isolating himself in this way had facilitated the opposite outcome. It seemed like a metaphor for life. Perhaps fate is, above all, a master of irony. (Did Shakespeare say that? Someone should. Hmm. Perhaps no more drinks tonight, I concluded).

Jake's opening this time was smooth: "My dear Othello, I would crave a word or two, the which shall turn you to no further harm than so much loss of time."

"Don't call me that," Kendrick snapped back. "That's over now. Everything's over. Finished. I don't want to talk to anyone."

He was evidently feeling very sorry for himself.

"Is that why you didn't phone back?" I asked.

"Why should I? I've already talked to the police."

"You probably don't know, Kendrick, but Mandy's father has asked us to look into this for him. That means we need to ask some questions."

"I've had enough questions for now. Just leave me alone."

"I cannot brook delay," Jake riposted. "Come not within the measure of my wrath."

Kendrick bristled slightly, but then almost immediately relented; I don't think he was up for a fight. "I'm sorry. Just can't believe what's happened. Any of it."

Jake rose from his stool and gave the man's arm a gentle tug. "Let us withdraw into the other room."

Kendrick didn't resist. As we headed to the back room, where stuffed chairs replaced wooden ones and the noise was reduced by half, Jake ordered two whiskies from a passing waitress (I declined). We found a table in a corner and sat quietly for several minutes, waiting for the drinks to arrive. Jake, hitherto so impatient, was showing surprising restraint.

Once the whiskies had arrived and were duly devoured, he began: "To show an unfelt sorrow is an office which the false man does easy."

It was the same sentiment he'd put to Helen, but unlike her, Kendrick could respond in kind: "I do affect a sorrow indeed, but I have it too."

This was all too pals-y for me. I felt ready to

explode. "You're trading quotations with us?!" I exclaimed at Kendrick. "Exactly how broken up are you?"

At this point, he really did break down, burying his face in his hands and sobbing violently. I felt horrible. I had done to him more or less what Jake had done to Helen – if you leave aside the personal slurs. Is there something in human nature that makes us more tolerant of the weaknesses of our own sex than those of the other?

I don't have an answer to that, but I do know one thing: however tolerant men might be of other men's foibles, that doesn't extend to the shedding of tears. Jake leaned toward him and softly muttered, "Do, I prithee, but yet have the grace to consider that tears do not become a man."

Kendrick rallied at the implied threat to his manhood. He exhaled deeply, then asked: "Can't you tell me how she was murdered? The police wouldn't say anything." It was a plea for some consolation; unfortunately, we couldn't give any.

"Sir, I can nothing say."

"It's not our choice," I added. "The police insist."

"But surely you could . . . ?"

"Listen, Kendrick, Jake and I won't be able to get very far if we get on their wrong side."

"Okay, I get it, but can't you at least tell me whether she suffered a lot?"

"It was quick, very quick; that's all I can say. Now

you tell us, why did you leave the party early last night? And why did you disappear this afternoon? Especially this afternoon. You must have known it would put you directly in their sights."

"Yeah, I suppose it does," he replied, "but I wasn't thinking about that. I was thinking about her. I'd only known her a short time, but the news really hit me hard. I just had to get away."

"How well did you know her?"

"Not well, really. We'd met at an audition and got together a few times after that to run through our scenes together." He took another deep breath and exhaled slowly. "I can't believe she's gone."

"I can see how it might threaten your career, your big chance."

"It's much more than that; you don't understand. She was so gorgeous, so incredible in every way. I think I was falling for her, believe it or not." His face became almost radiant as he spoke these words, then the radiance dissolved as his gaze returned to his near-empty glass.

"Falling for her?" I prodded.

"I know," he replied, still looking down. "It's crazy; I hardly knew her. But I couldn't stop thinking about her. I was even starting to get possessive about her, if you can believe it."

Yeah, I could. "When was that? You mean, at the party?"

"Yes, exactly." He raised his head and looked at

me. "I was looking forward to the party so much. Of course, it marked the beginning of our production, which is a big deal for us, as you know. For me, especially; it's my first leading role. But I also saw it as an opportunity to get to know Mandy better – you know, in a more relaxed environment."

"You mean, with a few drinks in her?"

He ignored the question, as did Jake. I think they took it as understood.

"But at the party," Kendrick continued, "she barely paid me any attention. Mainly, she was circulating, greeting everyone. Then I saw her in what looked like a serious conversation with Mike. It unsettled me. I was going to approach her as soon as they finished, but she left shortly afterwards without saying a word to anyone."

"So you followed her?"

"No, I didn't," he replied regretfully. "I just stood there like an idiot, trying to soldier on. But I couldn't pull it off; I was so upset at being slighted – if that's what it was. Some actor I am, eh? Anyway, I left the party maybe fifteen or twenty minutes after she did."

"When was this?"

"Hmm . . . about ten-fifteen, I think."

"Where did you go?"

"I wanted to find her but I had no idea where she might've gone. I don't know where she lives – lived. The only thing I knew was that she worked here.

I guess I hoped that maybe she'd left the party because she had a late shift. I even hoped that perhaps, if it weren't too busy, she and I could have a chance to talk – you know, just the two of us. It was a stupid idea, but I was desperate. I guess that tells you how bad I had it."

"And did she show up here?"

"No," he said wistfully. "I don't know where she went, but it wasn't here."

"So what did you do?"

"I just sat here and drank."

"When did you leave?"

"It was at least one o'clock, probably more like one-thirty."

It felt like time to let the man nurse his wounds in peace. "You've been a big help, Kendrick, and we really appreciate it. I have just one more question. How did you know that Mandy worked here? Did she tell you?"

"No. But I was brought here once by Fred when she happened to be on duty."

"Who is't you mean?" Jake asked. It was his first intervention in quite a while. I wondered what he'd been thinking.

"Fred? That's Winfred Gates. You know, the big-shot politician."

Yes, we certainly did know. "Tell me, Kendrick, where did you meet him?"

"At one of the auditions for the play. That was three or four weeks ago. He's been really helpful, taken me under his wing, so to speak. He seems to think I have potential."

So Gates really does have an interest in the theatre – or am I being naïve? Could there be some advantage for him in cultivating young talent? I'm embarrassed to say I also wondered about myself. Should I be insulted that he's never sought me out, or should I thank my lucky stars? A little of both, I concluded.

"Do you happen to know where he is now?"

"No, I don't. He was at the party last night. He left just as I was arriving, then later on I saw him here with the owner of this place. In fact, I sat with them for a while; it helped to take my mind off things. But I haven't seen him today at all."

By this point, Jake apparently had decided, as I had, that that was enough for the time being. "Well, sir, good night. We thank you."

"Are you really going to investigate this?" he asked. His tone, understandably, was one of disbelief.

"We are resolved," Jake replied, "and in this resolution here we leave you." He rose to his feet. "So again, good night."

Kendrick just nodded and lowered his head. I gave him a pat on the shoulder as we abandoned him to his grief. It felt like a lame gesture even as I was doing it, but I couldn't think of what else to do.

All the tables in the main room were now occupied, so we returned to the bar, where Jake promptly
ordered a carafe of white wine. Just as he was pour-
ing me a glass (I was too unhinged to refuse), he
spotted another acquaintance. This one was much
less welcome – to me, at least. Jake showed no such
reticence.

"And in good time," he whispered as he slid me a
glass, "here the Lieutenant comes."

Lieutenant Knutsen spotted us immediately.
"Benatsky!" he hollered.

"Lieutenant, is it you whose voice I hear?" Jake
was apparently in the mood for a little fun. "What
good tidings comes with you?"

Knutsen closed in on us rapidly. "Listen you little
shit, I told you to stay out of this investigation . . . ."

"Come, Lieutenant, I have a stoup of wine."

But the good Lieutenant was not to be distracted,
even at the prospect of a free 'stoup'. "Beat it," he
said. "Get out of here. Go on home."

"Not this hour, Lieutenant; 'tis not yet ten o' th'
clock."

Knutsen was undeterred. He pointed his finger at
Jake. "You've been questioning witnesses before I've
had a chance to get to them. That could be construed
as interfering with a police investigation. That's got
to stop."

"I'll do my best, sir."

"Good. Now, get lost or I'm taking you in."

Jake decided to take the high road – or at least the road that didn't lead to a night in jail. Beaming a disarming grin at Knutsen, he announced: "You are in the right. Good night, Lieutenant."

✻ ✻ ✻

As we were leaving, I invited Jake to my place for a coffee. A strange move, I know, but I was feeling too wound up to sleep; so much had happened. For the first time in my life, I had seen a dead body. And not just any body – the body of a woman I'd known. To make matters worse, I was now involved in investigating her murder. What do I know about murder investigations? Absolutely nothing. And this isn't just any run-of-the-mill killing, like a home invasion gone wrong. There may be powerful forces involved, people like Chiang and Gates who, for all I know, may be able to eliminate anyone who gets in their way. What chance would we have against people like that? To cap it all off, my partner in the investigation might actually be a madman.

"Tell me your mind," Jake said. He was installed in my favourite armchair, delicately nursing his coffee as if he weren't sure it was safe. Admittedly, it was only instant coffee; that's all I'd had the energy to make.

"What am I thinking at the moment?" I replied

disingenuously. It crossed my mind that it's probably not a good idea to express doubts about a man's sanity when you're alone with him at night and he's been drinking. But was I really concerned about that? In truth, I wasn't. I had a growing sense that this man sitting in front of me, whatever he was, wasn't out of his mind. I think I knew that when I invited him in. But I also knew he was not going to give up the investigation, despite the risk we might be facing and the odds stacked against us. "It's this. You weren't exactly frank with Knutsen, were you? You're not going to back off."

A slight smile creased his face. "I am constant to my purpose."

"But why?" I retorted. "Just because of what you said to Mandy's father?"

"I have promised, and I'll be as good as my word."

"I'm not sure that's what Helen wants. I think she would be happier if you just gave up." Suddenly, I felt my energy level crash. "God, I'm tired."

He seemed surprised. "How have you come so early by this lethargy?"

"Christ, Jake. It's been a long, difficult day."

He sat back and reflected for a moment. "I will weary you then no longer with idle talking. With what haste you can, get you to bed. The long day's task is done, and we must sleep."

Glad as I was of this response, I felt badly that I'd invited him in and was now ushering him out before he'd even had a chance to finish his coffee. Perhaps coffee isn't really his drink of choice. "Are you sure I can't get you something else?"

"I have heard it said, unbidden guests are often welcomest when they are gone."

That affected me somehow. He hadn't been unbidden, but I was definitely unbidding him now. I couldn't resist reaching across and touching his arm.

Again, the slight smile appeared. "I am so much a fool, should I stay longer, it would be my disgrace and your discomfort: I take my leave at once." And so he did. I was too tired even to think of calling him a cab, much less offering to drive him home.

As it turned out, I couldn't get myself to bed with any of the recommended haste. I had to get the evening down, even if only roughly. I opened my laptop, downloaded the voice recordings from my phone, and began to write.

In all, it required about forty-five minutes to enter the relevant facts – at least, those that seemed relevant (it wasn't always clear). Even then, I couldn't settle my mind; I kept wondering about Jake. It suddenly occurred to me that I should google him. I entered 'Jacob Benatsky' in the search engine. It produced, well, nothing of any value, so I tried just 'Benatsky'. It yielded a bunch of Czech websites, which suggested the surname might be Czech, but that was basically it. Perhaps his family escaped Czechoslovakia for Britain in 1938 when the Nazis marched in, I wondered, or else just after the war, before the Soviets took over the country and closed the borders?

Why was I being so fanciful? His roots are probably much more mundane. Yet I was still curious, so I tried Facebook. Again nothing. No luck, either, with any of the other social media sites I knew. I don't think I'd ever met anyone who was so entirely off the grid. In fact, it suddenly struck me, he doesn't even have a mobile phone, as far as I can tell. I really must find out more about him.

*T*UESDAY, JUNE 16. DAY.

I awoke feeling surprisingly refreshed. Perhaps it helped that I'd written out yesterday's events before I went to bed; I'd slept like a baby. There had been no further word from Walt or Eddie, so I assumed that the rehearsal would still take place and proceeded to what I now decided would be my morning treat – a double latte with an apricot croissant at Ingrid's. It was while I was indulging in this small pleasure that I received a phone call from Simon Catling.

Simon had moved on a lot since I was last in contact with him. He was now the reporter covering the city desk for the *Daily News*, which, despite all the competition from the internet, still commands a considerable following in the city. He is also married, which is sensible, I thought, since he always seemed to need someone and I knew fairly early on in our relationship that it wasn't going to be me. The call could only be about business, as indeed it was.

The *Daily News* was giving considerable play to the story of the beautiful young actress murdered just as she was about to appear in her first starring role, and when Simon saw my name among those who had discovered the body, he had all the ammunition he needed to take charge of the coverage. He was phoning to set up an interview. I explained that I didn't know when I could see him, since the rehearsals were still on – a fact he found interesting or at least newsworthy – so he settled for a few quick questions over the phone.

I was happy to oblige. It seemed to me that the more media coverage the story garners, the better; it would put pressure on the police to prioritize the case. It wasn't just that it might otherwise get bogged down through indolence or neglect. Suppose the murder actually did have something to do with Councillor Gates? Given his influence in City Hall, could the police be counted on to pursue the case effectively? And what if it also involved Chiang and other powerful individuals who turned out to have things to hide? We needed the press to get interested.

All it took was mentioning that the murder victim had been involved with Gates to conjure visions of Watergate in Simon's imagination. According to him, this could be the biggest thing to hit this town since . . . well, ever. They had already uncovered strong indications that the Councillor was up to his elbows in questionable dealings, but they'd never been able to find enough evidence to go into print with it. This could be just the opening they needed to get the authorities interested, or so he said.

He was reluctant to give further information, but

I pressed him. I may have made it sound like my cooperation was contingent on knowing more; in any case, he yielded a few tantalizing details under a strict promise of confidentiality. Their investigations had revealed a pattern in which development proposals backed by certain developers were favoured in the approval process, either by imposing less stringent demands in terms of social housing and public amenities, or by allowing variances from certain by-laws, particularly those involving allowable height and density. In addition, the careful tailoring of these proposals suggested that they may have benefitted from inside information as to what various city councillors were looking for, or at least what they would be willing to sacrifice.

It was all very flimsy, however. Every by-law variance, every reduced demand, could be justified in some way; nothing clearly rang out malfeasance. What was really needed was evidence that Gates benefitted in some way from any of this, but there the trail went cold. They hadn't been able to uncover any indication that he has, or had, a beneficial interest in any property development company, nor that he has ever received any kind of payoff. All that could be established is that he has a major stake in an importing business. It imports mainly from China, but whether that creates a conflict of interest with developers such as Chiang, who was born in Hong Kong and has family there, could not be determined.

Simon, nonetheless, was undeterred. He smelled blood. He insisted he had to interview both Jake and me in person as soon as possible. He also wanted me to tell him more about Jake. Who is he? Why did he want to accompany me to Mandy's apartment? I knew I couldn't even attempt to answer those questions, not even to myself, so I put him off by agreeing to arrange a meeting – ideally, for sometime today. It wasn't just deflection on my part. Since men tend not to take women seriously when it comes to politics, I figured that Simon might be more committed to pursuing the political angle if his source were another man. I made a mental note to approach Jake as soon as I could.

As I walked up to the theatre entrance, I could no longer prevent myself from wondering what was going to happen with the production. Could they really continue without their leading lady? Would I be asked to step in? Shortly after I arrived, I got the word. While the situation was still under evaluation, they'd temporarily given the Desdemona role to Mandy's understudy. She's very young, very sweet, and as was soon to become apparent, very much out of her depth. I have to admit I was disappointed not to have been asked; I'm far more experienced and have played roles of this magnitude before. It felt like another nail in the coffin – a rather unfortunate analogy in the circumstances, I know.

Throughout the rehearsal, Jake focused almost entirely on his own role. He has that annoying English way of speaking Shakespeare's lines so naturally that it makes every else's delivery seem just a little contrived and awkward. Well, he's had a lot of practice at it. Nevertheless, several of the cast members were clearly put out and few of them attempted to interact with him during the breaks. I did try, of course – several times, in fact – but without success. He seemed to resent any effort to strike up a conversation.

By the time the rehearsal ended – around five-thirty – I was feeling more optimistic. Perhaps it was that our new Desdemona had been so inept that it seemed inevitable that I would be approached about the role soon. Or perhaps it was just that I was acting again, living through someone else's emotions rather than my own. Jake's mood didn't seem to have changed much, but I was determined to break the ice. We had things to discuss.

I decided to take an upbeat approach: "What, ho, good Iago!" I exclaimed in a deliberately stagey fashion as I sat down next to him.

He looked up from the script he was perusing with single-minded intensity. (Who does he think he's fooling? He knows every line in Shakespeare). "I am glad to see you in this merry vein," he replied. His tone was tinged with that withering sarcasm the English do so well.

"But you seem a little less so."

"Indeed, I have been merrier," he admitted. "I have not that alacrity of spirit, nor cheer of mind, that I was wont to have."

"Are you afraid that the play will be cancelled?"

"I am not."

Okay, not that. "It isn't about last night, is it? I'm sorry I asked to you leave like that. It was just . . . ."

He raised a hand to forestall me. "You take things ill which are not so, or being, concern you not."

"It must be the murder, then. I think it's got everyone a little shaken up. Are you still determined to look into it?"

"I will die a hundred thousand deaths ere break the smallest parcel of this vow."

That seemed a little strong; he was truly in a grim mood. "If that's the case," I responded, "then I really would like to talk to you." I looked around at the general hubbub of sets being erected or adapted, wardrobes being fiddled with, and performers wandering about, gossiping and laughing. "But not here. We need somewhere more private."

He perked up at that suggestion. "Come with me. I will bestow you where you shall have time to speak your bosom freely."

Charming Jake was returning and I was glad of it. "Where do you have in mind?"

"The most convenient place that I can think of. I will lead the way."

The place was indeed convenient – a small French café, Chez Panisse, located just four blocks from the theatre. We settled at a table in a secluded corner of the inside dining area. Though the room was light and pleasant, his mood seemed to have darkened again. Remembering my preference for white wine, he proposed a French sauvignon blanc, *Veuve du Pape*. We waited quietly until it arrived. I used the interlude to pretend to check for messages, then placed the phone beside my napkin.

The wine arrived promptly and was at once put to the test. I knew better than to interrupt the absurd ritual of swirling, sniffing, and tasting that men seem to relish. With everything to his satisfaction, he spoke at last: "Sure, you have some hideous matter to deliver, when the courtesy of it is so fearful. Speak your office."

Speak my office? Why the sudden lurch toward formality? And why the apprehension? "It's not hideous at all," I reassured him. "In fact, I think it's good news. This morning I got a call from a reporter I know at the *Daily Mail*. His name's Simon Catling. He wants to look into Mandy's murder. He was fascinated to learn that she was involved with Winfred Gates. According to him, Gates is rumoured to be up to his elbows in corruption, graft – you name it."

"Rumour is a pipe blown by surmises, jealousies, conjectures," he declared dismissively.

"I think the information he has is a little more solid than that. Nothing incriminating as such, but it looks very suspicious."

"How so?"

I recounted what Simon had told me as best I

could. I thought the news would stimulate him as it had me, but he just stared icily at his glass. To relieve the awkward silence that followed, I launched into an extended account of the advantages of talking to the press. As I was making my final point, about us needing allies in case the police proved to be corrupt or corruptible, my phone rang. Jake sighed, grasped his glass and leaned back on his chair – universal signs that permission to take the call had been (grudgingly) granted.

It was Simon. He wanted to know whether I'd spoken to Jake yet. "We've just been talking about it," I replied. "He's here right now."

I extended the phone to him, but he wouldn't take it. "Who is it in the press that calls on me?" he asked disingenuously.

"It's Simon, the reporter I was just telling you about. He can provide more about the political side of this business. Will you hear him out?"

"I do not think it good."

This was awkward. "Jake, please. He can explain . . . ."

"I understand the business."

"But Jake . . . ."

"Look not so upon me. I will not yield."

I was going to have to ring Simon back. I made my excuses and hung up. "Jake, what's going on? I gave you good reasons why we should do this."

"Good reasons must, of force, give place to better,"

he replied.

"Better? What do you mean?"

"I mean, men may construe things after their fashion, clean from the purpose of the things themselves."

"You don't trust the press, is that it? You think they may have their own agenda, one that may not be consistent with ours? Sure, they want to sell newspapers," I acknowledged, "but wouldn't it be in their interest to reveal that a powerful figure in city government is involved in a murder? Even the publicity value of exposing Gates's close involvement with a big property developer should be worth their while. It's a win-win."

"I do not think so. 'Tis better as it is."

Why is he being so obstinate? I wondered. He's the one who's determined to solve this crime, yet here he is rejecting help from someone with much more investigative experience and a much deeper understanding of local government than either of us have, not to mention the power to mobilize public opinion, which could easily prove to be critical. It doesn't make sense. Not much about this man does.

My befuddlement must have shown, because then he said: "You throw a strange regard upon me, and by that I do perceive it hath offended you. To make a sweet lady sad is a sour offence; pardon me, sweet one."

I appreciated the apology, but it wasn't enough to

mollify me. Not this time. "You know, I'm not getting it. I don't understand you. You hide behind this weird Shakespeare thing and I can't get any real fix on you."

"You do seem to know something of me, or what concerns me," he responded.

"I know nothing!" I protested. Hearing the edge in my voice, I decided to ease off and try a more positive approach. "Let's mend that. Why don't you tell me something about your background?"

He shrugged. "What I have been I have forgot to know. 'Tis past, and so am I."

"Oh, come on," I smirked. "You expect me to believe you've forgotten your past?"

"I remember a mass of things, but nothing distinctly."

"Nonsense. That's virtually the same answer, just from a different play. You must think I'm an idiot."

"But I am sure I do not."

Is it only the English who can utter a line like that and make it sound ambivalent? "Then what's the problem?"

"If I should tell my history," he replied, "it would seem like lies disdain'd in the reporting."

"So you're just going to stonewall me – is that it?"

"I do not talk much."

"Give me a break!" I was getting pretty fed up by this point. This guy hides in the poetry like a sniper in the tall grass, and when he's cornered, he claims his right to silence as if he'd been taken prisoner. Next, he'll be spouting his rank and serial number. I was ready to give up on this whole ridiculous enterprise. My normal life, such as it is, was looking better and better.

He must have sensed my exasperation. "Pardon me, I pray you. I desire you in friendship, and I will one way or other make you amends."

"How?"

There was a slight hesitation, after which he declared: "Examine me upon the particulars of my life."

It seemed like an extraordinary concession, coming from him. I looked hard into his eyes, trying to see if he were serious. The problem, as so often, was that his expression was simultaneously intense and vacant. I decided to proceed with caution; this could be a minefield.

"Well then, let's see. Obviously, you're English. Do you still live in England?"

"Not now."

"So where do you call home these days?"

"I have none. No place will please me so."

"Really? So you just travel around, taking parts where you can?"

"Yes, in truth. I like the work well."

"Your work – it's mostly Shakespeare, I take it?"

"For the most part."

"And you have enough of it to make a living?"

"Ay, and more."

"Hmm. If you don't mind my asking, how is it that I've never heard of you – if you've done so much?"

"Follows it that I am known well enough, too?"

"I think it does."

"Well, then, I cannot tell what to think on't. It is a mystery."

"Really?"

He winced slightly. "I must confess, 'tis partly my own fault. I could be well content to entertain the lag-end of my life with quiet hours."

I could have quibbled about the 'lag-end' part – he couldn't have been more than forty – but an actor who preferred obscurity? That was definitely hard to buy. I sensed, though, that he wasn't going to yield much more along these lines – not yet, anyway – so I moved to what I thought would be more neutral ground. "Tell me this: are you married?"

He raised his glass and slowly drained it.

"Well?" I prodded.

"Wisely I say, I am a bachelor."

"Wisely? Why do you say that? Are you against marriage?"

He dismissed the notion with a wave of his hand. "That's as much as to say, they are fools that marry. You are too absolute."

"So you're not against marriage in general, just for yourself?"

"I'll have no wife," he affirmed with raised eyebrows. "I did never think to marry."

"All right, then, what about a relationship? Is there no special person in your life? A girlfriend?" Silence. "A boyfriend?" Still no reaction. "Has there ever been anyone?"

He paused for a moment. "There was a lady once. She was the first fruit of my bachelorship. Now I am alone."

Finally, an opening; I resolved to remember this brand of wine. "What happened?"

"'Tis an old story."

"I want to hear it."

He shrugged wearily. "Had time cohered with place or place with wishing . . . . She was too good for me."

"Oh, Christ!" I exploded. Just when I thought we were getting somewhere, he'd thrown out that corny old excuse. I was expecting a much classier level of obfuscation from this guy.

"Now my love is thawed," he went on, oblivious to my outburst. "Let that suffice you." He cast me a disconcerting glance as he refilled our glasses.

But it didn't suffice me. Something bothered me about what he'd said; I just couldn't put my finger on it. It wasn't the news that he'd once been in love – that made him seem more normal, more human.

Perhaps it was the finality of it. "Are you certain you won't change your mind about her? Or she about you?"

"No, it cannot be. I am sure of that."

There was a touching sadness in his voice. I wondered how far his abnegation would go. "Surely, you could still commit to someone else? I mean, if the right woman came along."

"Believe me," he responded, "there is no such thing in me."

That's it, I thought. What had bothered me was the idea that, for him, love was just a one-shot deal, an experience that could never be repeated. That's definitely not normal – not nowadays, at least. "So you'll just do without?"

"But is there no quick recreation granted?" he retorted archly, a slight smirk on his face. "As you know, no settled senses of the world can match the pleasure of that madness! And abstinence engenders maladies, so they say."

I couldn't help smiling. "I don't know about the maladies, but I can't argue with the madness part. But couldn't that madness lead to something more enduring – better, even?"

"Not so, sweet lady. Things won are done; joy's soul lies in the doing."

"Okay, I get it. You like the adventure, the thrill of the conquest, but once that's over, you get restless." Now he seemed only too human – too male. I decided to seize the high ground. "So, basically, you just move from one woman to another. As long as your sexual needs are taken care of, that's all you really want. Apart from the conquest thing, of course. In short, love'm and leave'm – with a little poetry thrown in to buff it up a bit."

"Heavens, how deeply you at once do touch me!" he protested. "Touch me not so near."

Surprisingly, he seemed genuinely hurt. (I say 'seemed' because it's hard to tell when he's sincere; he dissembles so well.) I pressed my advantage, nonetheless. "Well, it's true, isn't it?"

"Now do I see 'tis true," he admitted. "Such a one do I profess myself."

"Spoken like a true man."

It was a feeble attempt at withering sarcasm and he just shrugged it off. The contrition was over. "I am a man as other men are. However we do praise ourselves, our fancies are more giddy and unfirm, more longing, wavering, sooner lost and worn, than women's are."

"Men just want to have fun – is that what your saying? But what about companionship?" I persisted. "Sharing 'life's uncertain voyage'? You see no value in that?"

He sounded wistful as he replied, "In faith, I do not. I myself am best when least in company."

It was a beautiful line for a sad reality, I thought. "I certainly can't say that. But I have to admit, finding the right person is no easy task."

His mood seemed to change at these words. "Give me your hand," he said. Fortunately, he meant the hand that wasn't gripping the glass; otherwise, I might have resisted. Then he locked those intense eyes on me. "Make me acquainted with your cause of grief, for it is a way to make us better friends, more known."

How did he detect that there was any grief involved? Or was he just guessing, grasping at any straw that might allow him to shift the conversation to my life? I was more inclined to suspect the latter, but I also felt a need to get some things off my chest. Still, I hesitated.

"Come," he urged, using that same gentle tone of voice that he'd previously employed to announce Mandy's death, "quench your blushes and present yourself that which you are."

"What?"

"Speak freely what you think. I long to hear it at full."

"Okay, top me up first." He did, and I undid half his work in one quick move. "This is personal, you understand? Promise you'll keep this entirely to yourself?"

"If I do not, never trust me; take it how you will."

"That's not totally reassuring. This is difficult to talk about."

"A heavy heart bears not a nimble tongue."

He may have meant to sound sympathetic, but his remark came across as a little glib. I've never been one to confide my innermost thoughts and feelings to others, and it made me doubt whether he was the right person to receive them. "Maybe I shouldn't . . . ."

He said simply, "I do desire it with all my heart."

That was a much harder line to resist. "Well, here goes," I said, swallowing my reticence along with the rest of my glass. "Until recently, I'd been in a long-term relationship with a married man. Well, a separated man."

"What was't to you?"

"The relationship? Quite a bit, I guess. To tell you the truth, I thought it was going to be permanent; I wouldn't have got into it otherwise. Bruce seemed totally committed."

"So you thought him."

"Another typical male response," I retorted. "Shouldn't a man be what he seems?"

"Certain, men should be what they seem," he granted.

"But he wasn't. Not in the end."

"There's no trust, no faith, no honesty in men. The truth is, men's vows are women's traitors."

"Exactly!" I said. "Some of the lines you come up with really do nail it." This guy can be such a good sounding-board, I thought – when he's in the mood. I was feeling more than a little appreciative now.

He refilled my glass. "What was the impediment that broke this off?"

"Ultimately, he found someone else."

"Younger than you?"

I nodded.

"I thought as much."

"All too typical of men, if you ask me."

"They are not constant, but are changing still: one vice, but of a minute old, for one not half so old as that."

"Well, the time frame wasn't quite so compressed," I replied, chuckling despite myself, "but you're on the right track."

Although I'd agreed with him, something felt wrong. He seemed to be pushing the theme that men, himself included, are inherently less constant than women. How is it, then, that he could have had that great love, the one he implies can never be replaced? A bizarre thought fleeted through my mind: could it be that he claims to be fickle simply because Shakespeare provided so many good lines for it?

As I toyed with that bit of whimsy, he concluded, "Sorry I am to hear what I have heard. You have great reason to be sad."

I believed him. "You know, I think I am still sad about it. To be completely honest, I really . . . I feel the loss, even now."

"Some more time must wear the print of his remembrance out. Consider this," he added, "it is perchance that you yourself were saved."

"What do you mean?"

"I must needs say you have a little fault. You know not how to choose a man."

"What? You think I'm just some foolish woman who . . . ?"

"I, madam?" he recoiled. "I never said nor thought any such matter."

"Yeah, well, maybe you're right," I replied, conceding the point anyway. Resignation was increasingly overtaking my spirits. I couldn't deny that my choices in men hadn't exactly been stellar. I took another sip. How he knew it I couldn't begin to fathom, but it didn't really matter, I decided; the only thing for it now was to accept the logical implication of my dismal track record. "To tell you the truth," I said, "I think I should follow your path. Just give up on relationships."

Surprisingly, that wasn't what he wanted to hear at all. "Be not so rash," he admonished. "These are very bitter words. You will not do't for all the world, I hope."

But I was in the mood to be rash. "No, I mean it: relationships are impossible," I declared as I took another sip.

He shrugged. "A comfortable doctrine, and much may be said of it."

It was a patronizing assessment, but I didn't

mind. I'd probably merited the condescension. I knew I was saying things that I didn't really believe, but I'd dug myself in. "Top us up again," I said. "This wine is really growing on me."

"Most willingly." He's a good man with a bottle, I'll say that for him.

"Okay," I resumed, "I'm willing to admit that relationships can work – sometimes, for some people. But not for me. We're the same in that respect, you and I. So why shouldn't I just give up on them, like you have?"

"Patience, I say; your mind perhaps may change."

"Why should my mind change and yours not?" I countered. "Is it because I'm a woman and therefore more emotional? Or because relationships matter more for women? That's just crap, you know."

"Come, come. This is the way to kindle, not to quench."

"What?"

"Put not your worthy rage into your tongue. You know not which way you shall go."

"No one does! Not even you. But sometimes it's necessary to take stock of one's life. What I've learned is that, like you, I'm not the kind of person who can do relationships. They're not for me."

"Do you know what you say? Many a man would take you at your word."

"So what? Why should I care?" I was getting quite indignant now. "Your problem is that you still think that the only thing any woman really wants is to get a man. Those days are long gone, my friend. There are lots of women who choose to live their own lives. I'm beginning to think that maybe I'm one of them."

"Do not think so; you shall not find it so."

"No, you're not listening. I'm telling you the way it is."

He was clearly losing patience as well. "Shall I hear more, or shall I speak at this?"

"Speak away." I took another swig.

"I will tell no tales. This is your own folly."

"So you *do* think I'm a foolish woman, after all?"

"Pardon me, I am too sudden-bold, but 'tis no matter; better a little chiding than a great deal of heartbreak. Dangerous conceits are, in their natures, poisons."

"All right, Mr. Know-It-All," I snapped back, "what would you suggest I do? Join a dating service?"

"That's not my desire. Let me persuade you take a better course."

"What better course do you have in mind? 'Pray you tell me your remedy'." As sarcasm goes, it was an improvement. Quoting Shakespeare really helps, at least for that.

"Fortune brings in some boats that are not steer'd," he replied. "Be patient, for the world is broad and wide."

"That's it?" I exclaimed. "I should just leave it to chance because, eventually, my ship will come in?"

"Hear me with patience but to speak a word. I will be brief. Remember who you are. You are well favour'd, and your looks foreshow you have a gentle heart. Do not, for one repulse, forego the purpose that you resolved to effect."

There was a compliment in there, I knew, but also a rather arrogant assumption that he knew what I really wanted. Even if he were right about that, the strategy he proposed for getting it seemed unconvincing, if not completely senseless. "So what you're really saying is, just keep on doing what I've been doing all along. Just use better judgment when it comes to men and it'll all work out. Is that it?"

He looked at me intently for a moment. Then, as if deciding to forego further explanation, he simply said, "I speak no more than truth. Our remedies oft in ourselves do lie, which we ascribe to heaven."

"And you know this because . . . ."

"I have seen more days than you."

"That's it?! You know more because you're older and wiser?" I was almost sputtering. "That's just bloody-minded arrogance!"

"But yet I know you'll do as I advise."

"You don't know that!" I shrieked.

"So I do: what's the matter?"

"How can you possibly know?"

He shrugged. "I read your fortune in your eye."

"What!?" I cried incredulously.

But it was no matter. He glanced at his watch and began to rise. Evidently, having said his peace, he was ready to move on. "Let us depart, I pray you, lest your displeasure should enlarge itself to wrathful terms."

"Sit down! I'm not finished," I exclaimed. I made a deliberate and demonstrative effort to calm myself – the body-language equivalent of sarcasm. "Let me see if I understand this. First, you tell me how to lead my life better – which, by the way, is exactly the opposite course to the one you prescribe for yourself. Then, when I don't buy in to your game-plan, you decide that there's no point continuing because I'm too emotional to be reasoned with."

"Come, come, no more of this unprofitable chat. One cannot speak a word, but it straight starts you. Well, I have told you enough of this. I will speak no more: do what you will; your wisdom be your guide."

He got up again and tossed a couple of twenties on the table. No time to wait for a bill, apparently.

"Wait a sec! Are you leaving – just like that?"

"I will not stay to offend you."

"Jake, you can't just walk out."

"What other would you expect? You are strangely troublesome," he added with pointed understatement, undoubtedly meant to highlight my irrationality.

"But, but . . . ." I was definitely sputtering now.

"Enough of this; talk no more. It helps not, it prevails not, and so I take my leave. Madam, good night."

The message was clear: I'd overstayed my welcome, proven myself just another difficult woman. Well, so be it, but we needed a plan. "What about the case?" I objected. "We need to figure out what to do, don't we?"

It was his turn to be taken aback. But his expression was one of despair, not surprise. "In truth, I know not where to turn," he confessed, lowering himself back onto his chair. "My thoughts are whirled like a potter's wheel; I know not where I am, nor what I do."

I realized then that this may have been what really was bothering him: he was stumped about the murder. And with good reason, I reflected. The most likely suspects we have are Gates and Chiang, but there's no evidence of their involvement so far, nor any reason to believe either one of them wanted Mandy out of the way. All we know is that Gates had been dating her (if 'dating' is the word for it), and had helped her find work. About Chiang I have nothing at all. They're powerful men and it's unlikely that either would grant us an interview. To make matters worse, everybody else connected to Mandy (her father apart) has an alibi: either by virtue of attending Walt's party or, in the cases of Helen and Kendrick, by being at the Brown Pelican.

The Brown Pelican. Of course. "Perhaps we should return to the nightclub," I suggested. "Helen said that Gates goes there often. Chiang must as well, since he's the owner. We need to interview them, and that may be the only place where we can get near them."

He seized upon it immediately. "You are right; there is no other way. Let it be to-night."

"What time? I doubt Gates or Chiang would show up before nine."

"Very well, then. Between nine and ten." And off he went.

* * *

I remained at the table for a while, my emotions still roiling. Apart from everything else that was going on, Jake had managed to open up another front: my personal life. It isn't a front that I like to do battle on, even with myself. It didn't help that I had drunk so much. I felt embarrassment creeping in.

Then I re-considered. Who better to talk to about one's life than a virtual stranger such as Jake? With family and friends, I've always felt the need to be at least somewhat guarded. Even with my closest friends and – dare I admit it? – with you, dear journal. And especially with my mother, who feels the baby clock ticking much more than I ever did.

But with him, it's different. Who knows where he came from or how long he'll be around? If the play is cancelled, he may be gone in a flash. (I had the sense he does most things in flashes.) Even when he's here, it's like he's not totally here – there's an elusive, evanescent quality about him I can't quite fathom. Yet somehow it makes me feel I can reveal to him whatever I want.

There's something else as well. Maybe some of the stuff I'd said was over the top, but so were his comments. He'd tried to portray himself as a 'wham, bam, thank you, ma'am' kind of guy, but I'm not buying it. He cares. He cared about that past love of his, a great deal apparently, and he seems to care about my future – however patronizing he was about it. What's more, as annoying as he can be, I'm beginning to trust him. He gave up more than he knows in our little tête-à-tête.

What this all amounted to wasn't clear to me, but what was clear was that there was a debt that needed to be discharged. It was the debt he owed to Helen. He'd said she was owed much, but I wasn't sure he was including himself among her debtors. I wasn't prepared to wait to find out.

I doubt I could have walked a straight line if pressed to do it, so I left my car where it was and took a cab to the Pelican. I probably looked no worse entering the nightclub than most customers look leaving it – a small consolation at best, I know, but I could go with it.

Fortunately, Helen was already on duty. In fact, with the happy-hour crowd dissipating and the evening crowd yet to arrive, it was a good time to pay her a visit. I persuaded her to take a break and join me for a few minutes. I was well over my personal alcohol limit and she isn't supposed to drink on shift, so we settled for tea.

"How are you doing?" I asked.

"I'm holding up," she replied guardedly.

"Did you get any sleep?"

"Not much."

She looked it. I decided there was no point in beating around the bush. "Listen, Helen, I'm really sorry about last night. We didn't realize when we came here that Mandy was a close friend of yours."

"You couldn't have known."

"We could have broken the news better. Jake . . . he's a strange guy. I don't really know him very well."

"I meet a lot of strange guys in here. Well, actually, not so strange – I always know what they want. They just tend to be creepy or obnoxious."

"But he said some things . . . ."

"Yeah, he was more blunt than I'm used to, but what he said about me is what a lot of them are thinking. At least, he was open about it. And he wasn't trying to hit on me or anything – not with you there."

"I doubt that he would have tried in any case. . . .

Oh, that came out wrong. I don't mean that he's gay or that you aren't attractive. You're very attractive. Any man . . . ."

She cut me off; she didn't need to be reassured on that point. "That's what got me this job. So it's good and bad, if you know what I mean."

I did. I went on: "I still feel I should apologize for him. I had no idea he was going to behave like that."

"I was offended, sure, but not that much. I'm not a hooker; if I was willing to go that way, I wouldn't be slinging drinks here, would I? But some of the things I've done. . . . Let's just say, lots of people, ordinary people, wouldn't consider them all that different."

"But he shouldn't have been that aggressive." I was warming to her considerably. "You know, at one point he even called you a 'bed-swerver'."

"A what?!"

"Exactly. Who knows? But it does convey a certain impression." It felt like time to elaborate a little on his manner of talking. "I don't know how to explain this, but he . . . uhm . . . uses strange language sometimes. You see, we're Shakespearean actors and I suppose some of the language carries over with us."

As an explanation it was pretty lame, and I was expecting her to challenge it, but she didn't. "I'd rather be called a bed-swerver than a lot of other things. In fact, there's a certain . . . oh, I don't know . . . a kind of elegance to the way he talks. It's brutal at times, but it can also be very dignified, even charming. He's like a tall, cool drink that has a kick at the end of it. Or at the beginning. You know what I mean."

Indeed I did; it struck me as quite a lovely way to put it. There's a lot more to this woman than I'd given her credit for. She continued, "I can't believe I'm saying this. I hated Shakespeare in school. Well, I hated school in general." She smiled. "You know, you're lucky to have him."

"Oh, I don't have him. I only met him yesterday morning at rehearsal, and quite frankly, I don't know what to make of him. Just before I came here, we were having some drinks at a café. I was trying to find out a bit more about him, but before I knew it, he'd turned the conversation to me and was telling me how my life should unfold."

"No kidding?" she said, clearly intrigued. "What kinds of things did he say?"

"Well, he told me that I've been making the wrong choices in men."

"Been there, done that."

"Then he told me what I had to do to fix it. When I protested, he just told me I'd follow his advice anyway. Well, you can imagine how I reacted."

"I'm guessing you were a little ticked off." She grinned.

"More than a little." I was grinning, too. "Then he simply decided he'd had enough and walked out."

"And that's why you're here."

"Yeah, I suppose. You're the only one I can talk to who knows about Mandy and has some idea what he's like. And I really do feel badly about what he said to you when we first met."

"Well, he did mellow a lot."

"Still, the whole thing puzzles me. Was he really outraged at your . . . what shall I call it? . . . your lifestyle? If so, why did he become so sympathetic once you'd explained a bit about Mandy and you? He seems like a man of sudden, intense emotions, but it may have been just a ploy to get you talking. Or maybe – I hesitate to say this – maybe he's just crazy."

"To tell you the truth, I kinda like his style. A real man of mystery. And in a way, it distracted me from thinking about Mandy; I was too busy defending myself. Later on, when I did start to think, some of the things he said made sense."

"Really? What do you mean?"

"Well, I began to realize that I get through my day-to-day life by not thinking about what I'm doing. I know this place isn't where I want to be. The whole set-up is sleazy, really. I also know I can't last here much longer, even if I wanted to. They like'm young and perky here. Once that goes, I'll be out the door on my butt."

She became more reflective. "Mandy was getting out. This role in your play was going to be her ticket. Even if that didn't pan out, I don't think she was going to hang around here much longer. Gates

wasn't going to be in the picture much longer, either."

"They were going to split up?"

"She was an inspiration for me, I suppose," she
went on, lost in her own thoughts. "But where am I
going to go? I don't have her acting talent, nor any
rich patron to open doors. I'm stuck. Maybe Jake's
anger was the boot in the ass I need to get me going.
If only I could figure out where to go."

"Be careful," I warned. "He just might tell you."

We both had a good chuckle at that. It seemed like
a good place to stop; she had to get back to work and
I needed some down-time before the evening. I told
her we'd be back later on. She took it with a shrug,
picked up her tray, and headed off to greet some arriving customers.

T UESDAY, JUNE 16. EVENING.

It was around nine when I arrived back at the Pelican. The place was moderately full, more so than yesterday at this time but well short of its capacity. Soon it would get crowded, which wouldn't be good for our aims, either.

As I entered, my eyes were immediately drawn to a bar table where Jake was sipping a drink and chatting with Helen. I hustled over, arriving within earshot just as she was saying, "she was a nice girl when she started here; just someone trying to make a living while she worked on her acting career. Then she . . . "

". . . turn'd to folly," he suggested.

Panic seized me. Oh God, Jake, don't say the rest of that line! It's from *Othello* and I know it well. I feared that if he said it, we would be launched straight into last night's exchange of accusations and protests. The rest of the line is: "and she was a whore."

"Jake!" I cried. He looked around at me with mock-surprise. He knew exactly why I was agitated and was enjoying it immensely. That jerk! I swallowed my embarrassment and greeted Helen, who looked nonplussed. She was probably wondering why I had intervened so rudely just as he was describing Mandy's situation with such delicacy and understanding.

Fortunately, I had a pretext to move on. It was more than a pretext really; we needed to confirm that Kendrick had been here throughout the evening of the murder until at least one a.m. I was inclined to believe him, but we couldn't just take his word for it. We should have checked last night when memories would have been fresher; our only hope was that Helen or someone else at the nightclub could still recall it.

"Hi, Helen. While we have you, can you tell us whether Kendrick was here the night before last?"

"Who's Kendrick?"

"He's the actor who plays Othello – you know, Desdemona's husband – in the play. He's a black guy, good-looking, well-built, about six feet tall. We talked to him last night just after we spoke to you."

"Oh, yeah, I know who you mean. How could I forget him? Yeah, he was here Sunday night as well. He kinda had the hots for Mandy, right?"

"Yeah, you could say that. Do you remember how long he was here that night? Did he talk to anyone?"

"Sure. He came in around ten, maybe half past. Just after Mr. Gates and Mr. Chiang arrived. He went over to talk with them for a while, then they left and he returned to the bar and sat alone, drinking. He was here till pretty close to closing time, probably around one-thirty."

"You seem to remember it pretty well. Are you sure?"

"As sure as I can be; we don't get that many black guys in here. Besides, that police detective who came here last night asked me."

Well, well. Score '1' for Lieutenant Knutsen, '0' for us.

"I see. You wouldn't happen to know if Gates will be showing up tonight, would you?"

"No idea. Mr. Chiang will probably be here, though. Can I get you something?"

"No, thanks. I think I'll hold off for the time being."

She grinned, promising to check back later.

I turned to my colleague. "Jake, I've been wondering. What if Gates decides to stop coming here, at least for a while, now that Mandy isn't going to be around? It might be days or even weeks before . . . ."

"You need not fear it," he cut in, a smile of contentment stealing across his face. "Here comes the rogue, I believe."

I swivelled around to see for myself. It was Winfred Gates, all right; there could be no mistaking him. He's a man of middling age and height, with powerful shoulders supporting a portly girth and a massive head crowned by a mane of sleeked-back silvery hair. This imposing frame was encased in a charcoal gray suit of impeccable craftsmanship. Most striking of all, perhaps, are the large brown eyes that seem to take in everything. All of this cast a pall on the shorter, thinner, and considerably less well-dressed East Asian man accompanying him, whom I took to be Brian Chiang. They headed straight for the back room, followed immediately by Helen; I guess it doesn't pay to keep the boss and his powerful friend waiting.

We held back to allow them time to settle in and start drinking; the jollier their mood, the better our chances. They were well into their second drinks when we decided that the moment had come. Perhaps it was the waiting, but suddenly I felt a wave of doubt. "This won't be easy, you know," I cautioned. "These guys probably know how to handle themselves."

"But, I think, you'll find they've not prepared for us."

"Maybe not, but whatever you do, Jake, don't lose your temper."

"Why not?"

"Remember what Helen said about Gates. He's dangerous."

He patted my hand. "You are afraid, and therein the wiser."

"Aren't you?"

He leaned towards me and confided: "I have a heart as little apt as yours, but yet a brain that leads my use of anger to better vantage."

I took this as an indirect criticism of my be-haviour this afternoon. If I'd had a few moments more to think about it, I might also have seen it as a confession that his disparagement of Helen last night had been strategic rather than heartfelt. But I didn't have those moments because he'd already risen from our table and shot off towards theirs. I followed quickly, not feeling reassured in the least.

The two men looked up quizzically, almost sus-piciously, as he came within range of their table. "Pardon me, sir," he said to Gates. "Let me have audi-ence for a word or two. I will not long be troubled with you; nor the time nor place will serve our long inter'gatories."

A flash of perplexity crossed Gates's face, but it quickly gave way to an expression of bemusement. He had been around the Festival long enough to rec-ognize the quotation game, and he must have no-ticed that Jake was very good at it. I'm not sure he realized that Jake had already taken a shot at him.

"You're Benatsky, that English actor who's playing Iago, aren't you?" he replied. "Glad to meet you. Oh, and you . . . I know you," he added, referring to me. "You've been in one or two of our productions. Very good."

He pulled his bulky frame onto his feet, shook Jake's hand, and reached over to pull back a chair for him. Chiang remained seated. Neither of them bothered to offer me either a handshake or a chair, which didn't surprise me at all. I was a little put out that Jake hadn't covered that breach in etiquette – it seemed atypical of him – but his attention was riveted on Gates. I took the remaining chair anyway.

"Now, what can I do for you?" he asked.

"May I be so bold to know the cause of your coming?"

"To this night-spot? Well, I come a lot, as it happens. My good friend here . . . oh, I forgot, this is Brian Chiang – he's the owner of the establishment. It's a lovely place to socialize." He paused for a moment. Perhaps it suddenly hit him that he was talking to people, not just actors. "Oh, forgive my manners. Can I offer you something to drink? No need to be bashful – they're on the house, aren't they, Brian." (I'd put a question mark, only it didn't sound at all like a question.)

"Absolutely, Fred," Chiang replied. "I'm always happy to support the arts." He chuckled. I doubted the arts figured high in his list of needy causes, if he had one.

Jake, for once, passed on the offer. He reached into his jacket pocket, pulled out a copy of the program for *Othello*, opened it to the page showing Mandy's picture and bio, and placed it in front of Gates. "Do you know this lady?" he asked.

Gates glanced grimly at the photo. "Why, of course I do. That's Mandy. Amanda Bennett. She is – was – a very great friend of mine. And a very talented actress, I might add. A great tragedy, her death."

"I do beg your good will in this case. I would fain know what you have to say."

Gates smiled at the use of the word 'fain'. "Oh yes, that's right, you're poking into this thing, aren't you? Lieutenant . . . what's his name . . . Knutsen – yes, that's it – he warned me about you. Actually, he told me not to say anything to you. He seems to have formed the impression that you're a troublemaker. I must say, I can see where he's coming from."

He reached for his drink – by the looks of it, a whisky – swirled it gently and took another sip. "But you know what? I'm touched by your concern. This is a terrible business and – who knows? – maybe you can come up with something useful. I don't mind helping you out, if I can."

He leaned back in his chair and looked up towards the ceiling, as if what he had to say were so complicated and lengthy that he had to think about where to begin. I suspected that it had more to do with deciding how much he was going to reveal.

"Let me give you some background," he began, taking another sip from his glass. "I met Mandy at a party, oh, about six months ago. She was at loose ends. She had a real passion for acting, but all that had come her way were a few small parts – not nearly enough to live on. She was essentially broke, but very determined to make it, you know what I mean? Didn't want to have to go back home, dragging her tail between her legs."

He paused for a moment, as if relishing her vulnerable state when they first met. It must have been like shooting a large fish in a small barrel. "She was – how shall I say this? – very presentable from a male point of view," he went on, addressing this last observation to me, "so it occurred to me that she might make a suitable cocktail waitress here. I sent her to Brian, he agreed with my assessment, and that was that."

"I like to help struggling artists," Chiang explained, as if he felt an obligation to bear this heavy but necessary burden. He was clearly bemused by all of this.

But I wasn't. In fact, I'd already reached the limit on my bullshit meter. "It wasn't just a waitressing job, though, was it? What we've heard is, ..."

Gates cut me off before I could continue. "I can imagine what you've heard, Ms. . . . What did you say your name is?"

"It's Emma Marwick. Thanks for asking," I added with a good dollop of sarcasm.

"Listen, Ms. Marwick, I'm going to be frank with the two of you because I know you're going to find out anyway. Nothing illegal or improper is going on here. We . . . Brian hires attractive waitresses because it brings in the customers – people like me who enjoy the company of young, attractive women. Is that so bad?"

"It depends on what's expected of them."

"There's only one thing expected of any girl who works here."

"To greet a man not worth her pains, much less the adventure of her person?" Jake suggested.

Gates exploded with laughter. "The adventure of her person! What a delicious way to put it." He picked up a napkin to wipe some spittle from his lip. "But, no, it's not like that. No one is obliged to put the 'adventure of her person' on the line."

"Maybe not here, but we've also heard you organize private parties."

"I have friends – important friends – who have similar interests to mine, so we do occasionally throw parties and invite some of the girls along. But only those girls who are up for it – and believe me, lots of them are very up-for-it. If a girl plays her cards right, she can do quite well from these occasions."

"Then you live about her waist, or in the middle of her favours?"

He burst out laughing again. "Another good one, Benatsky. My goodness, you're quite the amusing fellow, aren't you?" Glancing my way again, he observed, "I can see why you're hanging around this guy."

I wasn't going to get side-tracked into explaining my relationship, or lack of one, with Jake – not to these guys. I decided instead to rub a little gloss off their sheen. "So what you're saying is, you use these women for a little casual prostitution. Is that about it?"

That seemed to knock him off his rhythm. Perhaps he had been expecting the kind of softball questions the press usually lobs his way. I don't think he quite knew how to respond. Jake pressed: "How say you, sir? Can you deny all this?"

"Prostitution is such a strong word," he replied, after draining his glass to the last drop. "And it's totally unwarranted. There is no prostitution here and I'm no pimp. Neither is Mr. Chiang. What we have are occasions when men and women . . . get together and enjoy themselves the way that men and women like to do. It's just human nature."

"That's a bountiful answer that fits all questions," Jake calmly observed. "I know not whether to depart in silence, or bitterly to speak in your reproof."

"Well, I can answer that one for you: you can depart in silence. Brian and I have more important matters to attend to."

"And yet I will not," Jake riposted. "Defend your reputation, or bid farewell to your good life for ever."

"What do you mean?" He was all attention now.

I decided to spell it out for him. "You say it's just men and women enjoying themselves, but I think it's really much more. I think you're using these women and these occasions, with their implied sexual opportunities, to trade favours and curry influence with powerful business interests."

He was dismissive again. "Oh, come on. We're just having a little fun."

"I'm not buying that. How often do these arrangements occur? Quite often, I'll bet."

He smirked a little and glanced over at Chiang, who looked back with a broad grin on his face. "Yes, it can be quite often, I suppose. But can one desire too much of a good thing?" he coyly asked.

"But these women . . . ."

"What about them? They come if they want. If they come, they know what to expect. If not, well . . . they're easy to replace."

Jake brought it to earth as only he (or Shakespeare) can: "Your affections are a sick man's appetite, who desires most that which would increase his evil."

I was startled by Gates's reaction: he burst out laughing once more. "Evil?! What's this talk of evil?" Then, gradually regaining composure, he explained: "There's no evil here. Sure, things may happen that the pope might not approve of, but in the final analysis, we're all just enjoying ourselves, like I told you." He and Chiang smirked at each other once more.

Jake wasn't buying it. "What manner of man are you? You speak like one besotted on your sweet delights. Have you forgot all sense of place and duty?"

"What's duty got to do with it? Listen here, I do my duty. I work very hard at it – and then I like to enjoy myself."

"Duty has everything to do with it," I snapped back, unable to control myself. "You've been 'enjoying yourself', as you put it, in cahoots with a prominent property developer, perhaps more than one. As the head of planning and building permits, aren't you supposed to maintain an arms-length relationship with these people? How do you think the public would react if they knew the government official who's supposed to be regulating and controlling these guys is actually in bed with them? I mean figuratively; I have no idea if it's true literally."

I hadn't intended to question Gates's sexual orientation – the metaphor had just popped into my mind and I was stuck with it – but even it didn't evoke a rise from him. He simply looked down at his folded hands.

"You are a pair of strange ones," Jake observed. "What is between you? Give me up the truth."

Gates looked up, his expression now one of defiance. "What do you mean, what's between us? My friend is a businessman; I'm an elected city official. We socialize from time to time. Despite Ms. Marwick's efforts to imply otherwise, that's all there is to it."

"Do you two know how you are censured here in the city?" Looking directly at Gates, Jake added: "You yourself are much condemn'd to have an itching palm."

It was a surprising accusation, given how dismissive he'd been of those rumours this morning. He must have been feeling desperate.

"Yeah, I've heard that one before," Gates replied, as cool as ever. "Let me give you some advice: watch what you say and who you say it to. You might find yourself facing an action for slander."

"That is no slander, sir, which is a truth."

"What makes you think you know the truth? You're an actor, for Christ's sake!" Quickly re-composing himself, he continued: "Listen, people say a lot of things – that's how they sell newspapers and put eyeballs in front of screens." I wondered whether this was a reference to Simon's interest in the case. "But here's the truth – the real truth: I've never taken a bent nickel from anyone and no one's ever going to prove otherwise."

"Can you think to blow out the intended fire your city is ready to flame in," Jake riposted, "with such weak breath as this? No, you are deceived. Corruption wins not more than honesty."

"This so-called fire – you know what it is? It's nothing but a bunch of whiners. People who hate change, who attack and demean politicians, no matter what. Fortunately, despite all their whining and moaning, I know how to make things happen."

"For which you are a traitor to the people."

"Nonsense! What a ridiculous accusation. Let me clue you in on some basic facts of life. When it comes right down to it, what most people really want is for someone to keep this city moving forward, and I'm that guy who does that. I'm just a public servant, like many others, but I'm one of the few who actually do serve. That's right, I serve. Maybe things don't get done exactly according to the book, but at least they get done. You should be giving me credit for that."

"'Tis more than you deserve. You sign your place and calling, in full seeming, with meekness and humility, but your heart is cramm'd with arrogancy, spleen, and pride."

"You're right about that last part. I *am* proud of what I've achieved. Why shouldn't I be? In my line of work, you've got to be relentless to get what you want. You've got to be able to push open doors, even when they're only slightly ajar. Even when they're locked and bolted. As it happens, I'm good at it."

"Think what you will; 'tis nothing but conceit. You are not worth the dust which the rude wind blows in your face."

Gates leaned forward and glared intensely at Jake. "Listen, my friend," he said, his voice low and menacing, "I'm won't take this crap from you or anyone else. Either you bugger off now or Brian has you thrown out. We're done here."

"Just a moment, Mr. Gates," I intervened hastily. Our strategy of trying to shake him up – if that's what it was – had failed abysmally; we had to get this back on track. "We're not here to discuss how you do your business – or the city's business, for that matter. That's for the voters to decide. We're here about Mandy. We just want to know where she fitted into all of this – for our investigation."

That seemed to appease him somewhat. "She didn't; that's the point. She wasn't like the other girls. She was beautiful, talented – she had everything, really. It was wonderful to spend some time with a young, vibrant girl like that. She had brains, too. I took her places and showed her things she never would have experienced on her own. We had a great time together. I was very sorry to hear of her death."

"You seem to be handling it well enough, if you don't mind my saying."

"Well, we weren't that serious, to be perfectly frank. In fact, we weren't serious at all. We both knew our relationship had run its course, or was about to; she was ready to move on and so was I. I don't like to get tied down in any one relationship for too long."

"Because there are so many other opportunities?"

"Well, yeah, basically. I admit it. Life is short – especially at my age – and I mean to take full advantage of every opportunity that comes my way."

"You smell this business with a sense as cold as is a dead man's nose," Jake observed. Not your everyday analogy, but most apt in the circumstances.

"Why are you so interested in Mandy, anyway?" Gates responded testily. "I suppose you had the hots for her, too. It wouldn't surprise me."

"I am well acquainted with your manner of wrenching the true cause the false way."

"Oh, I see," he sneered. "I've got it all wrong. You're just a concerned citizen. Well, we'll see how that works out for you."

Was that a veiled threat? I wasn't sure, but I knew we couldn't dwell on it; we still needed information. "If we could just turn to the murder . . . ."

"I know nothing about that."

"But you can see how it looks. . . ."

"What are you suggesting?" he snapped back. "That I did it? That's ridiculous."

"Are you a party in this business?" Jake asked.

"You mean, did I have someone else do it? Again, no. In fact, I'm extremely upset about what happened. I told you that and I mean it. That's the only reason I was willing to talk to you – the possibility that you might help solve it. Frankly, I don't have a lot of confidence in Knutsen."

"If that's so," I replied, "then help us out with a few details."

"Why should I? I no longer have any confidence in you, either."

Chiang snorted.

"Please, Mr. Gates," I said.

"What do you want to know? I'll give you five minutes."

"Let's start with the party at Walt's house Sunday evening. I remember seeing you there."

"That's right. I often go to these theatrical parties."

I resisted the urge to ask if that's because it's a good way to meet actresses; I was all business now. "Did you speak with Mandy?"

"Of course."

"Did you argue with her?"

"No, not at all. Why would we?"

I could think of a reason or two, but I had to keep to the straight and narrow. "Well, then, what did you talk about?"

"About the production, mainly. She was very excited; couldn't stop talking about it. She thanked me profusely for helping her get in the door."

"How much had you helped?" It wasn't relevant to the investigation, but I had to know. (So much for being 'all business'.)

"Listen, Walt and I go way back. I take a keen interest in live theatre – I know what you're thinking; it's not just for the women – and I've helped the Festival many times over the years. Not only with city money, either; I've contributed on my own account as well. I also serve on the Board. So when I come across an actress who has lots of talent – someone I think Walt should have a look at – he's usually willing to accommodate me."

"Accommodate you?" It sounded like another

weasel word.

"Again, it's not what you think. The Festival works because it's been able to maintain high standards, not just because it's subsidized by the city. That's down to Walt and the rest of us on the Board. No one would take on a performer who wasn't up to the role simply because I'd recommended her. My influence buys a girl a look, that's all. Mandy knew that and never asked for more."

"Getting back to the party," I said, "I can't recall when you left. It seems to me that it was early."

"Yeah, it must have been around nine-thirty or so. Not long after I'd had that chat with Mandy."

"Did you arrange to meet her later?"

"No. She said she would be going home soon to work on her lines. She was so nervous about it, I knew she wouldn't be in the mood for anything else; besides, I had some business to discuss with Brian."

"What business?"

"Oh, just some stuff about a project he's submitted for city approval. I can't talk about it, but it has nothing to do with this case."

I let that pass. It might be a thread to pick up later, but we needed to stay on course now. "So, you came here?"

"That's right. I arrived around ten. Brian was already here." Chiang nodded his confirmation. "We sat right at this table and talked till around eleven. The crowd was getting a little noisy by then, so we headed to my place. I had a decent half-bottle of whisky that was just begging for our attention."

"How late did the two of you stay there?"

"Oh, till around one, maybe one-thirty." He glanced at Chiang, who nodded his concurrence once more. Such helpful gents.

"And both of you were there throughout this time? Neither left for a while?'

"Oh, I think Brian had to take a leak at one point, but that's it." Chiang put on a mock-guilty look, as if he were embarrassed to have to urinate occasionally.

"And you never saw Mandy again? Either of you?"

They both shook their heads.

"And neither of you was in contact with her in any other way? Telephone, texting, e-mail . . . ?"

"Nope," Gates replied.

"Nada," chimed in Chiang.

Gates's manner was so matter-of-fact that I doubted seriously whether he'd really felt all that much for Mandy. Perhaps she hadn't been so special, just another easy mark for this powerful and vain man. But then he asked, "Now, you tell me something: how was she killed?"

"We're not allowed to," I said.

It was clear that he understood our reticence. As a city councillor, he'd probably got to know standard police procedure quite well. Still, he tried again: "Perhaps just a hint? It's not like you've been following police orders to any great extent so far, is it?"

"I'm sorry. They insist."

That seemed to satisfy him. "I suppose you don't want to step on Knutsen's toes any more than you have to. Doesn't matter, I can probably find out anyway." He rose abruptly to his feet. "Your five minutes are up. I've answered all your questions; any further communication I have on this matter will be with the police."

With that, he powered off towards what appeared to be a back office, Chiang in tow. No time, apparently, for any good-byes, much less a handshake (or, heaven forbid, two).

"He goes hence frowning," Jake observed, "but it honours us that we have given him cause."

I wished I could have felt as sanguine.

* * *

We sat quietly for a few minutes, trying to digest what had just taken place. My mind was whirling; I couldn't believe anyone could be so callous. Granted, Gates had shown a glimmer of concern over the loss of a woman he'd been sleeping with for the past several months, but really not that much, when it came right down to it. As for the other women he'd snared in his little circle of iniquity, they were clearly disposable, more like paper tissues than human beings.

Jake was evidently thinking along the same lines.

"Did you perceive how he laughed at his vice? I never knew man hold vile stuff so dear."

"I can't help wondering how a man like him could get where he is. Politicians inevitably have their critics, but as far as I know, his reputation is solid."

"I must confess that I have heard so much."

"That's not what you said to him. You made it sound as if people were ready to rise up against him."

"I would they were, but yet, alas, reputation is an idle and most false imposition, oft got without merit."

"But how does he pull that off, Jake? That's what I don't get."

He shrugged. "Custom hath made it in him a property of easiness. He turned me about with his finger and his thumb, as one would set up a top."

"Well, you didn't exactly use your anger to 'better vantage'; we both fell on our faces in that respect. But there must be plenty of people, influential people, who know much more about how his career is built, to some extent at least, on corruption."

"He is a privileged man. Plate sin with gold, and the strong lance of justice hurtless breaks."

"Now there's a sobering thought. You don't suppose it applies to murder as well, do you?"

"I do not know; I hope not." He glanced beyond my shoulder. "Look – here comes Helena."

I turned to see her approaching with a couple of glasses; we were getting our complimentary drinks, after all. I doubted Chiang would have been pleased.

"I thought you might need these." She placed the glasses in front of us, then scanned the room warily. "I didn't hear much you were saying – I stayed as far away as I could – but I hope you kept your promise not to let them know I've been talking to you. Mr. Gates wouldn't hesitate to have me fired if he found out."

"We have, I assure you," Jake replied. "For this relief much thanks." He nodded toward her and took a hearty sip from his glass. I followed suit eagerly.

She didn't seem assured at all. "You know, it's not just my job that's at stake if he finds out. He'd probably also make it difficult for me to get work anywhere else."

"If he fail of that, he will have other means to cut you off. How dangerous is it that this man goes loose!"

"The danger isn't just to me." She surveyed the room again, just to be sure. "If he's involved in Mandy's death, you're at risk, too. If you're smart, you'll forget about the investigation. Let the police handle it."

"The problem is," I replied, "we aren't sure that the police are capable of handling it. There may even be some senior officers under his control, for all we know."

"Listen, you two," she responded briskly. "Mandy was my best friend here and I want her killer found as much as anyone. But if what you say is true, Emma, it means that the risk is even greater than you think. I hate to say it, but you need to back off *now*."

She may well be right, I knew: the more we poked and prodded, the more cornered he might feel and the more dangerous he might become. "I understand what you're saying; maybe we should stop. It's not like we're making progress. All we've found out so far is that Chiang and Gates have alibis for the time of the murder – each other."

"What about you, Jake?"

"I am not made of stone," he replied, "but penetrable to your kind entreats, albeit against my conscience and my soul."

It was a nice attempt to reassure her without yielding an inch, but she wasn't fooled. "But you won't give up, will you?"

"His looks I fear, and his intents I doubt, and yet I'll venture it. He's a rank weed, a disease that must be cut away."

"But it's not your job to do it."

"If I bow, they'll say it was for fear."

"What's wrong with fear?" she retorted. "It can be a very healthy thing." He didn't reply, which told her that the cause was hopeless. "I've got to get back to work."

Before she could leave, he took her free hand and held it in both of his. "Let me peruse this face," he said as he gazed upon her with that disarming intensity of his. "I do in friendship counsel you to leave this place. You must do it soon." He held her hand for another second or two, then let it go.

She looked as if she were about to lose it totally. She turned quickly and bee-lined towards the women's bathroom. He followed her with his eyes. "I pity her. Nothing she does or seems but smacks of something greater than herself, too noble for this place."

I couldn't deny that sentiment, incredible though it still was to hear him express it. "Jake, she has a point. Let's face it: we aren't getting anywhere. All we've managed to do so far is to annoy some very dangerous men."

"If I could add a lie unto a fault, I would deny it."

"But you can't, so why not take her advice? I know what you're going to say: you gave your word. That was very noble of you, but it doesn't mean much if you can't deliver. I'm as suspicious as you are of these guys – Gates especially – but they're giving each other alibis that we'll never break, not unless we can somehow drive a wedge between them."

"It were a tedious difficulty, I think, to bring them to that prospect."

"I can't see it happening, either. They're as thick as thieves, and I imagine they know enough about each other to keep both of them quiet. Can you think of any other way we could get at Gates?"

"Believe me, I cannot, for the harlot king is quite beyond mine arm, out of the blank and level of my brain, plot-proof."

I couldn't help smiling a little; 'harlot king' was the perfect name for him. "Then we really don't have much choice, do we?"

He looked at his watch. "Let us go, for it is after midnight. The deep of night is crept upon our talk, and nature must obey necessity."

"You haven't answered me."

"I cannot tell what to think on't. We will have more of this to-morrow." He abruptly downed his glass and rose to his feet. "Farewell till then. Good night and good repose." And with that, he was gone.

WEDNESDAY, JUNE 17. DAY.

By the time I arrived home last night, I was too exhausted to bother making notes for this journal. I had time to do so this morning, however, because Eddie phoned to say that the rehearsal was cancelled. I called Walt to find out why. The official story was that they wanted to work one-on-one with Mandy's understudy to get her up to speed; in truth, he confided, that was just Plan A. Plan B was to scour other theatrical companies and agencies in the region to see if a more accomplished replacement could be found. I wasn't even Plan C, as far as I could tell. I'd declined the understudy role for the obvious reason (wounded pride) and, apparently, I'm to be punished for that. So be it.

After making some point notes, I began to delve into the voice recordings. As I went through them, my sense of discouragement grew. Gates had been crafty last night, craftier than I'd realized. He appeared to be levelling with us about the women, the parties, and so forth, but when it came right down to it, there was nothing especially useful to us. It's well known that he's acquainted with lots of prominent people and that he socializes a good deal; it's part of his public persona. We would need actual evidence of corrupt or illicit dealings to be a threat to him, and he seemed to realize fairly early on that we didn't have any. True, he left frowning, as Jake put it, but our efforts probably amounted to no more than an unpleasant turn to his evening, a minor perturbance at most. As for the murder, all we found out is that he has a solid alibi.

Just after noon, my mother rang, hoping to catch me during my lunch break. We usually have a chat on the weekend – calls which invariably end with an invitation for Sunday dinner – but she said she couldn't wait to hear how things were going. I had no doubt it was because she'd just heard about the murder of our leading lady; she was careful, though, not to bring it up. She probably didn't want to sound eager for me to step into the dead woman's shoes.

Unfortunately, it wasn't really possible to avoid the issue of replacing Desdemona, and as soon as I mentioned it, she had the opportunity she was waiting for. Why hadn't they turned to me as the obvious choice? she wanted to know. It was another variant of the 'why don't they see what a beautiful/talented/fantastic person you are?' comment that all children hate. These discussions generally take about half an hour to work through.

'Stepping into the dead woman's shoes' could have another meaning, however, and I was determined to steer as far away from that terrain as I could. Yes, it's a great tragedy that that poor girl was murdered, I told her. No, I don't know why, but (I embellished here) there is no reason to believe that it has anything to do with the play. Yes, that means I'm not in any danger. The last point involved more than an embellishment; it meant not mentioning my involvement in the murder investigation. As for Jake, I kept totally silent. Not only would he be impossible to explain, but any discussion would inevitably set the stage for another cycle through the 'why doesn't he see what a beautiful/. . .' routine. It seems that parents spend the first part of our lives protecting us from things they think we shouldn't know, and we spend the rest of their lives doing the same for them.

I'd no sooner finished that call when the phone rang again. This time it was Simon, still keen to pursue the story. He'd been unable to reach either Gates or Chiang (no surprise there); had we had any better success? I filled him in on our interview with them, including their alibis and our inclination to disbelieve them, and promised to let him know if we turned up anything further. I also suggested that he focus on finding solid evidence of corruption, if that angle really interested him. I knew it did, but I also sensed from his comments that his editor wasn't fully on board. Either the paper was concerned about a possible lawsuit, I surmised, or Gates had pull with it. Simon again asked me to arrange an interview with Jake; I knew it was hopeless, but I promised I'd try.

Speaking of Jake, it suddenly occurred to me that

I had no way of reaching him. I'd assumed that I would see him at the rehearsal, but it was now cancelled – for who knows how long? – and I had no idea where he lived. I didn't even have a land-line number. Talk about living off the grid! I wasn't even sure if he'd caught up with the twentieth century, much less the twenty-first. I phoned Walt to see if he could provide a number, but there was no answer. I then phoned Eddie, with the same result. They were probably in meetings, trying to sort out what to do about the play.

There was nothing else for me to do but wait till late afternoon and head over to the Brown Pelican. If Jake weren't there, I'd try Chez Panisse. As it happened, I was in luck; he was occupying the same bar table at the Pelican. It was good to know that in at least one respect, he's predictable.

He seemed lost in himself, but he came around quickly when he saw me approaching. "Welcome, fair one. Come, sit down."

"You seem to be in better spirits, today," I commented, sliding onto the barstool beside him. We were both facing the window, through which we could see pedestrians scurrying for shelter from the rain, which had just begun to pelt down with some earnestness.

"I am not merry," he replied with an ambivalent smile, "but I do beguile the thing I am, by seeming otherwise."

I noticed that he hadn't even ordered a drink,

which brought a quick end to my illusion about his predictability. I decided it was better left like that; we had some serious business to discuss. I lunged straight in. "I got another call from Simon this afternoon. He's still keen on the story, as you can imagine."

He cast me a look of extreme skepticism. "To what purpose have you unfolded this to me?"

"I think you're being hasty in dismissing him. He still wants to interview you and who's to say that his help won't . . . ."

He cut me off abruptly: "I do beseech you, take it not amiss; I cannot nor I will not yield to you."

"Why not? You were perfectly willing to throw corruption charges in Gates's face last night; don't you think it might have gone better if you'd found out beforehand what Simon and his colleagues actually have against him? He says there's quite a lot."

"Ay, but not enough."

"Not enough for them to go public, that's true, but if they start poking into it a little more, who's to say what they might find? If they can dig up enough to raise even a limited public outcry, it might embolden the authorities to put him under the microscope."

He wasn't buying it. "He sits high in all the people's hearts," he declared, "and that which would appear offence in us, his countenance, like richest alchemy, will change to virtue and to worthiness."

Well, maybe so, given his reputation as a skilled

manipulator of public opinion, but we wouldn't know for sure unless we tried. "Right now, Jake, he's the only suspect we have. There's also Chiang, but Gates is the one who was involved with Mandy. To make matters worse, they're providing alibis for each other that we have no way of breaking. If you're not willing to use the press, have you figured out some other angle we could try?"

"No, in good earnest," he admitted. "I yet not understand the case myself."

"So we're stuck where we were last night. Perhaps you should give some more thought to just giving up on this whole business. I'm sure you could find the right words to break it to Mr. Bennett."

"I cannot do it. I pray you, let it stand."

I'd expected as much. Several minutes passed, during which my mind scanned feverously for anything that might offer even a faint hope of gaining leverage on Gates or Chiang. Then something registered. "Maybe we need to come at this thing from a completely different direction," I said.

"How so?" He seemed intrigued.

"We'll never get Gates or Chiang, but suppose we don't need to? Suppose they're telling the truth: they were together at Gates's house, drinking his half-bottle of whisky, during the time of the murder. That would mean that someone else . . . ."

"Why, right!" he exclaimed. "There was a man. Alack, I had forgot."

I had, too, until a minute ago. "What did Mr. Lapierre say? If I remember correctly, he said that a young man came by that evening shortly after eleven-thirty and buzzed a unit. He figured it must have been Mandy's because the other residents are too old to be receiving visitors that late at night."

"And so he did. What then?"

"I think he said the guy drove off about fifteen minutes later."

He looked at me quizzically. "There is no more to say?"

"No, that's about it."

"Nay, but it is not so. There is more in it."

"More?"

"Ay, madam."

I needed only a moment, aided by the twinkle in his eye. "Oh, I see. If he'd continued buzzing, Mr. Lapierre would have heard it, so she must have let him in."

"'Tis likely, by all conjectures. And what follows then?"

"Well, to let him in that late, he must have been someone she knew well, maybe someone else she was involved with; you did say this has more to do with love than hate. The problem is, finding this man would be like finding a needle in a haystack. Mr. Lapierre couldn't give us much of a description; he wasn't even sure he'd recognize the man if he saw him again."

He pondered the matter for several moments before a grin slowly emerged. "I think I can discover him, if you please."

"You can? How?"

"'Tis nothing," he replied, nodding toward the bar. "Helena is here at hand."

I couldn't help returning his grin. He was absolutely right: if there had been another man in Mandy's life, who better to know about it than her best friend, Helen?

* * *

It took only the slightest glance from Jake to bring her scurrying to our table. He looked pleased; I think he likes women to respond on cue. (Well, what man doesn't?) "How do you, pretty lady?"

"Surviving," she replied, smiling briefly. "It helps to be working, keeps my mind off things. Mr. Chiang – he hasn't said anything to me, so that's good. How about you two?"

"We're managing as well," I said.

"I hope you've thought over what I said last night and decided to toss in the towel."

"I am sorry, madam," Jake replied. "I was not born a yielder."

She frowned. "No, I didn't think so. Does that mean you've made some progress?"

"It may be, very like."

"Really?"

"It's just a thought we had," I said. "Helen, was there anyone else interested in Mandy?"

She reflected for a moment. "You mean, apart from that cute black guy? Yeah, I suppose you could say so. There's Roddy . . . Roderick Chiang. He's Mr. Chiang's nephew."

"Is't possible? Sits the wind in that corner?" Jake muttered. "You know him well?"

"Not all that well. I know he works for Mr. Chiang, helping to run his rental business."

"I thought Chiang's in property development?" I asked.

"He is – that's the main thing – but he also owns several apartment buildings. Anyway, Roddy's been coming in quite a lot in the last few months. At first it was with his uncle – Roddy just turned old enough to drink – but since then it's mainly when he knew Mandy would be on shift. He seemed to have trouble taking his eyes off her."

"A sin prevailing much in youthful men," Jake observed, "who give their eyes the liberty of gazing."

"Yeah, so I've noticed. He seemed to idealize her, though – which is not the reaction we usually get around here."

"Let me ask you, Helen," I said, "do you think he could have had . . . what shall I call it? . . . evil designs upon her?"

"Evil designs? Oh, I do like that. You're beginning to get the hang of it. Watch out, Jake, she could be competition."

"Minds sway'd by eyes are full of turpitude," he pronounced gravely.

Helen struggled to suppress a snigger (as did I). "Okay, dude, you're still the king." She turned to me. "Getting back to your question – I don't think so. Actually, it was more like puppy love. He was infatuated with her. He knew about Mr. Gates but, like all young men, he assumed that a woman her age couldn't possibly be serious about an old guy like him. So he figured she was just biding her time till a suitable young buck like himself came along. And that was a problem."

"Why do you say that?"

"Because Mr. Gates is Mr. Chiang's key political connection for his entire property development business. There was no way Mr. Chiang was going to let his nephew mess with Mr. Gates's girlfriend. So he told me to fix it."

"Fix it?" I exclaimed. "What did you do?"

"I shouldn't be telling you this." She glanced around to make sure no one was paying attention. "Roddy was in here on Sunday night; he didn't know that Mandy wouldn't be showing up because of the party. Since I had him alone, I took the opportunity to disillusion him about her. I told him that he'd got her all wrong: she wasn't an angel, just a bar-girl –

you know, with all that implies."

"Did he understand what you meant?"

"Yeah, but he rejected it all. I couldn't leave it like that, though, so I went a little farther." Her expression darkened. "Too far, in fact."

"Really? What did you tell him?"

She looked down briefly, then directly at me. "I sort-of suggested she was not only . . . uhm . . . a free spirit, she sometimes took money for it."

"How did that go over?"

"Not well. He got very pissed off and refused to listen anymore. I figured he needed some time to calm down, so I suggested that we meet Monday morning to discuss it. I didn't want to, but I knew it had to be done. We agreed to meet at the coffee house across the street, but of course that was the morning when you . . . discovered her body."

"So he didn't show up?"

"Nope. Didn't even call."

"So what did you do? Did you just let it drop?"

"No, he'd given me his number, so I tried it a few times. I couldn't get an answer. Then you came in that night and told me about her. At first, my mind was totally on that, but then I started to get concerned about him. He'd really thought she was as pure as snow, then I'd told him about the bar-girl thing, now he'd learned she was dead. It had been a rough couple of days, as you can imagine."

"Do you ever manage to reach him?"

"Not till yesterday afternoon. He was in pretty bad shape. He didn't want to talk at all, but I got him to promise to meet me this morning. Again he didn't show up, so it was another wasted trip for me."

"But why did he swear he would come this morning, and comes not?" Jake asked. "You should for that have reprehended him." He seemed to take it as an unacceptable breach of etiquette, regardless of the circumstances.

"When he didn't show, I phoned him again – not to chew him out, just to see if he was all right – but he still wasn't answering. I left a message but he hasn't called back."

"Where is this rash and most unfortunate man?"

She shrugged. "I don't know . . . . Oh, you're not thinking he has anything to do with her murder, are you?"

"Nay, I know not."

"Listen, if you're thinking that, you couldn't be more wrong." She was clearly getting agitated, as if our suspecting him only compounded the harm that life – or rather death – had already done him.

"Helen," I said, "relax. It's okay. We only want to talk with him because he knew her, that's all."

"All right. In fact, it would be good if you could track him down. I'm still quite worried about him, to be perfectly frank."

"Maybe you can help us with that. Where does he live?"

"I don't have any idea. Sorry."

"Well, what's the name of the company he works for?"

"Uhm. . . . It's called Wentworth Properties or something like that."

"Okay. Could you give us his phone number?"

"Sure." She read it out from her phone and I entered it into mine. "I've got to get back to work. Can I get you anything?"

"No, thanks. We're going to get on this right away."

"Good. If you find him, please go easy on him."

I nodded as she hastened off to serve another table. Then I tried the number she'd given me. Still no answer. Texting it produced the same result, so I decided to track down his workplace. I found a Wentworth Property Holdings on the internet and tried their number. After going through the usual automated-menu maze, I eventually reached a human who informed me that Roddy Chiang did indeed work for the company, but that he hadn't come in that day. She didn't know – or wouldn't say – where he was. When I asked for his home address, she held fast to the standard line about not being able to give out employee information.

While I was engaged in these fruitless efforts, Jake approached the bar to ask the two barmen, who'd obviously caught some of the conversation. "Gentlemen, can any of you tell me where I may find the young romeo?"

They glanced at each other, smirked at his manner of address, but shook their heads. He returned to the table disappointed.

I again rang the number Helen had given me, with no better luck. Roddy clearly didn't have his phone with him or wasn't willing to answer it. I knew there'd be no point in trying to reach his uncle; after last night, he probably wouldn't even have taken the call, much less given up his nephew's address. Thinking about his uncle, though, gave me an idea.

"Jake, you don't suppose Mandy's apartment building is owned by Chiang, do you?"

A smile began to crease his face. "I know the reason, lady, why you ask."

"I was just thinking that since Gates got Chiang to give her a job, perhaps he also . . . ."

Just then Helen rushed up. "Did you get through to Roddy?"

"No, he's still not answering. Tell me, do you happen to know if the apartment building where Mandy lived is owned by your boss?"

"Yeah, it is. Mr. Gates arranged that as well."

"Thanks, Helen." She scurried off to another table.

I turned to Jake. "It's a hell of a long shot, you must admit."

"That's true enough."

"But we've got nothing to lose at this point. So it's

back to Mr. Lapierre? There'd be no point trying to do this by phone."

"No, indeed. Come, let's go."

He made off straight away for the door. I darted after him in hopes of securing the driver's seat, but my efforts were again in vain. The man is quick, I'll give him that.

❊ ❊ ❊

The reason we fixated on the apartment building's ownership is that, if Chiang owned it, it would mean that Mr. Lapierre and Roddy Chiang both work for the same company; it's possible, therefore, that they know each other. Admittedly, Mr. Lapierre probably wouldn't know Roddy's address, but he might know of other buildings that Brian Chiang owns; given the family connection, it's at least possible that Roddy lives in one of them. It was about as tenuous a lead as I could imagine, but at least it was something.

We arrived at the apartment building around five-thirty. Mr. Lapierre was in, fortunately, and agreed to talk with us again. He led us into the living room of his ground-floor unit, where he immediately opened the conversation by asking whether we'd made any progress with the investigation.

"Not a lot," I replied, "but maybe you can help us. We've found out that Mr. Chiang's nephew, Roddy, was interested in Mandy, so we'd like to talk with him. Do you know him?"

"You suspect him of being the murderer?"

"No, no, not at all." What led to that leap? I wondered. "We just thought that he might be able to tell us more about Mandy. He'd apparently got to know her quite a bit at the Brown Pelican. You do know him, don't you?"

"No, not really."

"But he works for Mr. Chiang's rental business. You also work for it, don't you?"

He nodded slowly.

"Then, you must have run into him occasionally."

"Yeah, I have," he admitted. "He's been here once or twice with Mr. Chiang. I've also talked to him a few times on the phone. You know, about problems with the building or the tenants, that sort of thing. But I can't say I know him."

The phone rang. While Mr. Lapierre was busy answering it, Jake whispered to me: "I do perceive here a divided duty; he is vex'd at something."

I shared his uneasiness. "It may be he's just uncertain about how much he should tell us. Obviously, he doesn't want to divulge any information that might get him into trouble with Chiang. We must be patient."

"I will be the pattern of all patience."

That seemed highly improbable, but any effort in that direction would be welcome. When Mr. Lapierre returned, I asked him: "Can you think of any other way we might get in touch with him?"

He hesitated for a moment. "Have you tried the office? They should know where he is."

"We had no luck there," I replied. "We've tried his mobile phone number as well, but he's not answering."

"Then I don't see what I can do."

"You don't happen to know where he lives?"

"No, I don't."

"This answer will not serve," Jake declared, his promised patience already beginning to fray.

I had to intervene quickly, before bad-cop Jake got going. "I understand your position," I said to Mr. Lapierre, "but the thing is, we really need to get into contact with him. He's not in any trouble; it's just that he's missed a couple of meetings, so we're a little concerned." I saw no point in adding that the meetings were with a cocktail waitress, not a business associate.

"I still don't see how I can help."

"Well, we're wondering . . . can you tell us which other apartment buildings Mr. Chiang owns?"

"I really can't answer that question, either. Sorry."

"And yet I would that you would answer," Jake countered, with a firmness that implied that responding was not optional. "If you fail in our request, the blame may hang upon your hardness."

I'm not sure if being accused of hardness did the trick, or if Mr. Lapierre concluded that Chiang's property holdings must be a matter of public record and hence safe to disclose, but whatever the case, he relented. "Here's a few other addresses you might want to check out." He reached for a scrap of paper and scribbled them down.

"I humbly thank you for't," Jake replied.

Mr. Lapierre hesitated again, then appeared to reach a decision. "There's something else," he said. "I shouldn't be saying this, but you might also want to check Mr. Chiang's own place. A few years ago, I was brought in to work on the renovation of a guest house at the back of the property. I wouldn't be surprised if that was for his nephew. The boy was being raised by his mother, but then she died suddenly. Some kind of car accident, I think. It was around that time that we worked on the guest house."

"Where does Mr. Chiang live?" I asked. In for a penny, in for a pound. Surprisingly, he told us.

Jake shot up from the sofa upon hearing the address. Giving him a lead is like waving a stick in front of a dog, I reflected. He grabbed Mr. Lapierre's hand and shook it vigorously. "Well, sir, I thank you."

Mr. Lapierre slowly rose to his feet, looking uneasy. "You don't have to tell anyone I told you, do you?"

"No, I have no reason for it. Fare you well."

* * *

"I'm guessing you want to try Chiang's place first," I said as we speed-walked back to the car.

"No question of that. The way is but short: away!"

There was no point in resisting; I just yielded up the keys. Even with him driving, it took us some fifteen minutes to reach the house in the steady rain. It wasn't a house really, more like an estate with a main building and three or four smaller buildings scattered around its extensive grounds. There was one car in the driveway, but no other indication that anyone was around.

We parked on the street and hastened up the driveway as quietly as we could; we didn't want to have to explain our presence to Chiang, should he be there. It didn't seem likely that he was – the car in the driveway was too modest to be his – but we couldn't take his absence for granted. At the end of the driveway, we came upon a former coach-house, now converted into what appeared to be living quarters. Its excellent shape suggested that it may well be the building that Mr. Lapierre had helped to restore.

Jake stepped onto the threshold and knocked quietly. The eerie silence that surrounded the whole area made me think of the last time we'd gone to find a missing person, so I was relieved when I heard a faint rustling emanating from inside. No one came to the door, though. After a few seconds, Jake announced, "Will you hear me, Roderigo? I do beseech you that I may speak with you."

Several more seconds passed without a further sound. Jake spoke again, a little more forcefully this time: "Open the door, or I will break it open." Again, no response.

I had no doubt he meant what he said about forcing the door, but I realized there might be a simpler option. I tried the handle. The latch released; the door hadn't been locked.

Jake pushed it open and barged in, with me trailing close behind. In the main room, we found a young man lying on the sofa under a blanket, cradling an ice pack against his left cheek. Even in the dim light of the cottage interior, I could see that he'd been beaten – badly. In addition to whatever damage the cheek had sustained, the eye above it was swollen over, and the chin and forehead were covered in abrasions. The fact that he made no effort to get up suggested that there might be considerable damage to his body as well.

"Let's see the boy's face," Jake said. He bent over the youth and examined his injuries closely. "What villains have done this?"

"No one," the young man responded. His voice was weak and raspy.

Jake wasn't prepared to take diffidence from the young man, even under the current circumstances. "I ask again, who was it? Tell who did the deed."

"It's no big deal. I got into a fight with some guy, that's all."

"Why, do you not know him?"

"No, I don't. What's it to you?" he added with what little indignation he could muster. "Who the hell are you, anyway?"

"I see, sir, you are eaten up with passion. Mend your speech a little, lest you may mar your fortunes."

"Just a moment, Jake," I intervened. "Roddy, I'm Emma and this is Jake. We knew Mandy from the play. We're sorry to burst in on you like this – you're obviously feeling unwell – but we've just learned that you also knew her."

With the mention of her name, he groaned and turned his head towards the back of the sofa. Though the body language was mildly off-putting, I was determined not to be deterred. I explained that her father had asked us to investigate. There was no reaction. I continued anyway: "Roddy, could you tell us a bit about her? We've heard that . . . ."

He cut me off abruptly. "That piece of crap! She can rot in hell, for all I care."

"What?!" Jake exclaimed.

"You heard me."

"Villainous thoughts, Roderigo. I am sure, though you can guess what temperance should be, you know not what it is."

I opted not to remark on the irony of Jake giving a

lesson in verbal restraint. The lesson was wasted in any case, for Roddy sharply replied: "She was just a fucking slut. End of story."

"By heaven, brat, I'll plague ye for that word," Jake uttered through clenched teeth, as though no such thing would ever pass his lips.

Sensing the interview was in danger of spiraling out of control, I intervened again. With my super-calm civil-service voice – the one I use for my students' parents – I continued: "We were just talking with Helen at the Brown Pelican and she . . . ."

Again, he cut me off. "She's just as bad. Screws anyone with a few bucks in his pocket."

"Now shame upon you, whether she does or no!" Jake seethed. "Speak not of Helena; let her alone."

Am I hearing right? I wondered. Is he actually defending Helen's honour against someone who'd just reacted essentially as he himself had done when he first met her? Who is this guy anyway?

I decided to shelve these existential thoughts for the time being and re-focus on the task at hand. "Listen, Roddy, . . ."

He cut me off a third time. "I don't have to listen to anything. If you don't like it, why don't you just go away and leave me alone?"

"Truly, for mine own part," Jake replied dismissively, "I would little or nothing with you."

Very helpful, Jake, thanks. I tried once more: "Roddy, we've heard a bit about you and Mandy.

How you were, well, infatuated with her and everything . . . ."

"Oh, God!" he cried, cringing with pain and despair. Though part of him clearly wanted to damn Mandy, Helen, maybe all women, there was another part, I sensed, that was bursting to talk about the anguish he was struggling so vainly to control. It felt like a torrent was about to be unleashed, and it was. "I wanted her so badly. I loved her. She was so gorgeous, so incredibly exciting. I hadn't felt so happy since my mother died."

I reached across and gave his arm a gentle tug. "Roddy, please sit up." Slowly and painfully, he did as I requested. "Did she feel the same way?" I asked.

He responded with a matter-of-factness that surprised me: "No. Well, I don't know. Not for sure. She was very friendly – we bantered, joked around whenever I went to the Pelican."

"Did you ever see her outside the Pelican?"

"Yes, we met a few times. Just for coffee. We hadn't been able to do that for a while, though, because she didn't have the time: she needed to work on her lines for the play. But it didn't matter so much. It was wonderful just to exchange a word or two at the Pelican whenever she could take a moment. The anticipation . . . not knowing when these moments might come or how long they would last . . . it was incredible. There was something magical going on between us." With these words, the modicum of composure he'd put together dissolved. His breathing seized up and he began to sob.

"He has strangled his language in his tears," Jake observed, glancing at me. The description could not have been more apt. It felt like torture to force him to continue, but Jake was undeterred. Turning back to the battered and anguish-ridden young man, he softly said, "But yet have the grace to consider that tears do not become a man."

Roddy panted heavily for a moment, then seemed to get a better grip on himself. He sniffled up the ooze that had begun to leak from his nostrils and wiped his eyes with his sleeve. I was momentarily stunned. I couldn't believe that line had worked again. Men are amazing – all you have to do is tell them that crying is unmanly and they stop. How is that possible?

After taking another deep, feverish breath, he resumed: "She wanted desperately to get her acting career going. And now it was taking off. I knew about her thing with Mr. Gates, of course, but this meant that he wasn't going to be around for long; she wasn't going to need him anymore. She told me so. Everything seemed possible for us."

He stopped again, not willing to abandon the spectre of infinite possibility that he – or they – had concocted. It fell to me to burst the illusion: "And then Helen told you something absolutely devastating – that Mandy had been putting it about, maybe for cash. Your vision of a golden future with this angelic creature was shattered."

"Yes," he wailed. "I couldn't believe it. I was crushed." Unmanly or not, the sobbing started up again.

The poor boy's state was heart-rending – almost unbearably so, in fact – but I was determined to follow Jake's unremitting lead. Besides, I don't like being cut off. "This was all on Sunday night, right?"

He nodded.

"What did you do after you heard this?"

Bringing the focus to the minutiae rather than the big picture seemed to help; he sat up a little more and resumed his account. "I didn't want to hear any more from Helen; I had to get out of there. So I walked around a bit, not going anywhere in particular. Then I realized that I had to get the truth from Mandy; it was eating me up. Helen had told me she was at a cast party, but I didn't know where it was and it wouldn't have worked to confront her there in any case. So I wandered around a bit longer, then returned to the Pelican."

Despite his silence, Jake had been following the conversation keenly. "Wherefore did you so?" he inquired.

Roddy took no notice of Jake's odd-sounding phrasing; his attention was riveted on finishing the story. "It was stupid, I know, but I guess I was hoping she might show up later."

"Couldn't you have phoned or texted her?" I asked. "You could have left a message, even if she wasn't answering. Or didn't you have her number?"

He cast me a guilty look. "The thing is, I did have her number, but she didn't know about it."

"How did you get it, then?"

"It's in her file at work. She was one of our tenants."

"I see. So you went back to the Pelican. What time did you arrive?"

"Oh, I don't know – about ten-thirty, maybe. I sat at the bar so that Helen wouldn't bother me anymore; we'd arranged to meet the next day, but I wasn't sure I wanted to talk with her ever again. I saw my uncle and Mr. Gates sitting at their usual table in the back room, but I didn't want to talk with them, either. Then this black guy joined them."

"Had you seen him at the Pelican before?"

"No, but I knew Mandy was playing opposite a black guy, so I figured this must be him. It had to be – why else would Mr. Gates be sitting with him? I know that doesn't sound real good, but that's the way I think of Mr. Gates. Anyway, I thought this might be a good sign – maybe the party was breaking up early and Mandy would be coming, after all. But then my uncle signalled me over. I didn't want to go, but I had to."

"Okay, so the four of you were sitting there . . . ."

"Not for long. Just after I arrived, the black guy took off."

"Did he leave the nightclub?"

"I don't know. No, wait. . . . He went back into the main room and sat at the bar."

"For how long?"

"Who knows? I had barely enough time to finish my drink before Mr. Gates suggested we all go back to his place and knock off some expensive bottle of whisky he'd been saving. This was even worse news – it meant I wouldn't get to see Mandy if she did show up. But I had no choice. When it comes to Mr. Gates, my uncle expects me to do what I'm told."

"So the three of you went to Gates's house. Did you all go together?"

"No. I'd come by car, so I followed my uncle. Mr. Gates had his own car."

"Where is the house?"

"It's on Thirty-Third, just west of Dunbar. You can't miss it. It's a huge place, almost as big as my uncle's." He nodded toward the mansion that dwarfed his little cottage.

"What happened then?"

"We just drank. They talked, mostly about business, but I didn't pay much attention. I was lost in my own thoughts. . . . Something was bothering me."

"What was that?"

"I realized that something didn't add up. I mean, how could she be sleeping around with customers at the nightclub, or whatever, if she was Mr. Gates's mistress? Why would he tolerate anything like that? He's not stupid; things don't happen behind his back without him knowing about it. If anything like that were going on, you can be sure he'd be all over it."

"Did you ask him about it?"

"Yeah, I did. He was talking about something he and Mandy were going to do and it sickened me, just thinking of them together some more. So I just blurted out what Helen had told me about her. My uncle kept trying to shut me up, but I just kept going. I was very drunk by this time."

"What was Gates's reaction?"

"He started to laugh. I couldn't believe it. It made me so angry that my uncle had to grab me to calm me down. Then Mr. Gates told me that I was right, he would never have put up with Mandy messing around while he was dating her; Helen must have exaggerated to warn me off. He also said that her warning hadn't been necessary because Mandy and he probably weren't going to last much longer. It didn't seem to be any big deal to him."

"But it was to you, wasn't it?" I could easily imagine how thrilled he would have been. "For you, it must have sounded like your dream had been reborn."

"Oh yeah, it was the best thing he could have said. The very best. I felt my spirits shooting up. But then he said something that really brought me down. He said that I shouldn't assume that once he was out of the way, I'd be the next in line. He said there's a lot of bees buzzing around that hive, or something like that."

"Did he mention anyone in particular?"

He paused for a moment, as if trying to recall precisely what had been said. "No," he replied. "No name was mentioned. But that's not the point. Whether or not there was anyone else at the moment – I didn't think there was, apart from me – I realized he was right about her in general. She was so beautiful. She had everything going for her. At the club, you could see that all eyes were on her; it was obvious. I used to be kinda proud of that – that she was taking time to shoot the breeze with me when there were so many other choices out there. Now I saw the downside: it meant she didn't have to settle for me – especially now that her career was starting to happen. She could do a lot better."

"So you felt dejected again. What did you do?"

"I got out of there as quickly as I could and came home."

"Straight home?"

"Yeah, I drove here and just collapsed on the sofa, too drunk to even take off my jacket or anything."

"Do you remember what time that was?"

"Uhm . . . I'm not sure. I think it was about one o'clock, maybe a little later."

"When did you hear about the murder?"

He started a little at the mention of that word. "The next morning. I got a call from my uncle. I thought he was going to chew me out for how I'd behaved with Mr. Gates, but he was phoning because he'd just heard about Mandy from the manager at her building."

"That must have been rough."

A look of total disgust came over his face. "You know what he said? He actually said that I didn't need to be bothered about Mr. Gates's girl anymore because she was dead. He seemed to think that made everything all right."

"How did that make you feel?" It was a lame line, but it was the best I could come up with. We needed to keep him going.

"Like fucking killing myself, if you want to know the truth," he replied vehemently. Then he became more reflective. "I don't have much. My mom died when I was seventeen, and after that, I really messed up at school. I'm still trying to catch up by taking on-line courses, but for the time being there's not much I can do. So I work for my uncle and live in his guest-house. I'm a fucking hanger-on. . . . You know, the family embarrassment you can't get rid of?"

"I'm sure it's not that bad."

"The only thing that gave me any sense of hope was Mandy. Now that's gone as well." He looked away as his eyes welled up and his chest wheezed.

"Come, come," Jake said. "You are a fool, and turn'd into the extremity of love. Enough of this." Apparently, he isn't tolerant of self-pity, even in the direst of circumstances.

"I mean it, I wish I was dead!" Roddy exclaimed.

"Nothing could be worse than this." He fell back on the couch and threw his arm over his eyes.

"But these are all lies," Jake calmly replied. "Men have died from time to time and worms have eaten them, but not for love."

This might be true, especially when the love affair existed mostly in the imagination of one of the lovers, but I also knew that Roddy wasn't ready for this brand of tough love yet. We were again in danger of losing his cooperation, and there was still one more matter to sort out.

"Roddy, I believe you," I said. "I can scarcely imagine what you're going through right now. You must be absolutely devastated. There's just one thing we need to ask you: who beat you up?"

"I told you," he replied, now angry and defiant again. "I don't know."

"All right, I get that. But how did it happen? And when?"

He expired deeply, as if having to explain were an unreasonable burden to place on someone in his condition. Well, perhaps it was, but we needed to know. After a few moments, he slowly sat up again, placed his elbows on his knees and buried his head in his hands. "Okay," he said, "By the time I got home from Mr. Gates's, it was around one-thirty, I think. I just walked in and flopped onto the sofa, like I said. I was asleep for a while – I don't know how long – when I was woken by the sound of the front door opening. I'd probably forgotten to lock it. Anyway, before I know it, this guy rushes over, grabs me up from the sofa, and starts whacking me with something. I was totally defenceless. Eventually, I must have passed out. When I came around, it was morning. There was blood on my clothes and vomit all over the bathroom. I could barely move."

"That's awful, Roddy. You've reported this to the police, I trust?"

"There's no point. I didn't get a look at the guy; it was dark and it all happened so fast. And nothing was stolen – well, maybe a few bucks, but there wasn't much else to take." He slumped down quite hard and rotated so that he was again facing the sofa back. His position was almost fetal. "They'd just fill in a report and file it somewhere."

"But still," I countered. "I mean, your uncle's a pretty influential man around this town and he's a friend of a powerful city councillor. Surely that would spark some interest from the police?"

"They wouldn't want to be involved, believe me," he said, addressing the fabric once more.

"You look like you were pretty badly beaten. I hope you went to the hospital, at least?"

He didn't reply.

"Christ, Roddy!"

"Why went you not?" Jake asked.

"What for? I'll be all right." He didn't sound as if he were glad about it. I can't say I blamed him.

* * *

We left Roddy to his misery and walked slowly back to the car. Though the rain was coming down even harder by this point, our minds were totally preoccupied with what we'd just witnessed. We sat silently in the car for a while, lost in our own thoughts once again. Finally, I asked him for his assessment.

"He is rash and very sudden in choler," he observed. "I would there were no age between sixteen and three-and-twenty, or that youth would sleep out the rest."

It seemed like a good idea to me as well. "He was certainly head-over-heels for her. He's young and inexperienced, of course, and she was beautiful . . . ."

"Young men's love then lies not truly in their hearts, but in their eyes."

"There's some truth in that, I admit. We're not talking about a mature love here. Still, I can't help feeling some sympathy for him. He's . . ."

". . . a peevish schoolboy, worthless of such honour," Jake countered. "A child that longs for every thing that he can come by." What is it with me today – will no one let me finish a thought? "What should such a fool do with so good a woman?" he added, a strong tinge of disdain in his voice.

He was being far too hard on the boy, I thought,

but I had to agree with this last sentiment. Roddy really did seem out of her league. Is it possible that he sensed it as well? Perhaps that's the reason the mere suggestion that there could be other contenders for her affections had upset him so. I decided to sound Jake out on this.

"Jake, do you think it strange that he could have become so distraught at the mere suggestion that there might be others interested in Mandy?"

"Good Lord, what madness rules in brainsick men, when for so slight and frivolous a cause such factious emulations shall arise!"

"Okay, I'll take that for a 'yes'." There was clearly no point in continuing this discussion. He seemed determined to take a harsh line on the boy, and was reaching rather deeply into his poetic toolkit to express it. I wondered why. I remembered the exchange we'd had on Monday when it seemed that we were each being more tolerant of our own sex than of the other; now, it was reversed. Yet here was a young man who had lost his mother just a few years ago and now had lost the woman he loved. Did it really matter that his love may have been immature and misplaced? Was I missing something?

Silence again descended on us. It felt oddly satisfying; at least I could be sure that no one would interrupt my thoughts. But I was wrong. Suddenly he asked, "What shall be done with him?"

I wasn't sure what he had in mind, but the question nudged me towards the realization that we had a responsibility in this situation. Actually, two. Not only should we report the assault, which is a serious crime in its own right, but we also had a duty to provide the police with any information that might be related to the murder. We couldn't be sure that the two violent crimes were connected, but we couldn't rule it out, either: they'd occurred on the same night to people who knew each other. Besides, it wasn't our place to judge; our duty was to report anything that might be relevant.

There was another reason to do so as well, a more self-interested one: we needed to keep the police on our side. Perhaps it was too late to win Lieutenant Knutsen over, but any brownie points we got from him might still be redeemable at some future point. "Jake, we need to let Knutsen know about this."

"But this is trifling," he replied.

"Perhaps, but it's also necessary." I explained my reasoning, which he appeared to accept. That's how I interpreted his grunt, anyway.

I opened my contacts list and selected Knutsen's direct line. As I expected, he was less than overjoyed to hear my voice. Before he could deliver another sermon about not interfering with a police investigation, I dropped the news about Roddy's infatuation with Mandy and the beating he had received by an unknown assailant on the night of her murder. Knutsen's tone moderated considerably. He knew about Gates's 'friendship' with Mandy, of course, but this other connection was entirely new to him. Ap-

E. P. MARWICK

parently, Gates hadn't mentioned it when he was interviewed.

Knutsen wanted to talk to Roddy right away, so I gave him the address. As he was writing it down, I turned to Jake to see if he had anything to add. He took the phone from my hand and greeted Knutsen. Before he could say anything more, the detective asked him to describe the seriousness of the assault. This was evident from the answer Jake gave: "Trust me, he beat him most pitifully." Another pause followed, which was terminated by the following request from Jake: "Do one thing for me that I shall entreat. See where he is, who's with him, what he does."

This seemed like sage advice, if only to prevent any further harm happening to the young man. As Jake returned the phone to me, I asked him, "Now that's taken care of, what's next?"

"Well, what would you say?" he replied.

I knew what I should suggest was 'give up', but I no longer wanted to: I felt the bit in my mouth. "I hate to say this, but I think we need to confront Gates again. I can't help thinking that he's behind everything. Maybe he wasn't as unconcerned about his relationship with Mandy as he claims to be. Maybe he really resented the fact that Roddy'd been trying to horn in on it."

"What follows then?" He seemed skeptical, but curious.

I thought about it some more. "Okay, suppose it played out this way. Gates knows the kid has been given a warning, so he has Chiang invite him over to their table at the nightclub, then he invites both of them to his house, just to see how the kid's taking it. When the kid challenges him about her, he knows the warning hasn't been enough. He's got to be taught a lesson, put in his place."

"And then?"

"Gates almost certainly knows that Roddy lives in the cottage at his uncle's, so he shows up late Sunday night and beats him up – or has someone else do it for him. Even if it were someone else, Roddy would know who's behind it – there'd be no point to the beating otherwise. But he's told that he better keep his mouth shut, if he knows what's good for him. You agree so far?"

"It may be so, I grant you."

"Really?" I felt encouraged enough to push it. "Then there's Mandy. Maybe Gates is angry at her for encouraging Roddy – or at least, for not nipping the flirtation in the bud. He might have intended just to give her a beating, too, but it gets out of hand. She tries to scream, so he throttles her with the scarf to shut her up. Except he does it too hard."

He reflected on this scenario for a few moments. "Of this I am not certain," he replied at last.

He was right, I realized: it was a huge leap. There was nothing solid to tie Gates to either act of violence, not to mention the fact that he had an alibi for the time of the murder. The alibi . . . could that be it?

"You don't suppose it might be better to confront Chiang instead? Tell him our theory that Gates may be the one who beat his nephew, or had him beaten. Maybe that would be enough to turn him against his buddy."

Jake tilted his head skeptically. "I cannot tell; I think not."

"Hmm. I suppose Gates is too valuable an ally – and too dangerous an opponent – to turn on him just because his nephew took a beating. What about my idea of trying to approach Gates himself, then? Or do you think that would be a waste of time as well?"

"No, madam, that's the next to do," he replied. "And let us do it with no show of fear."

"The question is, how do we get to him? We got lucky yesterday, but who knows when he'll show up at the Brown Pelican again? Even if it's soon, there'd be no guarantee that he'll talk to us, not after the way it went last time. He could easily have us thrown out."

"I'll undertake't: I think he'll hear me."

"But where? We can't just show up to his house and knock on the door." His silence told me that was exactly what he was intending to do. "But Jake, that's nuts."

"What cannot be avoided 'twere childish weakness to lament or fear," he replied. "He is a lion that I am proud to hunt."

"If Helen's right about him, it could be very risky."

This drew his attention, but only to the extent of stimulating his protective instinct. "It will be dangerous to go on," he acknowledged. "Wait on me tonight. You shall hear more by midnight."

I suppose there's still some part of me that hankers to be protected by a knight in shining armour – but only a small part. Besides, I don't like it when men decide to take control, even when my own trepidation invites it. I girded my loins and thrust myself onto my mount, lance in hand. "My dear comrade-in-arms," I said, "if you're determined to enter the lion's den, then I'm going in there with you."

W EDNESDAY, JUNE 17. EVENING.

I t's odd how a display of bravado is so often followed by a tremor of doubt. As the rain pounded down relentlessly on the car roof, I became increasingly preoccupied with the hollowness of my professed determination to accompany Jake. Confronting powerful and dangerous men with their crimes is not me, I told myself; I'm no knight in shining armour. Fortunately, Jake came to my rescue. "Is't near dinner-time?" he asked. "Shall I entreat you with me to dinner?"

"Consider me entreated," I replied.

We found a Thai restaurant a few minutes from the Chiang estate and dashed inside. It was virtually empty; too early for most patrons, I imagine, or just too wet. During the meal, Jake seemed totally lost in himself, which I hoped signalled that he was devising some sort of plan for how to tackle Gates. We were most of the way through our food when I broached the issue: "I trust you've figured out how we're going to do this."

He gestured nonchalantly with his shrimp-charged chopsticks. "We'll crave a parley to confer with him."

"What if he refuses?"

"That he will not."

I had my doubts about that, but I decided to play along. "Okay, suppose he does agree to see us. Then what? He didn't say anything useful last time; won't it just be more of the same?"

"It may not be, good madam, pardon me, for I will make him tell the tale anew, and this may help to thicken other proofs that do demonstrate thinly."

'Thin' was precisely the term for the evidence we had against Gates. We had a motive for the assault on Roddy and perhaps, at a stretch, on Mandy, but precious little else. "So, your thinking is, we'll just ask him to go through the events of Sunday evening again and somehow he'll reveal a detail or two that'll establish his guilt. What would induce him to do that?"

He smiled. "I am one of those gentle ones that will use the devil himself with courtesy."

I nearly choked on my Goong Pad Bai Gaprow (if that's what it was; it could have been anything). "Courtesy might get us in the door and might even get him talking," I allowed, albeit with more than a twinge of skepticism, "but why would it cause him to cough up anything incriminating? Besides," I started to snicker, "you'll explode, like you always do when you think you're not getting the full story.

You'll start damning and cursing him . . . ."

"Would you have me false to my nature?" he replied haughtily. "I mind to tell him plainly what I think."

"You'll take little delight in it, I can tell you."

Only when I transcribed this conversation much later did I realize I'd quoted Shakespeare again. That probably explained the slight smirk on Jake's face as he replied, "'Tis probable. There's reason he should be displeased at it."

"My point exactly." The conversation was becoming surreal. "Let's face it, Jake, this isn't much of a plan. I'll concede that sometimes your style does stir up some useful bits of information, but it failed the last time we talked with him, and this time he'll be on his own turf. We'll probably just piss him off – at the very least."

"If you think so, then stay at home and go not. I'll go alone."

"Not a chance, my friend."

Thus armed with a foolproof strategy, we drove to Gates's place. It was easy to spot, despite the pelting rain: there was one house two blocks west of Dunbar on Thirty-Third that dwarfed all the others in the neighbourhood. Jake parked the car, and without the least hesitation, walked up to the front door and knocked. I stood slightly behind him as we waited.

Several seconds passed without any response

from within. This was odd: the driveway held two rather large cars and, although the curtains were drawn, we could see that the lights were on in several of the rooms.

"I'll knock once more to summon them."

The second knock, though a good deal louder, produced no better result.

"Hoa, open the door!" he hollered as he hammered on it a third time.

That did the trick. The door was opened by a slightly-built man, presumably some kind of servant. "Yeah, what do you want?" he said.

"Commend me to your master," Jake replied. "Let it be known to him that we are here." The man hesitated, so Jake spoke again, as if to a simpleton: "Come, come, we are friends. Go and tell him, we come to speak with him."

The servant departed without a word, leaving us standing at the threshold. I'd seen enough *Masterpiece Theatre* to know that this was not what's supposed to happen; he should have asked our names and invited us into the entrance hall while he checked if his master was 'at home'. After a couple of minutes, the man returned and, without a word, started to close the door on us. This guy really needs to check out *PBS*, I thought. What's he been doing Sunday nights?

Jake's response was also outside the parameters of Edwardian drama: he blocked the door's advance by placing a foot firmly in front of the jamb. "Where's your master?" he asked, completely unruffled by the brusque treatment from the underling. "Is he at home? May we not see him?"

The servant shook his head slightly, but before he could make any further progress with the door, Jake flung his full weight against it, driving it open. The man stumbled backwards, nearly knocking over the hall table before falling sideways into the chair beside it.

"Out of our way, I say!" Jake proclaimed as he stormed past the astonished man. I followed quickly, before the man could regain his balance.

Heading in the general direction the man appeared to have come from, we came upon a door that was slightly ajar. Jake pushed it open to reveal a large den or study where Gates and Chiang were deep in conversation. Gates flashed a look of anger as we entered, but recovered quickly and gestured us into the room. He then signalled off the servant who was following fast behind. The man slinked away.

"Well, well, well," Gates said. "If it isn't our thespian-turned-sleuth. And the lovely Miss Marwick, you're here as well. What a surprise; I wasn't expecting to see you again so soon."

"Neither were we," I replied, "but we just came upon something rather disturbing. It couldn't wait."

"Oh, really? Well, you better take a seat and tell us about it. I hope it's not bad news about your investigation?"

I lowered myself onto the empty sofa, tugging Jake down with me. "Not exactly. We dropped in on Roddy this afternoon. You remember Roddy, don't you? He's Mr. Chiang's nephew."

"Of course I do," he replied, "but I don't find him all that disturbing." He chuckled in Chiang's direction. Chiang grimaced slightly.

"You might now. He's rather damaged."

"Damaged?" He looked puzzled. "What do you mean?"

"He's been attacked and beaten. Quite severely, by the looks of it."

"Really? Is he all right? When did this happen?"

"It happened late on Sunday night, the same night that Mandy Bennett was murdered," I replied, channelling my inner Lady Macbeth as best I could. "I think he'll survive."

"That's incredible!" he exclaimed. "Brian, did you know about this?"

"No, I didn't, Fred," Chiang responded gravely.

"Why, you were with him, were you not?" Jake asked.

Gates and Chiang looked at each other. Finally, Gates replied: "On Sunday? Yeah, that's right. We had a few drinks together. He was fine then."

"You do remember all the circumstance?"

"Well, let's see." Gates looked like he was trying to reconstruct a distant memory. "It was like I told you:

E. P. MARWICK

I was at Walt's party for a while, then I went to the Pelican around ten. I'd arranged to meet Brian there. Roddy showed up a little later, so we invited him over."

"That's one thing that's got us puzzled," I observed. "You didn't mention that Roddy was there when we talked to you before."

"I didn't think it was relevant. I thought you were concerned with what Brian and I were doing on the night of the murder."

"Nay, that follows not," Jake objected. "You should have said, sir."

"After all," I added, "you knew that Roddy was crazy about Mandy, didn't you?"

"Yes, yes, of course I did; it was pretty obvious. But it wasn't a big concern. Brian said he'd take care of it."

"But it gives him a possible motive . . . ."

"Listen," he cut in. "Roddy's just a kid. He's mixed up, sure, but basically harmless. I didn't mention him because I didn't want him to get sucked into your little investigation. He's had a tough enough time already."

I couldn't argue with that. "Okay, so what happened next?"

"We headed back here around eleven, as you know. I invited Roddy to come as well."

"Did you all come directly? Roddy said you had separate cars."

"We all showed up promptly, if that's what you mean."

"And how long did they stay?"

"Roddy was here till about one, then left. Brian stayed a little longer – maybe half an hour?" He looked towards Chiang for confirmation. Chiang nodded.

"When Roddy was here, did he raise the issue of your relationship with Mandy?"

"Yeah, as a matter of fact he did. Someone had told him . . . ."

"That was Helen," Chiang interjected.

"Yeah, Helen. Apparently, she'd told him that he should give up on Mandy because she wasn't the innocent thing he thought she was. That was your doing, wasn't it, Brian?"

Chiang nodded again.

"Well, as a matter of fact, she wasn't all that innocent – I can vouch for that," Gates continued, a wry grin contorting his face. "But not in the way Helen had said. Anyway, he was extremely upset by what he'd heard. And confused. He couldn't figure out how I could be involved with her, if that's the way she really was."

"How did you respond?"

He shrugged. "He was right, of course; there's no way it could have been like that. It was a stupid thing to have told him." He glanced severely at Chiang. "So I set him straight."

"You set him straight?"

"Listen, I told you I was very fond of Mandy, and I was. But getting the female lead in *Othello* meant that the affair was coming to an end. She would either succeed, which would mean she didn't need me, or fail, in which case she intended to try her luck elsewhere, somewhere with more opportunities. She told me as much; we were quite frank about these things. Besides, as I told you, I was ready to move on."

"Yet we have only your word for any of this," I countered. "We can't help wondering if you might not have been more upset about losing her than you're letting on." He flinched a little at this suggestion. "Or perhaps you don't like being rushed. Perhaps you decided that the boy needed to be taught a lesson in patience."

"Oh, I see," he replied, smirking with incredulity. "You think I roughed him up to warn him off or put him in his place. Listen, if I want to teach someone a lesson, I don't resort to violence to do it. I'm a powerful man in this town, but I'm not a gangster. You should know that much, Miss Marwick."

I didn't know that at all, but now was not the time to take it up. "Still, someone must have done it," I pointed out.

"But how could it have been me? I was with his uncle at the time."

"Not quite. We know that Roddy was attacked

at his home sometime after your drinking session with Mr. Chiang."

"So you're suggesting that I went to Brian's place after he'd returned there, broke into the guest house located just behind his house . . . ."

"No. There was no evidence of a break-in."

"Well, then."

"However," I added, "there was no need to break in. The door was unlocked."

"Was it?" He thought about that for a moment. "But I wouldn't have known that, would I? Think about it. The only way I could have attempted to get into Roddy's place is if I had a key; breaking the door in would have made too much noise. So would banging on it to wake him up from his drunken stupor. But how would I have a key to Roddy's place?" Turning to Chiang, he asked: "Did you ever give me one, Brian?"

"No. Why would I?"

Gates turned back to us. "Did either of you ask Roddy if he'd ever given me a key?"

Jake and I remained silent.

"Of course you didn't." He bristled with indignation at having to deal with such incompetence. "Here's some advice. Check your facts before you start making accusations. When you do ask Roddy, you're going to find that the answer is no. I scarcely know the boy."

"So, basically, you told Roddy that Mandy wasn't a

tart and that your relationship with her would soon be coming to an end. That's it? Nothing more?"

"What more could there be?"

"You didn't, for instance, tell him that there might be others interested in her?"

"I may have mentioned something of the sort," he conceded after a slight pause. "My concern was that Roddy might get his hopes too high. He understood that she wasn't going to need me, and he was glad to hear me confirm it; what he didn't understand was that she wasn't going to need him, either. Quite frankly, they'd be lining up in droves once the play got going."

It wasn't the right time to point out the problem with that metaphor. "Was there anyone in particular you had in mind?"

"Anyone in particular?" he bristled. "How could there be anyone else? Between acting, waitressing, and seeing me, she had no time for anyone else. Besides, I may cheat on women; women do not cheat on me."

"What about Kendrick Page?"

That sparked his interest. "Are you saying he was keen on her? Well, I suppose I shouldn't be surprised; they were playing opposite each other. But nothing had developed, that's for sure. If anything had, I'd know about it."

Sad as it seems, I believed him. Gates was not someone you'd want to cross, especially if you were aiming at a successful stage career in this town. "So, what was Roddy's state of mind when he left that night? Was he angry? Worried?"

Gates grimaced as he searched for the right word. "I'd say he was just mixed up. And drunk, of course. He'd been told a lot of stuff in the last few hours and it was going to take him some time to sort it out. He left shortly after we had that conversation."

"And neither of you have seen him since then?"

Chiang responded first. "That's right."

Jake seemed incredulous. "Not see him since? Sir, that cannot be."

"It's true," Chiang replied. "I was at the office Monday morning when I received the news of the murder. I checked with the rental office, but he hadn't come in yet, so I phoned him at home. He was upset when I told him what had happened, of course, and also very hung over, but he said nothing about being beaten."

"Didn't you check in on him when you got home? He lives on your property."

"I decided to leave him in peace. It was only today that I found out he hadn't been at the office this week, but I figured it's probably best he takes a few days off. I had no idea he'd been roughed up."

"I didn't hear a peep, either," said Gates. "Poor bugger."

These expressions of sympathy were a bit much to take, and Jake, I could tell, was approaching his limit. He leaned forward to signal that he was going to take over the questioning. I was more apprehensive than relieved.

"The clock upbraids me with the waste of time," he declared. "I do now let loose my opinion; hold it no longer."

"Jake, please!"

"Be quiet, and do not interrupt me in my course," he replied. "Patience is stale, and I am weary of it." Then, staring directly at Gates, he let it fly: "I think you have killed the poor woman. What say you to it?"

Gates reacted with predictable indignation: "How dare you come into my house and throw out an accusation like that?! I told you before, I did NOT kill her. Any suggestion that I did – or had any involvement at all in her death – is utter nonsense."

Jake was unfazed. "Nay, 'tis most credible. You have killed a sweet lady, and her death shall fall heavy on you."

"Fall heavy on me? What the hell does that mean?" His gaze became steely cold. "What can you possibly do?"

"Lingering perdition," Jake replied, "worse than any death can be at once, shall step by step attend you and your ways."

It was a delightfully vague line and it clearly had Gates perplexed. Did we have some evidence against him? Were we threatening to go to the media with what we knew or suspected? You could have almost seen the wheels turning behind those sharp, glistening eyes of his. "Listen," he said, "let me give you some advice. . . ."

"We need no more of your advice."

"Can you cut with the self-righteous bullshit? We need to reach an understanding."

"What compact mean you to have with us?"

"You've got it pretty good here. Why don't you just . . . ."

"I care not for good life," Jake cut in again. "I think it rather consists of eating and drinking." His flippancy would have tried a saint's patience.

"Well, it also consists of being able to make a living," Gates countered. He was on more familiar turf now. "That play of yours – you know it hangs in the balance right now. I can tip that balance one way or the other."

"It's true," Chiang noted. "Around here, the Councillor gets what he wants."

"You are never without your tricks," Jake countered, unmoved by the threat. "I knew what you would prove: my friends told me as much, and I thought no less. You do yourselves but wrong to stir me up."

"We can make life difficult for you on other levels as well," Gates pointed out. His tone was increasingly menacing.

"Say no more: howe'er the business goes, you have

made fault i' the boldness of your speech."

"It won't be just the boldness of my speech you'll have to worry about."

"There is no terror in your threats, for I am arm'd so strong in honesty that they pass by me as the idle wind, which I respect not."

"God dammit it, Benatsky, you fucking . . . ."

"Ill deeds are doubled with an evil word."

"Okay, that's it. Out! Now!" Gates rose to his feet, followed immediately by Chiang. He then moved forward and positioned himself right in front of Jake, who remained seated. "Benatsky, this is the deal: you keep your mouth shut." He smiled cruelly. "For your own good – and hers."

If this threat bothered Jake, he showed no sign of it. He calmly looked to me and said, "Let's take leave of him." As he rose, he offered Gates one parting thought: "We'll leave you to your meditations how to live better, and deal with others better."

With that, he proceeded serenely towards the door. I scurried behind him with considerably less grace. That's how it felt, anyway.

We walked quickly to the car, as if dogs might be loosed at any moment. For once, Jake took the passenger seat, leaving me to drive my own vehicle. I didn't, though – not at first. Anger was surging up inside of me, anger over too many things to know where to begin. It didn't help that Jake showed no signs of sharing my turmoil. In fact, he seemed almost placid.

"I see your brows are full of discontent," he observed after several minutes of awkward silence.

"'Pass by me as the idle wind'?" I exploded. "I can't believe you said that." It felt like only sarcasm could temper my fury. "What were you trying to do in there? Was it, like, some new kind of comedy shtick – insult the target as much as you can and watch him go bananas?"

"Come, these jests are out of season," he responded. "Reserve them till a merrier hour than this. I am not in a sportive humour now."

"Then why did you play the fool in there?"

He looked shocked at my shrillness. "Shall I tell you why? His insolence draws folly from my lips. But I did proceed upon just grounds to this extremity. I am not sorry neither."

"For Christ's sake, Jake, that's nuts!"

"What means this passionate discourse?" He looked as if I'd just told an off-colour joke at a funeral. "You must confine yourself within the modest limits of order. We will talk no more of this matter."

So here was the fucking voice of reason again! I'm sorry for the language, dear journal, but the mere act of writing up this conversation up causes my blood to boil. This has got to be the most exasperating man alive. Somehow, I managed to calm myself enough to say: "Jake, these guys are serious. There could be consequences – bad consequences – for us if we don't back off."

"I know not what may fall," he allowed. "Much that I fear may chance."

These frank words brought home to me the realization that his passion, as he would call it, may have damned us both. Like a true Shakespearean heroine, I wanted my downfall – if it must happen – to be my own doing. I wanted to be Juliette, not Ophelia. "Well, I don't want to be sucked into this," I responded.

"Nor would I wish you."

"But what about you? Did you see how he looked at you when you accused him of murder?"

"I did so. His cheek look'd pale, and on my face he turn'd an eye of death."

Exactly, I thought; I couldn't have put it better. "Jake, I think we've reached the point where we can't go on alone. It's become too risky. We've got to go to the police. If you won't, I will."

"No, do not, I prithee."

"What? That's really nuts!"

"Why, my negation hath no taste of madness," he protested testily. "The law protects not us: then why should we be tender to let an arrogant piece of flesh threat us, play judge and executioner all himself?"

"So what are you suggesting we do – carry guns around so that we can shoot it out, if we have to? That makes no sense. If you're not going to go to the police for protection, then we'll have to go into hiding."

"You may do so; I will not."

"So you're just going to continue doing whatever you please, not even letting the police know of the danger . . . ."

"Let's reason with the worst that may befall," he interrupted.

"All right, the worst is that Gates is a vicious, corrupt, arrogant, powerful city official who'll stop at nothing to prevent anyone from accusing him of murder. How's that?"

Rather than answering, he stared vacantly through the windshield for a minute or so. "Can this be true?" he muttered at last.

"Of course it can."

He continued to stare off into the night. Very soon, my impatience got the better of me. "Jake, I . . . ."

He held up his hand. "Enough; no more. Until I know this sure uncertainty, I'll entertain the offer'd fallacy."

The offered fallacy? At first I didn't understand, but quickly it became clear. He was going to take Gates's deal, after all. He'd say nothing against him, whatever he might believe – until he had the evidence to back it up.

"Do I have your word on that?"

"So you have."

"I'm glad to hear it; I just wish you'd told him that. Even then," I added wearily, "it may not be enough."

"What's to come is still unsure, but that's no matter," he declared, "for I am fresh of spirit and resolved to meet all perils very constantly."

If these bold words were intended to reassure me, they failed utterly. Grit may be admirable at some times, but at others it just irritates. I felt more confused and conflicted than ever. "On that upbeat note, I think I'll pack it in," I said.

"What is the time o' the day?" He checked his watch. It was about eight-thirty. "There's something else to do."

"You mean, now?"

"Yes, indeed, I do."

I couldn't agree. I was feeling absolutely drained; it seemed to me that we needed to slow down – at the very least. "Whatever it is, couldn't it wait till tomorrow?"

"I would not have things cool."

"Why not?"

"Trust me, it shall advantage more than do us wrong."

That cryptic reply put me over the top again. "How can anything advantage us at this point?" I exclaimed. "We know that a very dangerous man, Gates, is behind these crimes and there's nothing we can do about it."

"You look but on the outside of this work," he declared. "Our indiscretion sometimes serves us well, when our deep plots do pall."

I was startled. "What are you saying? You think that something useful was revealed by your so-called indiscretion in there?"

His head tilted slowly. "I cannot speak, nor think nor dare to know that which I know."

"What does that mean? If there's something you've figured out, something that might . . . ."

He slapped his forehead. "I forgot to ask him one thing; I am a fool."

"Who? Gates? We can't go back in there . . . ."

"No, not he."

"Who, then? I don't understand. You're not making any sense."

He looked at me at last, as if emerging from a daydream. "If I chance to talk a little wild, forgive me. I do spy a kind of hope."

"Hope?! You need to explain that."

"Madam, not yet. Let's go learn the truth of it."

"At least tell me this: do you have another suspect in mind?"

"As yet, I do not."

"But you have something – is that what you're saying? Jake, you got to tell me."

"'Tis no time to talk. Wherefore stay we?"

"Because I don't know where we're going," I

snapped back. But, of course, I did. "Oh, let me guess . . . back to the Pelican. There to meet with . . . ah, the fair Helena."

"So be it," he replied with a smile, "for it cannot be but so."

Damn him. He was enjoying this.

✻ ✻ ✻

As we drove to the nightclub, I couldn't help but ruminate some more about Jake's verbal assault on Gates. It seemed absurd from every angle. The strategy, I thought, had been to get him talking in hopes that he would give up a crucial detail or two that would weigh against him, or at least that would advance our investigation in some way. And we did get him talking – until Jake decided to accuse him point blank of being the murderer. It certainly had aroused Gates's anger and thereby placed us in peril, but what had we gained? Absolutely nothing, as far as I could see.

Yet, I couldn't help wondering if something useful had been revealed after all, something I'd missed entirely. Jake had implied as much when he claimed to 'spy a kind of hope', but was that just to lift my spirits? I resolved to push him till I got the truth.

"Jake," I said as we passed through the entrance of the Pelican, "I don't think it's fair for you to leave me hanging like that. If you've actually got something, anything at all, you got to . . . ."

"Never make known what you have seen tonight," he whispered in my ear.

"What?"

It was too late. He was already striding over to a bar table, where a well-oiled Lieutenant Knutsen was surrounded by a gaggle of empty glasses.

"What's the matter, Lieutenant?" Jake proclaimed with an air of well-honed conviviality.

Knutsen broke off the concentrated gaze he was casting on the one remaining glass with anything in it and raised his head. He looked as if his worst nightmare had just arrived, which may well have been the case. "I just got a call from the chief of police, Benatsky, who's just had a call from Councillor Gates. He's . . . ."

"Come, come, you're drunk," Jake declared soothingly.

"I've had a drink or two . . . ."

"Good wine is a good familiar creature," Jake observed, "if it be well used." Which clearly wasn't the case here – or did he think otherwise? I've often found it amazing how men have total sympathy for one another's drunken stupors, however intolerant they may be of other vices. With women, it's generally the other way around.

"You saying I'm drunk?" Knutsen retorted. He reached across the table to grab Jake by a lapel, but he missed by a wide margin and only narrowly avoided falling into the array of empty glasses.

"Nay, good Lieutenant; I pray you, sir, hold your hand." He was smiling broadly now; for men in bars, this was all good fun.

Or should have been, according to the code of men in bars. But Knutsen was annoyed, really annoyed. He steadied himself and took a wild swing at Jake. Jake dodged it easily, but by doing so, removed the one object of resistance that might have kept Knutsen upright. The Lieutenant fell to the floor so quickly it looked like a dive.

"Good Lieutenant!" Jake exclaimed, smiling so broadly now I thought his face would crack. He bent over to help Knutsen up; I'm not sure he would have made it otherwise.

"Are you hurt, Lieutenant?" he asked as he steadied the officer on his barstool and brushed off his jacket.

"I'm fine. Lemme go," sputtered the abashed but resentful officer. "You really know how to mess things up, don't you?"

"What mean you, sir?"

"You just can't go around interrogating powerful members of the City Council. Now I've got the chief of police breathing down my neck. My fucking career is on the line here. We need to solve this case and fast."

"I am for it, Lieutenant," Jake declared, "and I'll do you justice."

"That's what I'm afraid of," Knutsen replied. "Please, please . . . just stay out of it." He was almost whimpering now.

I had to break up this emerging love-fest. "You're tired and a bit drunk, Lieutenant," I said. "You need a good night's sleep. I'm going to get one of your officers to drive you home."

"As Heaven is my judge . . . ." replied Knutsen. "Oh, fuck it, I'm going home."

Jake threw a few bills on the table while I guided Knutsen toward the street, where I'd noticed a squad car stationed. I guessed that this was not the first time that the Lieutenant had allowed liquor to assault him so brazenly.

On re-entering the club, I spotted Helen loading up her tray with the glasses from Knutsen's bar-table so that Jake could make use of it. They were clearly pleased to be in each other's company, although neither was saying a word. When I think of how their initial meeting had gone, I couldn't help but be amazed.

I decided that Jake's admonition to say nothing didn't apply to Helen, so I launched in as soon as I reached the table. "Hi, Helen, we've had quite an evening," I said in response to her greeting.

"What happened?" she asked. There was a slight but unmistakeable note of apprehensiveness in her voice.

"First, we managed to figure out where Roddy lives. We went there and found that he'd been attacked and beaten."

"Oh my God! Is he all right?"

"It was a quite a bad beating, but he'll be fine. He's more upset about Mandy."

"Well, he would be. Who attacked him?"

"He either doesn't know or wouldn't say," I replied. "He's clearly frightened of something or someone."

"You're not still thinking he might be involved in her murder, are you?"

"We never did, not really, and now that he's been attacked, it's even less likely. In fact, we found out he has an alibi: he was here with his uncle and Gates until about eleven on Sunday night . . ."

"That's true. He was with them for a while. I remember now."

". . . and then all three of them went back to Gates's house and stayed there until about one a.m. We know that the murder took place between ten and one, so he's off the hook."

"I'm glad," she responded. "He's a little spoiled – well, who wouldn't be, with an uncle like that? – but he's basically a decent kid. The last few days must have been hell for him."

"That's for sure. Unfortunately, his alibi reinforces that of Chiang and Gates. I see no reason why your boss would be involved in the murder, but

I'm much less sure of Gates. We've just come from his house . . . ."

"You went there?!" she exclaimed.

"Yeah. We stopped by for a little chat. We suspect him of having done the beating, or having had it done, to teach the kid a lesson. If so, he may have taken it out on Mandy as well. So we confronted him. Well, Jake did." Both of our gazes averted to his face, which glowed with an expression of benign equanimity.

"You're kidding!" she cried. Her alarm was clearly rising. "What happened?"

"Gates got a little upset. As you've been telling us all along, he has a vicious streak."

"His liberty is full of threats to all," Jake concurred. "To you yourself, to us, to every one."

Helen looked just as rattled as she had the last time. Jake, however, seemed much less sympathetic. "Why are you silent?" he asked. "Alas, why gnaw you so your nether lip? Some bloody passion shakes your very frame." That much was obvious, but what he said next was not: "You look as you had something more to say."

I was surprised; it sounded like he knew something about her that I didn't. She seemed more than surprised; 'stunned' might be a better word.

"No," she hesitatingly responded, "it's just that I'm afraid of him, of both of them. You didn't tell them I'd talked to you, did you?"

"Nay, yet there's more in this."

That comment surprised me further, but not so much as did Helen's reaction to it. Slowly, her composure began to dissolve. She kept her focus fixed on the table, avoiding eye contact with either of us. I could feel my anxiety level creeping up. Something was definitely going on here that I didn't understand.

"Well, well, come on: who else? Who is it?"

After a pause that seemed interminable but probably lasted only a few seconds, she expired deeply and began to speak. "Okay, I haven't been totally honest with you. There is someone else. Someone Mandy was interested in. Very interested, if you know what I mean. I should have told you about him before."

"Indeed, I should have ask'd you that before," he reassured her. "Who may that be, I pray you?"

"He's a real nice guy, so much nicer than the sort we usually get in here. I didn't want to get him into trouble with Mr. Gates; he's in a vulnerable position. Who knows what Mr. Gates would have done?"

The tension was unbearable. "Well, who is he?" I asked.

She looked up at me. "He's someone from the play. He's come around here quite a few times. Once when Roddy was also here, which was a little awkward. Fortunately, he didn't come around when Mr. Gates was here."

"Helen, please, . . . who?"

"His name's Mike. You must know him; he's playing the part of Cassio, I think it is."

"She false with Cassio!" Jake blurted out. "Well, well, as 'tis the strumpet's plague to beguile many and be beguiled by one." He appeared to be highly amused.

"I wish you'd stop using that term," I said.

"Pardon me, madam." His face now sported a look of mock-contriteness.

I can't say what mine sported, but I knew how I felt: dumbfounded (again). "Helen, are you sure about that?"

"Oh yes, I'm very sure. They met at an audition for the play. It was like a thunderbolt. They . . ."

". . . no sooner met, but they looked," Jake intoned, "no sooner looked, but they sighed; no sooner sighed, but they asked one another the reason; no sooner knew the reason but they sought the remedy."

"Yeah, pretty much," she agreed with a faint smile.

"Besides," he added mischievously, "the knave is handsome, young, and hath all those requisites in him that folly and green minds look after."

"Do you have to go into it in such lyrical detail?" I snapped at him.

"Why, what's the matter," he retorted, "that you

have such a February face, so full of frost, of storm and cloudiness?"

The patronizing bastard! I couldn't find any words; I just wanted to scream. Though he must have seen my perplexity, he didn't let up: "Why are you breathless? And why stare you so? You have seen Cassio and she together, and so have I."

"Yes, of course, we have. Everybody at the party last Sunday saw them talking together. Why should that matter?"

"You know the cause," he replied bluntly. He was looking much more solemn now, those disturbing eyes bearing down on me with full intensity.

"What do you mean?" I exclaimed, flustered by this sudden turn of events. It felt as if I'd been thrust onto the hot seat. "It's just that Michael seems . . . I don't know . . . so straightforward and guileless. It's hard to imagine him chasing Gates's girlfriend behind his back."

"Yet there's more in this," he countered.

It was the same thing he'd said to Helen. He does know a lot more than he's let on, I thought. But what?

"Okay," I admitted, "Michael's a friend of mine and, like Helen, I'm worried where this might lead to. Listen, we all know where the evil lies in this business: it's with Gates. Maybe also Chiang, but certainly Gates. If we now throw the spotlight on Michael, what's going to happen? The investigation will be diverted towards him and he could end up wrongly accused, especially if the police feel they can't get enough on Gates or Chiang – or if they're under their control."

"Ay, do you fear it?" he replied. "Then must I think you would not have it so."

"Of course I wouldn't have it so! Wait a sec, what do you mean by that?"

He declined to answer. All he said was, "Let's not confound the time with conference harsh. I'll leave you, lady. Good night." With that, he started to drift toward the bar.

"Hold on!" I exclaimed, grasping his sleeve. "You can't just leave it like that. We've got to talk about this. How could it be Michael? I can't believe it. I mean, what would be the motive?"

"You are too indulgent," he replied. "To-morrow morning let us meet him then."

"But Jake, we know who the murderer is. You said so yourself."

"The event is yet to name the winner: fare you well. What you have said, I will consider; what you have to say I will with patience hear. At nine i' the morning, we'll meet again. So please you, let me now be left alone."

"What are you going to do?"

He smiled. "I will see what physic the tavern affords. Once more, fare you well."

❋ ❋ ❋

I was more than willing to leave Jake to his 'physic'. He was being deliberately obtuse and I no longer had the will, nor the strength, to continue wrangling with him. I decided to return home, relax a little and try to make some sense of this turbulent day. And perhaps take some physic of my own.

I noticed the message light flashing on my land line as soon as I walked in. I checked it immediately; I figured it would be news about the play. Indeed, it was (nice to be right about something!). Walt had decided that our new Desdemona was now ready to rehearse with the rest of the cast, so we were expected on stage tomorrow at nine o'clock. . . . Damn it, that's when Jake said we'd meet. How did he know?

I was still puzzling over this when my mobile phone rang. It was Simon, my reporter friend. Although I was bushed, I decided to take the call. My concern was for Roddy; suppose whoever had attacked him decided to come back to finish the job? Jake had asked Knutsen to keep tabs on him, but I could see no particular reason to expect the Lieutenant to take that request seriously. Perhaps casting more public attention on the assault would reduce the chances of a recurrence. It was worth a try.

I quickly filled Simon in on the attack and, to a lesser extent, on our confrontation with Gates. I chose not to bring Michael's name in it; we had no evidence against him, and besides, any mention in the press of an actor as a suspect might truly scupper the play.

Simon, for his part, had little to contribute. He promised that the assault would be reported, but he saw little hope of getting the paper to re-open the investigation into Gates's conduct in office. His editor refused to allocate any resources for it, given the absence of new evidence and the past record of failures to make headway against the powerful councillor. I couldn't say I blamed him; we ourselves had nothing on him, despite all our efforts. True, we'd found out at first hand that he's a nasty piece of work, but making that public would be, as he'd noted, slander – or in this case, libel. I knew that Jake's reply had been a bluff: it's not enough for something to be the truth to avoid such a charge; you had to be able to prove it. We couldn't, period.

We ended the call with vague promises to keep each other informed. I then popped a cork (I always keep an emergency bottle of Chardonnay in the fridge), sliced a generous wedge of sharp cheese, and sat down in my favourite chair. I was well into the second glass before I could feel my nerves yielding to the anesthetic. As they did, my anger slowly melted away. It wasn't just the wine taking over. The more I thought about it, the more convinced I became that we had little to fear from Gates. He's too shrewd and cunning an operator, I reasoned, to risk bringing on more trouble than absolutely necessary. To avoid his wrath, all Jake has to do is stick with the deal. And he would, I was sure. It wasn't just that he'd promised; the more pressing reason is that he seemed to have moved on. 'The event is yet to name a winner' he had said, as if the field were now wide open.

Why had he said that? There can be only one sensible answer: he must think that Michael Calthorpe is the murderer. But how did he reach that conclusion? I roused myself from my chair's cozy embrace and grabbed my phone. I couldn't go through all the interviews I'd recorded – it would take most of the night – but I could at least scan through the key exchanges. The answer must lie there.

I began with the interview with Gates. The critical passage in that interview had to be when I asked him if he'd told Roddy about any other men in Mandy's life. I reviewed that portion of the recording carefully. There was a slight pause before he denied it, but nothing else of note. That pause would seem to be a slim basis for Jake to infer anything.

Then I remembered a strange moment that occurred when we were sitting in the car after that interview. Jake said that he'd forgotten to ask him something, but he wasn't referring to Gates, so who did he mean? It had to be either Roddy Chiang or Mr. Lapierre, the only other males we'd interviewed that day. It took a fair bit of time (and another glass of wine) before I realized that it wasn't Roddy I should be focussing on, but rather the manager: we never asked him if the younger man he saw at the apartment building Sunday night might have been Roddy. I checked the time. It was around ten p.m., not too late – at a stretch – to place a call.

"Hi, Mr. Lapierre, it's Emma Marwick. Jake and I were talking to you earlier about Roddy."

"Did you find him?"

"Yes we did, thanks to your help. There's just one thing we forgot to ask you."

"It's quite late. . . ."

"Yes, I know. I'm sorry. It's just this: I know you didn't get a good look at the man who came to the building late on Sunday, but could it have been Roddy Chiang?"

"No, it wasn't him. I'm sure of that. The man I saw was much bigger and definitely not East Asian."

"I see. Thank you so much. Good night."

It was what I expected, given what Gates and Chiang had told us, but I was glad of it, all the same; the poor boy had enough troubles already. But the larger issue still remained: why is Jake focussing on Michael? He seems the most improbable of suspects. Apart from his basic nature – I shared Helen's instinct about that – the obvious problem is that he was at the party Sunday night. Or was he? I remembered that he'd stayed for quite a while – longer than Kendrick or Gates, certainly – but not till the end. Did Jake observe him leaving early – early enough to have gone to Mandy's apartment and kill her? Is that the clue that makes him so sanguine about this line of investigation?

It still didn't make sense, though. Even if Michael had left in time to have done it, what would be his motive? It's easy to imagine that Gates, the soon-to-be ex-lover, might have been angry enough; Roddy, the youngish would-be rival, could conceivably be a candidate as well, although that seemed a stretch. But if Helen's description of the attraction between Mandy and Michael, particularly as captured by Jake's Shakespearean lyricism, were true, what possible reason would Michael have had for killing her?

To the contrary, one could say that it's surprising that he himself hadn't been assaulted or even murdered. Maybe that's it. Maybe Jake is thinking that if Michael were innocent, he should have been a victim of some kind of attack, as Roddy had been. Yet, he didn't seem to be following that logic with Roddy – it was I who'd suggested that Roddy couldn't be the culprit because he'd been attacked. Did Jake agree with that observation? I checked the recording. No, he didn't say a word. So what is he thinking?

That's a good question to ask in general, I reflected. Jake's behaviour, as usual, had been perplexing. Particularly the sudden rages. They brought to mind a book I remembered reading at university. It was written a long time ago by Norbert Elias; the title, I believe, is *The Civilizing Process*. The basic argument, as I recall it, is that the development of Western civilization – perhaps all civilizations?

– is characterized by an increasing ability to control impulses and achieve ends in more rational, planned ways. For instance, whereas noblemen in Shakespeare's time might have drawn a sword at an insult to their honour (this kind of flash of anger is common in Shakespeare's plays), nobles in the eighteenth century would have challenged their insulters to a duel to be conducted at another time according to strict rules, and contemporary men would probably let it pass, at least for the time being. They might try to get back by outfoxing their opponent in business or even sleeping with his wife – not necessarily more admirable, but certainly more deliberative and cold-blooded. (Of course, I'm discounting road-ragers with guns under their car seats; as far as I can tell, the civilizing process has passed them by.)

Jake reminded me very much of the sixteenth-century version of men. Emotions surge over him quickly and with little apparent control. Anger, especially. It can flare up without much in the way of overt provocation, but it can also disappear just as quickly, leaving little residue. His initial encounter with Helen is a perfect example. When he first met her, he was damning her to hell-fire, then following the briefest of explanations, he decided that there was ... what was it? ... 'more owing her than is paid'. The encounter at Gates's house also fits the pattern. Almost out of the blue, he exploded with rage, flinging out an accusation of murder, then once we had left the house, he immediately lapsed into a state of eerie calmness.

Could it be, I wondered, that he uses Shakespearean language as a device to mask his somewhat outmoded emotional and mental make-up? In fact, it may not even be a conscious strategy. Perhaps he just feels an affinity for Shakespearean dialogue because it lends itself so well to his underlying dispositions? He may even have gone into classical acting for precisely that reason.

Seductive though this diagnosis is, I realized almost at once that there's a major problem with it (quite apart from my total lack of qualifications to make it). The point about controlling impulses is that it's generally better for achieving goals; people who can't manage it usually lose out to their more calculating counterparts. Yet, so far, Jake's style had been remarkably successful. At times, his outbursts had threatened to terminate interviews prematurely, but in the end we'd generally found out more than we had any right to expect. The one exception might be tonight's interview with Gates, but even here he appeared to have got more from the interview than I – not the sign, I would have thought, of someone governed by passion.

I wrestled with these thoughts for some time, eventually reaching the conclusion that the whole exercise was pointless. I'd been trying to put him in a neat little box, and it served merely to diminish him. He's far too complex to fit any simple classification or characterization. All I could say for sure is that he's driven – driven to achieve whatever goal he's set his mind to, which for now was solving the murder of Mandy Bennett. For some equally opaque reason, I'd been brought along for the ride, and no matter what frustrations or trepidations that entailed, I didn't want to get off. Not yet. Not till we were done.

Oh, there's one other thing I was sure of: he's absolutely the last man any woman should fall for. It's bound to happen from time to time – the poetry thing alone would see to that – but when it does, it can only end badly. Whatever charms the poor woman may possess, they could never be enough to pin him down. Nothing could.

*T*HURSDAY, JUNE 18. DAY.

I arrived at the theatre shortly before nine, somewhat groggy from a night of troubled and disjointed sleep. I was looking forward to getting back to familiar territory – acting. There wouldn't be a great deal of it, given the role I had, but it would still feel good to be someone else for a while.

Jake approached as I was chatting with Ollie and Stan. He appeared somewhat dishevelled, doubtless because he was more than a little hung over. My companions promptly made their excuses and withdrew. It may have been Jake's rough state that drove them off, but I'm more inclined to suspect the fear of another thrashing in the quotation game.

"How have you slept?" he enquired.

"Not so well, to be frank. I couldn't help thinking of yesterday's developments. I'm still very uneasy about them. How about you?"

"'Twas a rough night, I confess."

"Perhaps a little too much celebrating after having discovered Michael's connection to Mandy?"

"It is not vain-glory for a man and his glass to confer."

"Well, that's true enough, I suppose. But it isn't glory, either."

He ignored my comeback. His eyes were scanning the stage area.

"There's something I want to clear up," I continued. "I spoke with Mr. Lapierre last night. He confirmed that the man he saw arriving at the building late on the night of the murder wasn't Roddy. That's the question we forgot to ask, isn't it? But what I don't get is: how did you know the answer?"

"Not now," he replied. "I pray you, pardon me. Here is the man."

He shot past me towards the far stage entrance, where Michael had just appeared. I followed with a good deal less eagerness.

"How now, Cassio!" he announced as he came within range of his prey. "I am glad to see you."

"Oh, hi, Jake. Emma. What's up?"

"Let me ask you a question," Jake said.

"What's it about?"

"You may guess quickly what."

"Not the murder, I hope."

"It is indeed."

"Why, what's that to you?" he snapped.

"You probably aren't aware of this, Michael," I said, "but Jake and I have been asked to look into the case."

"The police asked you?" He sounded incredulous.

"No, not the police. It was Mr. Bennett, Mandy's father."

"I can't believe it – are you saying you're private detectives now?"

"We are not, sir, nor are we like to be," Jake responded.

"If you don't mind," I resumed, "we just have one or two questions."

"The time is very short," Jake added. The chaotic milling about of the cast and crew was indeed beginning to take on some coherence. The rehearsal would be starting any moment now.

"I don't really want to do this," he replied. "She was such a fantastic person . . . well, I don't need to tell you. . . ." He started to waver, then took a deep, almost feverish breath. "Listen, I think it would be better if we just put it out of our minds and concentrated on the play, don't you? I find it all so very sad."

"Nor come we to add sorrow to your tears," Jake reassured him.

"It might help if you could tell me how she was killed. The police won't say anything, but you must have a good idea, since you were there."

"Yes, we do," I admitted, "but I'm afraid we're obliged not to say anything for the time being."

"Then why should I . . . ?"

"Michael, please," I cut in. "We just have a few simple questions. It would really help us."

"Well, I suppose. What do you want to know?"

"Remember the party on Sunday night? I recall that you were there, but I'm not sure when you left, exactly. Do you remember?"

"Let's see. . . . I don't know exactly, either, but it was fairly late. Mandy had already left and so had Kendrick. By the time I got home, it must have been close to one a.m."

"Really? I seem to remember you leaving earlier than that. Did you go straight home?"

He looked surprised. "No, I was restless – probably anxious about the play. I'm not sure; I just knew I didn't want to be in company. So I just drove around for a while until I calmed down, then went home."

"So you have no witnesses for what you were doing after you left the party?"

"Witnesses? Why would I need witnesses?"

"Listen, Michael, the reason we're asking is that we've heard that Mandy and you . . . ."

"Mandy and me what? You think we were involved? Oh, come on, Emma. I'd only just met her and . . ."

". . . ever since, you loved her?" Jake suggested.

"That's nonsense! Apart from everything else, I knew she was going out with Winfred Gates, one of the Board members. Why would I attempt to interfere with that? It could have cost me my career."

"Love's reason's without reason," Jake remarked

with a shrug.

"What?"

"We all are men," he explained. "In our own natures, frail and capable of our flesh; few are angels."

"That's crap!" Michael cried. I thought so, too, but for a different reason.

"In what have I offended you?" Jake calmly inquired.

"You're accusing me of being involved with Mandy, and I don't like it. Why would you even suggest such a thing?"

"But for a satisfaction of my thought; no further harm," Jake assured him. He does a wonderful line in disingenuity, I had to admit.

"Look, you're barking up the wrong tree. I liked Mandy – she was fantastic, like I said – but that's it." He appeared to be reaching the limit of his patience. Fortunately for him, Eddie was calling for everyone's attention. The rehearsal was about to begin.

"I do not like this fooling," Jake commented as Michael hastened to join the others. "Could he say less? What is the matter, think you?"

"Maybe you *are* barking up the wrong tree. Maybe he's got nothing to say."

He grimaced, although whether it was because of Michael's replies or my concurrence with them, I couldn't say.

* * *

After a few anodyne comments from Walt, the rehearsal began in earnest. Since my character is Desdemona's lady-in-waiting, I appear in many of our new heroine's scenes, which meant that I had to endure the unpleasant experience of observing her work at first hand. I couldn't help feeling . . . well, if not exactly insulted, then certainly under-valued. But I was determined to let it 'pass by me as the idle wind', to quote Jake/Shakespeare.

On the upside, my character also appears quite often with Jake's, since they're husband and wife in the play. It was weird to see him doing what he always does, but following a script this time. Our characters don't like each other very much, which had the effect of making me think of how much I actually do like him, in spite of everything. They say there are great truths in Shakespeare, but I don't imagine he could have anticipated this one.

Around mid-morning, work began on scenes in which my character doesn't appear, so I took the opportunity to phone Mr. Bennett. I wanted to arrange a meeting to see how he was doing; the memory of his distress on Monday morning still lingered in my mind. I also hoped he could tell me more about Mandy. What was she really like? Was she just a young kid angry about the death of her mother and anxious to strike out on her own? Or was she the hyper-ambitious aspiring actress prepared to do whatever it took to get ahead? Either way, it shouldn't matter for our investigation and wouldn't,

I was convinced, but I had to know. We agreed to meet at Chez Panisse at twelve-thirty.

More scenes came up in which my character appeared, but also more breaks. I looked for a chance to use one of these to talk to Kendrick. Since he was playing the lead role, the opportunities were infrequent, but late in the morning one of them appeared and I seized upon it.

"Hi Kendrick, may I have a word with you?"

He looked uncomfortable for an instant, but then recovered and agreed. We moved over to an empty corridor near the stage. "How's your investigation going?" he asked immediately. "Are you making any headway at all?"

"Some," I replied. "How are you coping?"

"It's been a bit rough, to tell you the truth. I mean . . . it's not that Mandy and I had anything going. She was friendly and so on, but really, it was just a hope on my part. Maybe there was something on her side as well, but I couldn't be sure."

Was this humility speaking, I wondered, or just an attempt to throw attention away from himself? "I think we're all affected by her death," I said. "Part of it is that we don't expect it to happen to people our age, or in her case, younger than us. And certainly not violently."

"Are you sure you can't tell me how she was killed?"

"I have a feeling it's going to come out soon," I replied as neutrally as I could. It still struck me as odd that everyone needed to know that.

"What you just said about the young dying . . . . You're right, you know. At first, I was preoccupied by the loss of my hopes of some kind of relationship with her, perhaps the possible loss of my first real acting break as well, but then I realized it wasn't about me at all. That's not the tragedy. The tragedy is that a young woman has lost her life. It's the unfairness of it all, that's what's so hard to get over."

Kendrick had always seemed a cut above many of his age and gender, but my appreciation of him was now growing considerably. "I'm wondering, is there anything you know about her that might help us find her murderer? I mean, any detail that you might have forgotten to mention?"

"I've been asking myself the same question over and over, but no, there's nothing. I didn't know her that well, to be frank."

"Did she ever mention any men in her life?"

"No, not at all. In fact, that's one thing that gave me hope. A woman like Mandy is bound to have someone, I figured. But the fact that she hadn't mentioned anyone told me I had a chance; it was like she didn't want to discourage me."

"You didn't know about her relationship with Gates, then?"

"She was involved with him?" He seemed genuinely surprised. "If I'd known, I would never . . . ."

"No, I don't imagine you would have."

Nor would she have mentioned Roddy or Michael, I thought. I doubt she saw Roddy in that way, and as for Michael, their 'thing' was probably too new and uncertain to mention. Kendrick would find out about these other men sooner or later – probably sooner – but I didn't want to be the one to bring them up, so I let the matter drop. I asked him one or two questions about how he felt the play was going (carefully avoiding the Desdemona issue), after which we both headed back to the main stage.

✻ ✻ ✻

The morning session went on a little longer than I'd anticipated, which meant that I wasn't able to get to the café until close to one o'clock. Mr. Bennett was still there, staring blankly at nothing in particular. I walked over and greeted him. He seemed glad to see me, but in a cautious way. We quickly perused the menu and placed our orders.

With those preliminaries done, he thanked me for phoning him and asked straight away if that charming man he'd talked to earlier would be joining us.

"I'm sorry, Mr. Bennett . . ."

"Please call me Henry."

". . . Henry, then. Unfortunately, Jake is tied up with the production right now. He has a bigger part than I have, you see. Anyway, he sends his best wishes. He'll be talking to you soon."

It wasn't entirely untruthful; Jake did have a larger part than mine and he probably would be talking to Mr. Bennett at some point in the near future. But there was another truth I wasn't mentioning, which was that I wanted to do this interview alone, without being forced to act as the monitor of Jake's moods. I couldn't fault the way he'd handled our first talk with Mr. Bennett, but I wanted to get a feel for our victim that wasn't guided by his agenda (if that's what it was).

Henry seemed disappointed, but he put that aside. "Can you tell me if you are making any progress in the investigation? All the police have said is that it's still early days."

"We are learning things," I said guardedly, "but we're not quite there yet. What we'd like from you now is a little more background on Mandy." I let him think that deep background is the assistant detective's job.

"What would you like to know?"

"Perhaps you could discuss what she was basically like. I mean, as a child growing up. How her mother's death affected her. Why she left home. That sort of thing." I was trying my best to make it sound professional.

"She was pretty much a normal kid," he began. "Sweet, full of energy, mischievous at times, I suppose, but really no worse than any other kid. Adolescence was the usual mix of moodiness and sullenness, with occasional moments of exuberance. She drifted away from us and into her own music, gossip, and activities, but again I don't think it was anything out of the ordinary. No drugs or anything, as far as I know." Reminiscing was bringing some life to his voice.

"What about boys?"

There was a pause that suggested I was pushing into territory no father wants to explore. "Well, in truth, I didn't hear much about that. She may have confided in her mother, but not much got through to me. I suppose that's par for the course." He paused again. "I don't recall her being heartbroken over any boy; of course, with her looks, I wouldn't have expected rejection to be an issue. But whatever she got up to, nothing disastrous happened. No diseases, no pregnancies."

In other words, none of the things that give fathers nightmares. "Then her mother died," I prompted.

"Yeah, that was devastating for her. For me, too. I'm afraid I withdrew into my own pain just when I should have been there for her."

"It must have been difficult for you."

"It was, but I should have done more. Before my wife passed away, she asked me to look after Mandy. I promised I would and I failed her. Failed both of them."

It looked like he was going to lose composure, just

as he had when we'd first talked to him with his dead daughter lying a few feet away. "I'm sorry to raise this, Henry. These memories can't be easy."

He soldiered on as if I hadn't spoken. "She didn't drop out of school or anything. Didn't even miss a day, which was a little disturbing, to be frank. She never talked much about her mom, or about anything else, for that matter. Didn't seem to spend time with her friends, either. Occasionally, she didn't come home at night, which really upset me, but she always refused to say who she'd been with or what she'd done. I didn't know what to do. So we drifted apart."

"How did she do in school?"

"Her marks did suffer, as you can imagine, but she got through. Part of it was the acting. It's the one thing she really threw herself into. She took the drama course in high school, joined the drama club, and got into a couple of the school plays – even got the female lead in the main production in her final year. Then, without telling me, she applied to the City College drama program."

"Really? When did you find out?"

"At the end of her final year of high school. I pressed her about her plans and she replied that she was going to attend the College, starting in September, and that she would be moving out."

"What was your reaction?"

"Well, I wasn't pleased about the moving out. It

seemed to underline the fact that I'd failed to con-
nect with her after her mother's death."

"But you didn't try to stop her?"

"No. What could I do? She was eighteen. Besides,
I was pleased in a way that she had a goal, however
unlikely it was that she could ever make a career of
it. . . . That's not a criticism of her talents, mind you.
It's just a tough business, as you must know." I certainly did.

He went on: "So she found herself a room in a
student apartment and moved out. Didn't even ask
for financial support. When I asked her about it, she
just said she'd work part-time, which I guess is what
happened."

"How often did you see her?"

"Rarely, to be blunt. She'd phone on my birthday
and she generally came home for Christmas and
Thanksgiving dinners, but that's about it. She was in
a number of the College drama productions, but she
would never tell me about them. Eventually, I figured out that I could go to the department website
and check upcoming productions; if I saw her name
in the cast, I'd get a ticket in the back."

"In the back? So she wouldn't know you were
there?"

"Yes. It seemed clear that she wanted to keep me
out of the loop. The one exception was this play,
Othello. When she got the part, she phoned right
away to tell me about it. I couldn't believe how ex-

cited she was. It felt like she'd finally turned a corner."

I had to stop now; the thought that his daughter had been brought down just as she was about to escape her demons had finally pushed him to the breaking point. "Henry, I'm afraid I have to get back to the theatre. You've been an immense help and I know it's been difficult." He bowed his head slightly. "Please hang in there. Jake or I will be contacting you soon. I have a feeling this case is going to break very quickly."

"Is that what he thinks?"

"Absolutely."

Another lie. What was becoming of me?

I realized as I headed back to the theatre that my impressions of Mandy had been mistaken. While she was alive, I'd viewed her primarily as a competitor, a woman whose looks and youth had allowed her to steal a role that should have gone to me. She'd been merely a device that registered the passing of my own youth, not a person in her own right. Now I'd begun to see the world from her perspective and it wasn't what I'd expected. We tend to assume that youth and beauty are automatic tickets to happiness, but it hadn't been so for her. Life had thrust her into a morass of pain, from which acting – no matter what the price – represented the only salvation.

What I hadn't gotten from Henry was any sense

of her relationships with men. Clearly, her attractiveness had had the expected effect of drawing them like ants to honey; she never needed to be alone. But which one did she really want?

The affair with Gates was the easiest to read; he offered wealth, influence in the theatrical world, and even – according to Helen – some modicum of charm. Yet he was definitely short-term; neither a bother nor a solution. There was no real attachment there, at least on her part.

What about Roddy? That seemed an unlikely relationship, yet they may have found a powerful bond based on the common experience of having lost mothers as teenagers. Roddy was the more vulnerable: he was younger, the loss was more recent, and he hadn't found a way to strike out on his own. Mandy may have seen in him a fellow-member of the walking-wounded, someone to whom she, limping less seriously, could lend a shoulder. That common burden may have brought them together in a way that no other relationship could have. It wasn't love, not for her, but it might still have been very powerful, nonetheless.

Then there was Kendrick. He's only a few years older than her, and is both handsome and a talented actor in his own right. My inclination was to believe his claim that things hadn't gone very far, but who knows how she really felt? Might something serious have developed if circumstances had permitted? Or was it just wishful thinking on his part?

Finally, there was the real puzzler: Michael. I was much more inclined to believe Helen's account than his; there definitely had been something going on between them. Like Kendrick, he has looks, talent, and a love of acting, all of which she might have found appealing. If she hadn't been killed, would she have chosen him? We'd probably never know for sure, but I had to admit he was the likeliest bet.

✽ ✽ ✽

I made it back on stage by two o'clock. Walt chewed me out for being late, but it was half-heartedly delivered and received – we both knew my part was too minor to get worked up about. If I'd been less experienced, he probably would have come down harder – chalk it up as the one benefit of my new status as a 'mature' actress.

Jake was curious about where I'd been, so I told him I'd met with Mr. Bennett to see how he was coping. I also mentioned that he'd asked about the state of the investigation and that I'd promised that he, Jake, would fill him in as soon as possible. Thus I managed to cover most of my half-truths – at least to my satisfaction, if not to Jake's.

Before the rehearsal could start up in earnest, we had an unexpected interruption. A trio of police officers burst onto the stage, led by our dear Lieutenant Knutsen. He was clutching a sheaf of papers in his hand.

"Some news is come that turns their countenances," Jake murmured to me.

I had the same impression; they appeared to have something to announce. I couldn't tell from their faces whether it was good news or bad, but the furtive glance Knutsen shot in my direction make me more than a little uneasy.

Jake didn't wait for an announcement; he strode up to Knutsen and asked: "How do you now, Lieutenant? May I be bold to ask at what that contains, that paper in your hand?"

Knutsen clearly didn't appreciate this attempt to steal his thunder, but he rallied well. "This paper, Mr. Benatsky," he replied, addressing us all, "contains the results of the autopsy on Amanda Bennett. There is no longer any reason why the cause of death cannot be released."

This comment hushed most of the cast and crew, some twenty or so strong, and provoked audible intakes of breath. Knutsen was having his moment, after all. He scanned his audience and continued, "The cause of death is . . . strangulation. She was strangled in her apartment between eleven p.m. and one a.m. on Sunday night."

"Were there any other signs of violence?" Stan quickly asked. He seemed shaken; he'd probably been hoping for something less painful, like a gunshot to the back of the head.

"No," Knutsen replied, "there were no other signs of violence. That includes sexual assault."

'Thank God for small mercies' was the thought running through everyone's mind, or so I assume. Certainly through Stan's.

"There's more," Knutsen announced. He needn't have scanned the audience again; he had their total attention. "The murder weapon was a very expensive white silk scarf." He turned to one of his officers, who handed him a clear plastic bag containing the offending item. "*This* scarf," he declared, holding the bag up over his head for all to see. The scarf became in that moment a sacred token, an object of rapt awe.

"We were not able to extract any physical evidence from this scarf, apart from that of the victim," he continued, "but that doesn't mean we don't know anything about it. Our investigations have found that it was purchased last week from the men's accessories counter at Nordstrom's department store. As it happens, the item sells so rarely that the clerk on duty remembers the sale. In fact, she was able to give us a very good description of the woman who bought it." He scanned the stage once more, relishing the aura of dread and expectation that enveloped his audience. "She was white, in her early to mid-thirties, average height and weight, with medium brown hair and blue eyes. The clerk is confident she'd recognize this woman if she saw her again."

"I have heard better news," Jake muttered. So had I; it was a description that matched me in every detail.

"Master lieutenant, pray you, by your leave, ..."

Knutsen raised his hand to pause him. "Mr. Benatsky, I trust you appreciate that this lead is the product of careful, diligent police work. Work done by trained professionals, not amateur, self-styled detectives. Now, do you really think you have something useful to contribute?"

"So I have."

"You better make it brief."

"Well, sir, to do you courtesy, this will I do." He pivoted sharply towards Michael. "How came you, Cassio, by that scarf?"

Michael's face froze in an expression that melded astonishment with fear. He looked as if he had taken a direct hit from a stun gun.

"I' th' name of something holy, sir, why stand you in this strange stare?"

It was to no avail; Michael remained speechless. I think my level of anxiety had risen just as much as his, but I could put voice to it. "Jake, for Christ's sake!" I cried. "How can you possibly suspect him? Have you totally flipped out?"

He must have felt my frustration, but he remained unperturbed. "You speak a language that I understand not," he declared.

Under normal circumstances, I might have burst out laughing at that comment, but these weren't normal circumstances. "What?!" I exclaimed. "Jake, this is crazy."

"I understand a fury in your words, but not the words," he calmly replied. "Alas, what ignorant sin have I committed?"

"What sin have you committed?! You're pointing the finger at Michael without a shred of evidence. Just because the police announced that the murder weapon is that scarf."

"I suspect without cause, mistress, do I? He alter'd much upon the hearing it," he added, gesturing toward Michael, who still looked transfixed.

"Of course, he did!" Aware of how shrill that sounded, I made a conscious effort to lower my tone. "Why wouldn't he? He's suddenly been accused of having the murder weapon in his possession – without any evidence whatsoever!"

Jake's patience, never thick to begin with, was already wearing thin. I'd become a hindrance, not a help. "Do not talk to me, Emilia. You shall have no cause to curse the fair proceedings of this day."

"Excuse me, but I . . . ."

"Go to, hold your tongue."

That arrogant bastard! I was not about to be dismissed like some hysterical woman. "I will not hold my tongue!" I declared. "You have absolutely no reason to suspect him. All we know is that he and Mandy may have been involved, or perhaps were beginning to get involved. That's no basis for asking him how he acquired the murder weapon."

Jake's reply was just as sharp: "Why ask I that? You have seen nothing then? Nor ever did suspect?"

At this point, the Lieutenant, whose silence had been won thus far by his total befuddlement, managed to find his voice. "Just a moment here. Did you say that this guy was involved with Ms. Bennett?" He looked anxiously from Jake to me. He'd been scooped, and he didn't like it one bit.

I was too wrapped up in the argument to pay any attention to his remonstrations. Moderating my tone to a soft, pleading murmur, as if I were coaxing a deluded schizophrenic to take his medication, I said: "Where's this coming from, Jake? Being involved with Mandy, if that's what it was, makes him a person of interest, certainly, but nothing more. There's no foundation for what you're implying. You must see that."

"I could have told you more," he admitted. "I pray you, pardon me; I will hereafter make known to you why I have done this."

Though he hadn't accepted my point, I appreciated the apology nonetheless. Our peace-making, however, served only to amplify Knutsen's frustration. "Listen, you two!" he hollered as he tried to insert himself into the space between us. "I want you to tell me what the hell's going on right now."

But it did no good. The Lieutenant continued to be shunted aside as Jake rotated to bear down upon Michael. "Good sir, say whether you'll answer me or no."

"Jake, please," I pleaded again.

"If not, I'll leave him to the officer," he replied, nodding over his shoulder toward Knutsen. "This must be answer'd either here or hence."

"Hence?" Knutsen recoiled, more puzzled than ever. Events were still escaping him and he was desperate to catch up. "What do you mean by that? Are you saying, he either answers or we take him in for questioning? You can't tell us . . . ."

"It can't be him," I interjected, now more resigned than anything else.

"Let it be who it is," Jake countered. "How say you, Cassio? I must be answer'd."

But Michael remained tongue-tied; events were moving far too fast for him as well. Pointing toward the evidence bag, Jake prodded in a gentler, more dispassionate manner: "Cassio, whence came this? Come, tell me true."

At last Michael managed to mutter, "I . . . I never saw this before."

It was one of the lines his character delivers in the play; was he aware of it, I wondered? Perhaps at some level, for he quickly found his own voice. "Didn't the cops say it was a woman who bought it? Why do you think I had it?" he asked querulously. "Just because of the expression on my face? That expression was one of shock; it had nothing to do with guilt. I never had that scarf and I'm not guilty of anything. And you'll have to find a better reason to . . . ."

"I have more cause," Jake cut in abruptly. "I have good witness of this." He swung around to face Kendrick. "Did you see the scarf?"

Kendrick was caught off guard at first, but then he looked more closely at the evidence bag and nodded. "Yes, I saw it." All eyes were on him now.

"Where was this?" Jake asked.

"It was at the party last Sunday night. He was holding it in his hand." He tilted his head toward Michael, who looked as if the second stun-gun round had connected with his solar plexus.

"At what hour?"

"Around ten or so. He was talking to Mandy, then he went towards the hall closet and came back with the scarf. I thought it was odd that he should be carrying a scarf at this time of year."

This is incredible, I thought. When the police first announced the murder on Monday, Michael revealed that Kendrick had left the party early, in effect making him a suspect. Now Kendrick was returning the favour. Both were infatuated with Mandy and each was trying to implicate the other in her murder. They were like two stags in rut.

"Just a moment, Kendrick," I said. "Why didn't you mention this earlier when we interviewed you?"

"Why would I? I didn't know it was the murder weapon."

Lieutenant Knutsen had reached his limit. He turned on Michael and shouted, "Listen, you little shit, I'm having no more of this. Where did you get the goddam scarf?!" He was shaking with rage.

Realizing that total denial was no longer a credible option, Michael improvised. "All right," he replied with a shrug, "I think I know what's going on. I did bring a scarf and jacket along that night, since it was raining and a bit chilly. But it wasn't this scarf. The scarf I had was an old one I'd found in my bedroom, behind a chair. Probably left by some woman I was dating. It could have been there for quite a while; I'm not very good at tidying up."

Ad-libbing is not something he does well; he works much better with a script. Jake lost no time in jumping all over this patent fabrication: "A likely piece of work, that you should find it in your chamber, and not know who left it there! This is not strong enough to be believed."

"No, really!" Michael insisted. "The scarf I had was older, more cream-coloured . . . ."

"The one I saw was new, like that one," Kendrick countered. "In fact, it was that one, I'm sure of it."

"No more light answers," Jake admonished Michael.

"Who the hell are you to question me anyway?" Michael exploded. "You play the great detective, quoting from this play and that, but you have no idea what you're doing. You're just throwing accusations around. I had a scarf, yes, but not this one. And I gave that scarf to Mandy at the party, just as she was leaving. I never saw it after that. End of story."

"You praise yourself by laying defects of judgment to me," Jake responded, "but you patch'd up your excuses."

Michael again looked dumbfounded, but he had a point. "Wait a sec," I said. "We need to take what he says seriously. If he had a scarf but gave it to her, that would mean he's innocent."

Actually, it wouldn't, I realized as soon as I'd spoken. He might have gone to Mandy's apartment, got into an argument, saw the scarf and killed her with it. Jake once more seized upon the vulnerability. "You would say so," he stated sarcastically.

"What do you mean by that? Are you saying I'm *biased*?" I shot him a hostile glare, made all the more awkward by the blush that I could feel expanding rapidly across my face.

"How now? What's the matter?" he prodded in a deliberately provocative manner. "You look angerly, and your colour, I warrant you, is as red as rose."

I fought to regain my composure. All that mattered was to establish that Michael had not left the party with the scarf. Although it wouldn't prove his innocence, it would mean that he was no more likely than anyone else to be guilty: anyone who was at Mandy's apartment that night could have seen the scarf and used it to kill her. I looked at Kendrick, who now seemed somewhat abashed. "Kendrick, the scarf you saw in Michael's hand at the party – did you see him give it to Mandy?"

"No," he replied, "I can't say I did."

Whether he was telling to truth or just trying to keep Michael in the soup, I couldn't tell. I decided to cast the net more broadly: "Did anyone else see Michael give a scarf to Mandy at the party?"

I looked around the stage. There was no response, apart from some shaking of heads.

I tried another angle. "Well, did anyone see Mandy leave the party with a scarf?"

Again, no luck. A presentiment of dread was creeping over me. I tried one more sally: "How about Michael? Did anyone notice whether he had a scarf with him when he left the party?"

Same result. It meant that Mandy might have left with it, but that was a small consolation at best.

"Have you no more to say?" Jake asked. "An honest tale speeds best being plainly told."

The implication of guilt in Jake's remark was now so obvious that even Knutsen couldn't miss it. "It appears you have something to tell us, Ms. Marwick. I want to hear it – now."

It embarrasses me to make this admission – I mean, what kind of person misleads the police as well as her partner in detection? Nevertheless, the fact is, I hadn't been totally honest with either of them. Not about Michael. I'd been doing everything I could to keep him out of this investigation, so convinced was I that he couldn't have been involved in any way with murder. I was still convinced, more or less, but my strategy had backfired. The only way I could help him now was to tell the truth.

"Lieutenant, I have a confession to make."

"What do you mean? Are you going to tell us that you're the murderer?"

I decided to ignore his juvenile sarcasm. "I think you know that I'm the one who bought that scarf."

"Do I, Ms. Marwick?"

Coyness doesn't really suit him either, but again I chose to rise above it. "Well," I said, "if you didn't know by this point, you'd find out soon. It was a gift for Michael's birthday last week."

"Well, as it happens, Ms. Marwick, we did figure out that it was you who made the purchase. We also figured out that you must have given it to someone because there are witnesses that support your story that you remained at the party throughout the evening."

"But . . . ."

"What we didn't know," he went on, ignoring my attempt to intervene, "is that Mr. Calthorpe is the one you gave it to. Nor did we know that Mr. Calthorpe had the scarf with him on the night of the murder. That changes everything."

"Why do you say that?"

"Come on, Ms. Marwick," he responded, his tone withering, "surely you can see that it puts him squarely in the frame for the murder."

"No, you've got it all wrong!"

He just smirked at my distress. "So I have it all wrong, do I? Well then, why don't you tell me how it really is. And don't give me any more nonsense about another scarf, cream-coloured or otherwise. There was no other scarf."

I didn't have much choice. I took in a deep breath and began. "Michael had the scarf at the party – that scarf – just as Kendrick said." Michael hung his head sheepishly. "But he didn't leave with it. He's telling the truth about that. I saw him give it to Mandy as she was leaving."

"Hmm. Funny that Mr. Page, who noticed the scarf in Michael's possession, didn't see that, nor did anyone else at the party. Apart from you, that is." He paused for a moment, then added: "Let me ask you this: if this is the truth, why didn't you tell us earlier?"

A very good question indeed. I realized how foolish I'd been all along. "I didn't want suspicion to fall on Michael. I'm sure he couldn't have done it."

"Why is that, Ms. Marwick?"

"I know him. He's a good friend."

"Nonsense. I'll tell you why. You're involved with him. Admit it. That's why you gave him the scarf."

I was cornered and I knew it. "Okay, it's true. The scarf was a token of more than just friendship. We've been going out for the past few weeks."

"And now you're saying that you saw him give it to Ms. Bennett, even though no one else at the party did. Do you really think anyone's going to believe that? At this point, Ms. Marwick, you're no more credible than he is."

"No, wait, there's more to it than this." I was now frantic; everything was going wrong. I could see only one way out. "Let me explain. The scarf is the first thing I'd ever given him. It signified . . . well . . . the connection, the bond that I felt between us. I was so pleased when I saw him arrive with it at the party; it meant he felt that connection, too. Then I saw him give it to Mandy as she was leaving. I suddenly became enraged. It felt that . . ."

". . . to give't away were such perdition as nothing else could match."

I stared at Jake. He knew exactly what I'd been thinking. "How did you know?" I asked.

"You think none but your sheets are privy to your wishes?" he replied.

It was typical Jake. First, the perfect quotation to capture the mental state, then the perfect line to obfuscate the reasoning that led him to it. But I was in no position to complain. I looked at him contritely. "I should have told you," I confessed.

"You have broken the article of your oath, which you shall never have tongue to charge me with."

I could have pointed out that he'd also held back information, but since what he'd held back was knowledge of what I was holding back, this objection, too, would have been hollow.

Knutsen wasn't interested in the status of our mutual disclosure pact, of course; what he wanted was the rest of my story. "Enough of this," he declared. "What happened next?"

"I was furious, as I said. I confronted him, demanding to know why he'd given my gift to her."

"And what did he say?"

I looked at Michael, then back at Knutsen. "He claimed he did it simply because it was cold and rainy that night."

"Mandy was very nervous about it," Michael explained. "She was afraid she'd catch something just before rehearsals were about to start and blow her big chance." Turning to me, he added, "Honest, Emma, that's all it was."

Jake wasn't fooled in the least. "That is the way to make her scorn you still," he retorted, nodding towards me.

He was dead on. Michael's repeating of that stupid excuse had made me angry all over again. I decided to go full bore; there would be no holding back now, no matter the consequences – for him or for me.

"I was annoyed and perhaps a little drunk," I resumed. "I told him he was insulting my intelligence by trying to sluff me off with such a feeble excuse. Even if it were true, it wouldn't be acceptable – that scarf should have meant more to him than that. I told him that, as far as I was concerned, he'd ruined everything."

"Love is blind, and lovers cannot see the pretty follies that themselves commit," Jake observed.

"Who are you talking about?" I snapped back. He raised an eyebrow but said nothing.

"Don't stop here, Ms. Marwick," Knutsen prodded. He was less credulous now; he sensed the story was swinging back in his direction.

"After that confrontation," I resumed, "we didn't talk any further at the party. Michael pleaded with me, but I wasn't prepared to listen to him anymore. Then, he left."

"When was that?"

"Let me see. . . . Mandy left around ten and Michael and I had our row right after that. My impression is that he stayed around for an hour at most, so I'd say he left around eleven, perhaps a little earlier."

"That means he could have committed the murder," Knutsen observed, glancing toward Michael.

"Yeah, he could have . . . technically," I agreed. "But I never believed it, not even for a moment."

"Why not? Are you telling me you didn't recognize the scarf wrapped around the victim's neck when you found the body?"

"No, I did recognize it. But like I said, I saw Mandy leaving the party with it, so I knew it could have been used by anyone to strangle her."

"So you say. To anyone else, however, it'll look like Michael's the murderer and you've been covering up for him."

"You don't understand," I pleaded. "That row we had – that was the end. Michael and I are done. I have no reason to try to cover up for him. That's what I'm trying to tell you."

Knutsen summoned over one of his officers to confer. The quiet as they did so was almost unbearable; every pair of eyes seemed riveted on me. "The thing is, Ms. Marwick," he said at last, "no one seems to have noticed this big row you claim to have had, either. It's not mentioned in any of the witness statements. It's hard to see how that's possible, if you're telling the truth."

I looked around the stage, hoping that someone would jump in to support me. Finally, Jake said: "I think I did, sir."

"Yeah, right," Knutsen replied, his voice dripping with sarcasm. "You didn't mention it, though. Why is that?"

"'Twas but a bolt of nothing, so I thought."

"In my experience, couples don't break up in a bolt of nothing."

"Obviously we couldn't have a big blow-up, not in front of everyone," I started to explain. I didn't get any further, however, because just then, Knutsen's phone sounded. After a moment's hesitation, he held up a finger to pause me while he took the call. I glanced over at Michael. His head was still bowed, his mind probably racing to find some way to escape this mess. If that's what he was hoping for, he couldn't have been more deluded.

During the call, which lasted several minutes, Knutsen emitted a number of uh-hmm's and oh-yeah's, punctuated by sizeable silences, an occasional 'are you sure?', and a final 'well, thank you very much, Mr. Lapierre, I'll be calling on you soon'. By the time he'd stowed the phone, the air of anticipation on the stage was almost palpable; he was in his element again.

"That was Mr. Lapierre," he announced, as if anyone could be in any doubt. "He's the manager at Ms. Bennett's apartment building. Apparently, he was watching the noontime news on a local television station today." He paused for dramatic effect. One beat. Two beats. "On the broadcast, they did a report on the murder of Amanda Bennett which featured interviews with some of you people, probably done when you were arriving at the theatre this morning." Another two-count. "Mr. Lapierre phoned because he thinks he recognized the man who visited Ms. Bennett just before midnight on the night of her murder." An extra long pause, at least four beats. "The person he identified is . . . you, Mr. Calthorpe."

Following Knutsen's lead, all eyes swivelled toward Michael, who looked like he might melt on the spot. "It's funny, Mr. Calthorpe," Knutsen noted disingenuously as his gaze bore down on his victim, "you didn't mention this at all during your interview."

"Really, no. I mean, I don't know what to say,"

Michael stuttered. "I'm sure the manager is mistaken. I never went there. He must be confused about that – with the shock of finding the body and all."

"No, he seems quite certain," Knutsen responded acidly.

That was disputable, I knew. "Lieutenant," I interjected, "when we interviewed Mr. Lapierre, he expressed considerable doubt about whether or not he'd be able to recognize the visitor."

"Not anymore, Ms. Marwick," he replied tersely, his eyes still fixed on Michael. "He's sure now."

He stepped closer to his target. "According to your statement, Mr. Calthorpe, you left the party late and arrived home around twelve-forty-five a.m. You also stated that it took you about twenty minutes to drive home."

"That's right," Michael replied weakly.

"But it's not right, is it? We now know you left the party much earlier. That leaves a lot of time unaccounted for. I think you'd better explain."

"Well, I was feeling a little restless, so I drove around . . . ."

"No, Mike . . . I can call you Mike, can't I?" Taking silence for consent, he continued: "Start from the beginning. I want to hear everything. And I want the truth this time."

Michael glanced hesitatingly around the stage. There were still some twenty of us, each hanging on every word that was uttered. "Can't we do this in private?" he pleaded.

Knutsen considered the request for a moment, then looked over to Walt and asked if there were some other room that they could use. Walt signalled for us to follow him. Well, not exactly 'us', but as the officers led Michael in that direction, Jake and I simply tagged along.

The room Walt led us to was one of the equipment rooms, filled mainly with spotlights of various sizes and other electrical paraphernalia. As soon as Michael entered the room and turned around, he registered our presence. "I thought we were going to do this in private," he remonstrated. "Isn't that my right?"

"No, not really," replied Knutsen coolly as he opened a folding chair and slowly lowered himself onto it. "Since Ms. Marwick and Mr. Benatsky are the ones who have unveiled your lies, I think it would be good to have them here – just to make sure you're not going to spin any more yarns." He folded his arms and leaned sideways against some shelving.

Michael looked thoroughly resigned. Walt had left, but Jake and I were clearly staying. He unfolded a chair and sat down, leaning forward to place his elbows on his knees. He looked up at me as if waiting for me to be seated as well, but I didn't oblige. Neither did Jake.

"You're right, Emma," he began. "I was . . . taken with Mandy. We met during the auditions, as you know. We don't have many scenes together, but I was asked to read opposite her in one of the auditions. I couldn't believe how beautiful she was. I was mesmerized."

"How far did it go?" I quickly asked.

"Not far . . . I mean nowhere," he replied. "There was clearly something been us, a connection – call it what you will. But I was going out with you, and, though she didn't talk about it, I could tell that she was in a relationship as well."

"So you both decided not to take it any further because of your other commitments? How noble!" I retorted. "Frankly, I'm not buying it. I told you: we've heard that things went a good deal further than that."

"From who?" he replied.

I said nothing.

"Listen, whatever you've heard, you've got it wrong."

"Oh, yeah?"

"Let me explain . . . ."

"You two love-birds can sort out your little problems later," Knutsen cut in. "What I want to know is . . . ."

"The truth is," Michael resumed, ignoring the Lieutenant entirely, "we hadn't really had a chance to get to know each other. We'd had coffee a few times . . . ."

"Oh, give me a break!" I exclaimed.

"Okay, I did show up at the Brown Pelican a couple of times in hopes of talking to her, but it was always when she was on duty. There wasn't much chance to talk; she couldn't even sit down and have a drink."

"Yeah, right!"

"Okay, okay. She sat down once or twice when she was on a break, but it was only for a few minutes." He hesitated. "In fact, one of the nights there was another guy hanging on her every movement. He and I sat a few seats apart at the bar and studiously avoided each other. We scarcely exchanged a glance; it was bloody awkward."

I looked at Jake. I could tell that we'd both reached the same conclusion. "Was this guy a young East Asian guy?" I asked.

"Yeah, that's right. He couldn't take his eyes off her." He said this with an unmistakeable undertone of disdain; how could anyone dare to covet what he coveted? Then he twigged. "You know him?"

"Never mind that. Just tell us what happened next."

He hesitated a moment. "It was bizarre. She seemed to show more interest in him than me. At least, she was more flirtatious with him. He was just a kid."

"You don't know much about women, do you?" I replied sarcastically. The man's ego was beginning to revolt me.

Jake decided to relieve the confusion that was

written all over Michael's face: "She did show favour to the youth in your sight only to exasperate you, to awake your dormouse valour, to put fire in your heart."

Thanks, Jake. That was, again, most helpful.

"Well, maybe so," Michael responded. He seemed to warm to the idea. "Anyway, it upset me a lot at the time. Then this party was arranged and I knew she'd be there. I saw it as an opportunity to get to talk with her in a more relaxed setting."

"You mean, when she had some liquor in her," I suggested. He hadn't been the only one to have that idea.

"Yeah. . . . No, not that. I mean, when neither of us was working or rehearsing. You know."

"I'm afraid I do," I answered. "Remember, I was there." He looked abashed. He couldn't twist this tale any which way he wanted.

"Love-birds, if you don't mind," Knutsen intervened again, "it's all very touching, but could we please get back to the sequence of events."

"Right, sorry," Michael replied. He seemed relieved. It was almost as if he preferred to be questioned by Knutsen than by me, which was rather odd in the circumstances. "At the party, I waited for her to arrive, then as soon as I could without attracting too much notice, . . ."

"You mean, from me."

He ignored that and continued: ". . . I approached

her."

"Oh bravo!" I exclaimed. "And then?"

"She started with the usual party chit-chat – probably because all these other people were around – but I was in no mood for it. So I asked if we could speak seriously for a couple of minutes."

Knutsen broke the momentary silence. "Well?"

"Well, she said she was really tired and just wanted to head home and go over her lines some more for tomorrow. Could we do it another time? she asked. But I couldn't let it go. This whole thing with the young guy, with her other relationship – if there was one . . . . I guess I just needed to know where we stood." He looked at me again. "I'm not saying I would have ended it with you if she'd expressed an interest. In fact, as I look back on it, I can't believe I was even tempted . . . ."

Before I could reply with even more bitter sarcasm, Knutsen cut in again. "Yeah, all right, you're a match made in heaven. Now go back to the party. You had to know where you stood; what did she say?"

"Basically she said, we need to talk, but not now. She actually said those words: 'we need to talk'! I was stunned; I couldn't believe it. It was like the ground was being yanked from under me."

"But words are words," Jake interjected brusquely. "I never yet did hear that the bruised heart was pierced through the ear."

I'm not sure that's true – I can recall some words that bruised my heart – but it certainly put Michael in his place. He looked crestfallen.

"Then what happened?" Knutsen prompted. He had no intention of easing up.

"I didn't know what to do next. I wanted to do something to make it better, but all I could think of was to offer her the scarf. I went to the hall closet, got the scarf and tried to give it to her. She said she didn't want it. I followed her to the door, begging her to take it. In the end, I think she took it just to appease me." He looked back at me. "The next thing I knew, you were barrelling my way. I could tell from your expression that you must have seen everything. I expected a tongue-lashing, but what I got was . . . dumped. I couldn't believe it. I tried to talk to you about it, about us, but you wouldn't have it."

"So what did you do, Mike?" Knutsen asked. He was checking his cuticles intently. Any moment now, I expected him to start pantomiming a violin being played.

"At first, I tried to put it out of my mind and stay at the party," he replied. "But I couldn't. I had to get out of there. What was whirling around in my head was the thought that, in the space of just a few minutes, I'd managed to lose both women. . . . Or had I? I didn't know if I would be able to patch things up with you, Emma, but I needed to clean the slate with Mandy, one way or the other. I had to know if she was dismissing me or just postponing me."

He had Knutsen's full attention now. "So you . . . ?"

"So I drove around, like I said. But my driving somehow ended up with me at her place."

"How did you know where she lived?" I asked. If he'd been there before, I said to myself, he might be leaving this room a eunuch.

"Once, after an audition, I'd given her a drive home," he responded. He looked up at me and added, "Nothing more! Honest."

I wasn't sure I believed him, but I had to give him credit; it was a pretty good dodge.

"So you rang her buzzer," nudged Knutsen.

"Yeah, I did."

"What happened then?"

"She let me in." He shrugged. "Then she set me straight. Yes, she likes me, finds me attractive, she said. But she's involved with someone – nothing serious, but that's the way she likes it. She's not looking for anyone else. Wants to concentrate on her career. Hopes we can remain friends. You know, the usual baloney."

"I'm willing to bet you weren't delighted to hear this news," Knutsen surmised.

"No, I wasn't. I accused her of leading me on. She admitted she'd been flattered that an older, more successful actor like me had taken an interest, so she may have given off the wrong signals. As the date of the first rehearsal approached, she said, it became clearer to her that she didn't want any complications in her personal life. She was even uncomfortable that I'd given her the scarf at the party. Asked me to take it back."

"So you picked it up and then you wrapped it around her pretty little neck and strangled her with it," Knutsen suggested. He was entirely too smug for my liking.

"No, I didn't!" Michael burst out. "I didn't even take the scarf; I just ran out. She was alive and well when I left. That's the truth!" He fell forward onto his knees and grasped both of my hands. Sobbing, he squeezed them tightly and said, "I'm so sorry." He bowed his head.

"I don't know what to say to you," I replied. My emotions were roiling. Part of me went out to this anguished man who, notwithstanding the foolish lies and evasions, was in the frame for a murder I was sure he hadn't committed. The other part felt no sympathy for him at all.

"Whate'er you think, good words, I think, were best," Jake advised.

Easy for him to say. I had none. All I could manage was, "How could you do this to me?"

"I'm sorry, so very sorry, that you've suffered all this," he replied. He looked intensely into my eyes. "I mean it. The truth is, I wouldn't wish any companion in the world but you."

I was speechless; I couldn't believe what I was hearing. Knutsen wasn't, though. "Well, you're not going to get that wish any time soon," he pronounced summarily. Then he addressed the other two officers: "Tell him his rights and take him in."

While Michael was being cuffed and led out, Knutsen honed in on us. "You two – I want you at police headquarters at eight-thirty tomorrow. Especially you, Ms. Marwick."

"I don't know if we can," I objected. "We'll probably be having a rehearsal tomorrow."

"Oh, isn't that sweet? Still trying to polish up your Desdemona, just in case? Screw the rehearsal; you be there."

T HURSDAY, JUNE 18. EVENING.

J ake and I had little opportunity to talk during the remainder of the afternoon. The police had no sooner left than Walt hustled us all onto the stage to resume the rehearsal (reading Cassio's lines himself). The session didn't wrap up till around seven o'clock, at which point Jake walked over to me and said, "We must needs dine together." Exhausted though I was, I was more than willing.

We found a table at the back of Chez Panisse. Jake suggested a bottle of burgundy this time. Although I'm normally a white wine drinker, it sounded good to me. The stronger the better. After filling our glasses nearly to the rim, he launched in. "I see this hath a little dash'd your spirits."

"Yeah? Well, that can happen to a woman when she finds her boyfriend has become infatuated with another woman – a young, beautiful . . . ."

"Say not so in bitterness. This is a mere distraction."

It felt like bitterness was all I had. "And then he had the gall to say it's really me he's wanted all along. I'm to be his life's companion."

"It pleases him to call you so."

"Well, of course it does – now that the other woman's dead!"

"You are too tough. Good phrases are surely, and ever were, very commendable. In truth, I think 'tis no unwelcome news to you."

I realized only later, in transcribing this passage, what the comment about good phrases was alluding to – Michael's profession of devotion had consisted of paraphrased lines from Shakespeare. At the time, it was the latter remark that drew my attention. "Oh, you think I should be happy, do you?" I said. "Whoo-pity-do! My man's come back!"

"I care not for such words," he replied. Like most people, he seldom has much use for sarcasm that's not his own. "A woman sometimes scorns what best contents her."

If that observation was intended to calm me down, it failed miserably. I was seething. I'd had to deal with Michael's crap this afternoon, now I was getting another dose of it from Jake this evening. Well, not anymore. I abruptly rose and grabbed my coat.

"Stay, madam, I must speak a word with you," he said, reaching for my arm.

I glared back at him. His eyes had that deep, slightly unfocussed look that I find so strangely beguiling. "What?"

"Do not seek to take your change upon you, to

bear your griefs yourself and leave me out."

I sat down again. Whatever his peculiarities, he could be a good sounding-board and at that point, I badly needed one.

"I just can't believe this is happening," I resumed after taking a large gulp from my glass. "How can he possibly admit he was 'taken' with Mandy, had to know where he stood with her, but still come out with that stuff about wanting me all along?" It was a wound I just couldn't leave alone.

"You rub the sore, when you should bring the plaster," Jake observed, somehow guessing the metaphor I had in mind. "I would your spirit were easier for advice, or stronger for your need."

"What do you mean?"

"'Tis not a time for private stomaching," he replied. "You and he are near in love."

"Near in love?! I don't know where you get that idea." I took another sip of the surprisingly appealing wine. "Sure, we'd started something. And sure, it was promising. When we met, he seemed kind, decent, even charming at times – the kind of man I could take seriously. It was a welcome change after . . . well, you know, my recent romantic history."

"Saw you no more?"

"Well, to be honest, I suppose I was beginning to believe that we could build a future together. But that's not going to happen now."

"What horrible fancy's this?" He refilled our glasses.

"I mean it. The guy's a complete idiot. I mean, if you're going to lie, at least make the lies believable." I took another sip. "I still think he's innocent, of course – of the murder. But going to her place after the party to beg her not to dump him – I never imagined he would have done that. As far as I'm concerned, we're finished."

"Wherefore should you do this? This is the very ecstasy of love, whose violent property fordoes itself and leads the will to desperate undertakings."

"I'm not desperate!" I exclaimed, sounding about as desperate as I possibly could. "Jake, you've got to understand," I continued, calming myself with another sip of the most excellent wine. "The last thing I expected from him was that he'd be tempted away by another woman. I thought he could be trusted. Do you realize that he didn't even apologize – until he was cornered?"

"But that's no fault of his. How could he see his way to seek out you?"

"Well," I conceded, "I suppose I made that difficult by refusing to talk to him anymore. He probably thought it best to keep quiet and hope it would all blow over." I sipped once more, spilling a little on the table. "But he can forget about that now."

"I prithee, lady, have a better cheer."

"Don't prithee me!" I responded with a sharpness

that startled both of us. I was really wound up, I could feel it. "Remember that conversation we had the other day? You said I don't know how to choose a man. Well, I've thought about it a lot and I think you're right; that's exactly it. I don't know how to pick them at all." I reflected further as I took another sip. "Or maybe I'm not the type who can inspire devotion and loyalty. I'm the type men take on for the time being, until something better comes along. It's like I have 'pump and dump' tattooed across my forehead."

He burst out laughing. "Well said: that was laid on with a trowel."

I shot him an angry glance; maybe I preferred him silent after all. "It's my fault, really," I went on. "I think I read too much into relationships. And what happens? Ultimately I get betrayed. That's what happened with Bruce and that's what's happened here."

"Prithee, have done . . ." he began to say, but I shot him another quick look that froze him in his tracks.

"I probably don't deserve loyalty. I mean, look what I've been doing this week. I'm supposed to be helping you with the investigation, but all the time I've been hiding from you my involvement with someone who has to be considered a suspect, someone I'd even given what turned out to be the murder weapon. You probably think that's why I agreed to help you – so that I could cover up for him."

"I never thought it possible or likely."

"Well, I hope not, anyway." I paused to lubricate

once more; this was thirsty business. "And how did that end up? He's now the prime suspect and I'm possibly considered an accessory. I've messed up everything, absolutely everything."

"You are too tough. Bear with patience such griefs as you yourself do lay upon yourself, for who is so firm that cannot be seduced?"

"Aha, there it is! I knew it. In the end, you men all hang together. All you really want is to be able to get away with it. What did you call it the other day – a little 'quick recreation'? And to think I considered you my friend."

"What mean you, madam? You have no cause to hold my friendship doubtful."

"Well, what kind of friend would try to convince me to take back a philanderer – and a very stupid one at that? Or is this just you having a little fun?"

"You mistake the matter. I am more serious than my custom; you must be so, too."

"All right, then, let's look at what's been going on – seriously. Yesterday, we were convinced that Gates was behind the murder, maybe Chiang as well; then you discover that Michael, though involved with me, was tempted away by Mandy. So what do you do? You try to convince me to forgive him for straying, while at the same time doing everything possible to ensure that he's well and truly fitted up for the murder. Some friend you are."

"How shall I understand you?" he recoiled. "Will

you blame and lay the fault on me? I have made no fault; the fault's your own."

My spirits suddenly crashed, which is precisely what I deserved. "You're right," I acknowledged. "This is all my doing. I guess I just needed to unload on someone."

He reached across and took my hands in his. "When I spoke that, I was ill-temper'd too. I did not think you could have been so angry."

It was a kind gesture, but not one I was prepared to accept. "Jake, it's not your fault that I've made such poor choices in men." He was about to object, but I shushed him. "It's not your fault, either, that I kept vital information about the murder from you and the police. I've been wrong at every turn, and all I've achieved for my efforts is to make a mess of everything."

"Let me see your eyes. Look in my face," he said. Before I could react, he reached up and placed his hands on my cheeks, then lifted my head gently so that our eyes met. "A friendly eye could never see such faults. The worst fault you have is to be in love."

I began to cry. He released my face and reached into his pocket to extract a handkerchief. I couldn't help smiling; he must be the only man in North America who still carries one. "Sure, there's some wonder in this handkerchief," I said, quoting from *Othello*.

He smiled, too, as he handed it to me. "Have you not sometimes seen a handkerchief?"

"Not since I was a kid." It's funny how little it takes to change the mood. I could feel my spirits reviving.

He took the handkerchief from my hand to dab a few tears I'd missed. "Be comforted," he said. "There is hope all will be well."

It was what he'd hinted at yesterday. Even the smallest glimmer of hope would be good at this point, but I was suspicious. "Are you just trying to make me feel better, or do you really see some way out of this?"

He licked the tips of a couple of his fingers and pushed back a strand of hair from my forehead. "Peace, I say. All shall yet go well."

"You *have* figured something out! Jake, you've got to tell me."

"Press me not, beseech you, so. You shall know more hereafter."

"But . . . ."

"Quarrel no more," he responded curtly but with an unmistakeable undertone of sympathy, "but be prepared to know the purposes I bear." He leaned closer to me still. "I'll have this knot knit up to-morrow morning."

"Tomorrow morning!?"

"If tomorrow be a fair day, by eleven o'clock it will go one way or other," he specified. Then he rose and reached for his jacket.

"Where are you going?" My head was spinning. "I

thought we were going to have dinner."

He shrugged apologetically. "I must leave you. Be not dismay'd, fair lady; take no offence. There is something in the wind, and something to be done immediately. I had forgot."

He sounded sure of what he was doing, or at least resolved, but I suspected he just needed to be alone; it seems he can take only so much emotional intensity at one go. I tried to stand up, but he placed both hands firmly on my shoulders and guided me back down.

"Keep good quarter and good care to-night: the day shall not be up so soon as I, to try the fair adventure of to-morrow." He leaned over and kissed me on the cheek (fortunately the drier one), threw a couple of bills on the table, and headed toward the door.

"Jake, wait! What do you mean – the fair adventure of tomorrow? Tomorrow I may be in jail!"

He turned back. "Nay, that you shall not."

"How do you know?"

"Many likelihoods informed me of this before, which hung so tottering in the balance that I could neither believe nor misdoubt. Yet do not fear: that is now answered. I will speak with you further anon."

"You put me off last night; now you're doing it again. Couldn't you just explain some of what you're thinking?"

"Nay, pray, be patient. Doubt not but success will fashion the event in better shape than I can lay it down in likelihood."

"Please, Jake, give me something. Anything."

He walked back and kissed me again, this time on the top of my head. "Not till you have slept. Adieu till then."

❊ ❊ ❊

I decided to stay at the restaurant. It was partly enervation over Jake's abrupt departure, but mostly the realization that I was rather drunk. What I needed was food. And water. Lots of water. And time to think.

I still believed everything I'd said, including the blame I'd levelled on myself. In all my calculations, I'd never anticipated that Michael might have gone to Mandy's apartment that night. Even after we recalled that the manager had seen a young man arriving at the building, the possibility never crossed my mind. I'd been a complete idiot.

Was I wrong about his innocence as well? It's a question I had to ask myself. He certainly had seemed stunned when I told him at the party that it was finished between us; was it really so unimaginable that being dumped by another woman that same night might have pushed him over the edge? Try as I might, I still couldn't buy into it, but how could I know for sure?

The first thing that occurred to me was that if he

had strangled her in a fit of rage, there ought to be some traces of his presence in the apartment. Knutsen hadn't mentioned finding any, but of course the forensics people might not have had a copy of Michael's prints or DNA to compare with, since he hadn't been a suspect until today. Presumably, that's been taken care of by now and we may find out tomorrow that signs of his presence were detected everywhere. But suppose his prints or DNA weren't found at all. That's possible if he's innocent: he might have been shown in, had a brief, disappointing conversation with her, and then headed straight out the door without touching anything but the door handle, which she would have touched later when she opened the door to her killer. Yet that wouldn't be conclusive; he might have killed her and then wiped the place down before he left.

I pursued the train of reasoning further. Suppose he strangled her, then wiped the place down. If so, today had really been a disaster for him. Granted, we'd put a lot of pressure on him, but ultimately there was no reason he need have confessed to being at her apartment that night. The testimony of the manager was shaky and he knew it – I'd pointed it out – so he could simply have maintained that he was driving around all evening till one a.m. The authorities might not have believed him, nor believed my testimony that I'd seen Mandy leave the party with the scarf, but what could they have done? Their suspicions alone would not have been enough to convict him, probably not enough even to bring him to trial. It would have been incredibly stupid of him not to have realized this.

Could he have been that stupid? It was another question I had to ask, but this time the most likely answer reassured me right away. If he had been cold-blooded enough to remove any traces of his presence after having killed her, there was no way our questioning would have rattled him into making such a blunder. It didn't add up. Assuming nothing is found to place him in the apartment, the only reasonable conclusion had to be that he didn't do it. But would the authorities see it that way?

That seemed doubtful. More than doubtful, in fact. They had the murder weapon in his hands (discounting my evidence as biased), his admission to being at the crime scene, and a plausible motive for committing the offence. He was done for, I realized, unless we could come up with some real evidence to exonerate him or point the finger at another suspect. Jake seemed to have a lead on that, but I was baffled.

Speaking of Jake . . . what should I make of him now? Yesterday, he was gung-ho to take on Gates and Chiang; today he played a pivotal role in blowing apart Michael's story. In fact, he seemed to delight in doing so, while at the same time trying to convince me that, despite the lapse with Mandy, Michael and I are meant for each other. Presumably, he would only do so if he were convinced of his innocence, but if so, why had he worked so hard to put him in the frame?

There was another thing as well. He castigated me for holding back the information about Michael and the scarf – which is valid, no question – yet he was holding back, too. And not just his suspicions about Michael and me. If he's going to have the case wrapped up tomorrow, there must be a lot else he hasn't revealed. That definitely would be a violation of our agreement, if it's true. And if it isn't true – if he said it just to cheer me up – then he was lying, and rather cruelly, at that. Either way, I concluded, he has a lot to explain.

I'd reached the point where I could no longer speculate, no longer worry, no longer even think. I had to go home. As raw and reckless as I was feeling, though, I still couldn't bring myself to follow Jake's lead and just throw a couple of twenties on the table. But I did leave a respectable tip.

When I arrived home, I immediately settled down with a mug of tea and a box of chocolates. There was no message about tomorrow's rehearsal, so I decided to check in with Walt. I imagined he already knew where things stood, but I couldn't take it for granted. I managed to reach him right away. Yes, he'd heard that Michael was being held overnight for questioning – it had been reported on the evening news – but he didn't know if he'd be back in time for tomorrow's rehearsal. I caught him up on that, including the fact that Jake and I had been ordered to be at police headquarters in the morning.

Walt said he wasn't worried about Michael's role

or mine; he'd be able to work around our absence since there are plenty of scenes in which neither of our characters appear. I know it was perverse of me, but I couldn't help taking that as another unwelcome reminder of how unimportant our parts are. He said nothing about Jake, who has a much more central role; I suppose he regards him as such a natural that rehearsals aren't so essential. He wouldn't be wrong about that.

Then Simon phoned. He was much more chipper this time; with Michael having been taken in for questioning, he finally had something juicy to report (apparently, mere assaults don't count for much). Sure, it wasn't the political bombshell he was hoping for, but it would do for the time being – especially if he could get the real dope on Michael. He offered an inducement – I give him the inside track on the investigation, he'll make sure my name and picture feature prominently in the paper.

It didn't seem to have occurred to him that if I were going to pass on confidential information, the last thing I'd want would be to be associated with it. When I pointed it out, he promised anonymity, even cash. I replied, somewhat testily I admit, that I don't know what the real dope is and that even if I did, I wouldn't be passing it on to anyone. We left it at that. I was pretty sure I wouldn't be hearing from him again.

I didn't get much further with my cup of tea before the phone rang again. It was Henry Bennett this time. He, too, had seen the news. He wanted to know if this meant the case was solved.

"No, I'm afraid not," I replied. "Mr. Calthorpe has only been taken in for questioning. I don't think you should read too much into it at this stage."

"Oh, I see," he responded, clearly disappointed. "What does Mr. Benatsky think? Does he see any hope of progress?"

I was angry enough at Jake to dump him in his own soup. "Mr. Benatsky says he'll have it all wrapped up tomorrow."

"He does?" Henry exclaimed. "That's fantastic! That makes me feel so much better. I can't tell you how difficult it's been. I don't know why I cling so much to finding the murderer, but I do. It's all I think about. I need to know why my daughter had to lose her life. There has to be some reason for it. And some reckoning."

"I understand what you're saying," I replied. "Believe me, we're doing everything we can to bring this to some resolution."

"If you're going to wrap it up tomorrow," he persisted, "then you must have some idea who the murderer is. Can't you tell me? Please."

"I'm sorry, Henry. The truth is, I have no idea."

That seemed to stun him. There was an awkward silence, which I ended by promising to contact him as soon as I knew anything for sure. He thanked me and bid me good night. I did the same, for all the good it would do.

I didn't feel happy about being so blunt with him, but I didn't feel happy about much by this point. It was time to download my recordings, make some short notes on the day's misadventures, and crash.

By the time I'd finished my notes and reviewed a few of the conversations I'd recorded, I was feeling a little better. One thing that stuck out for me in the recordings was something that wasn't mentioned. In our extensive exploration of Michael's involvement with Mandy and possibly with her murder, no one had given any consideration to the assault on Roddy. That assault had to be related to the murder, I felt sure; it couldn't be just a coincidence that one of Mandy's suitors was attacked on the same night as she was killed.

What did that mean for Michael? I reckoned it was positive. It didn't seem plausible that he could have gone to Mandy's place after the party, lost his temper and strangled her, then got into his car and driven to Roddy's cottage to thrash him. How would he even have known where the kid lived? He was just someone he'd seen once in a bar. This wasn't proof, I knew, especially as he had no alibi for the time of the assault, but it opened the door to doubt, which had to be worth something.

I was just about to turn in when another thought occurred. I returned to my laptop. This thought had to be added to the day's record, much though I hated to do it. The thought was this. Suppose Michael's admission that he'd visited Mandy after the party hadn't been gratuitous. Suppose he'd been stupid in another way: he'd actually killed Mandy in a fit of jealous rage and then fled from the apartment in a panic – without cleaning up the murder site.

At first, he might have thought he was in the clear: no one knew about their flirtation except me – and I wasn't telling. Then, everything changes when Jake establishes that he had the scarf that night. He's now an object of suspicion. The police have grounds to take his fingerprints and a sample of his DNA, and when they do, they'll quickly find out that he'd been at the apartment. So he figures, why not get ahead of the story? Not just by admitting that he'd been there at some point; that wouldn't do much since the police would be able to prove it anyway. No, the smarter course would be to admit he was there on the very night of her murder. Since there's no other convincing evidence for that – given that reasonable doubt could be cast on Mr. Lapierre's identification – it would make him look like he has nothing to hide. After all, what murderer would willingly place himself at the crime scene at the time it occurred? He would appear to be a little naïve and foolish, perhaps, but no killer.

I wrestled with this scenario for some time, but all I achieved was to make myself thoroughly depressed. I got out my emergency bottle of sleeping pills. Everything hung on whether physical evidence of Michael's presence had been found in the apartment. I hoped not, but I needed to know. What Jake was up to I couldn't even guess, but my next step was clear.

F RIDAY, JUNE 19. MORNING.

I woke up groggy again. Too much liquor or too much happening – probably both. It was a spectacular late-spring day, one of the best so far, which depressed me even further. Would the no-doubt equally spectacular sunset find me in jail as well? I wondered. Jake had tried to reassure me on that score, but how could I count on that? The fact that he wouldn't reveal his reasons suggested to me that he might not have very good ones – if he had any at all.

I arrived at police headquarters at eight-thirty, as ordered, and after some preliminaries, was shown to an interview room where Lieutenant Knutsen was interrogating Michael. Knutsen's victim looked like he'd been through hell. He was in yesterday's clothes, sweaty and unshaven. Couldn't they have let him take a shower, at least?

"Hello, Ms. Marwick," Knutsen greeted me cheerily, "how are you today?" When I didn't reply, he continued, "Welcome to our modest quarters. Mike and I have just started our little chat." It looked more like the little chat had been going for hours. "Please take a seat and join us." He gestured towards an empty chair.

I nodded discreetly to Michael as I sat down. It was hard to believe that this man, recently so dear to me, could be a violent killer. Between philandry and murder lies a huge gap, I knew, however tempting it might be at times to minimize it. Diverting my gaze from his sad eyes, I launched straight in. "Good morning, Lieutenant. Before you go any further, I'd like to know if Michael has been charged with anything."

"He has," replied Knutsen smugly. "With murder."

"In that case, shouldn't he have a lawyer present during questioning?"

"Relax, Ms. Marwick, he's been informed of all his rights, including the right to a lawyer. He declined."

I looked over at Michael, who kept his eyes fixed on his lap. By every outward appearance, he'd given up.

But I hadn't. "I have a couple of questions, Lieutenant Knutsen, if you don't mind."

He hesitated for a moment, then acquiesced. "Well, Ms. Marwick, I can imagine that you might have one or two things you'd like to clear up." He seemed content to humour me for the time being.

I smiled to indicate my gratitude. "The first question is simple."

"Always my favourite kind."

No surprise there. "Have you discovered any forensic evidence – fingerprints, DNA, that sort of thing – that places Michael at Mandy's apartment?"

"Why does it matter? We know he was there on the night of the murder; he said so himself. You're not thinking that his admission can be retracted or discredited in some way, are you? It can't, believe me."

"But you did check, didn't you?"

"Yes, of course we did. It's part of standard procedure."

Well," I persisted, "what did you find?"

"Very little; the place had been wiped clean. All we could come up with were a few hairs. They're undergoing analysis now, but it doesn't look like they're a match to Mike. Nevertheless," he cautioned, "that makes absolutely no difference at this point. He has admitted being there that night. As I said, that cannot be taken back."

I wasn't interested in doing so. The fact that the place had been wiped clean meant that the worst-case scenario that had obsessed me last night wasn't true. Michael hadn't been smart to make that admission; he'd been stupid. The right kind of stupid, the kind that's not guilty of murder. The logic was flimsy, I knew – many things could break it and, even if it withstood scrutiny, it didn't amount to evidence of any kind. Nevertheless, it gave me some hope. It's funny, I thought; I've never wished for a stupid man before.

"Let's move on, Ms. Marwick. By the way, where's

Benatsky? I thought I told him to be here, too."

He did, but I wasn't going to confirm it. All I said was, "I haven't seen him."

"He'd better show up soon or I'll have him picked up. What's your other question?"

"Oh, I was just wondering, how do you see Mandy's murder connecting with the assault on Roddy Chiang?"

"Connecting? What do you mean 'connecting'?" He seemed surprised; perhaps he thought the case against Michael was so airtight that there was no reason to link it to any other crime.

"Well," I said, "think about it. We have the murder of a woman and an assault on a man who was infatuated with her, both on the same night. That can't be just a coincidence. The two events have to be linked in some way."

"Wait a moment," Michael objected. "Who are we talking about?"

"Now that you bring it up," Knutsen cut in, "that's an interesting point. Tell me, Mike, how much bad blood was there between you two?"

"None in the world," he declared, "nor do I know the man."

"Stop it, Michael!" I said.

"Stop what?"

"Stop using Cassio's lines from *Othello*. You've got to start talking for yourself, not your character."

"Hold it! If Jake can . . . ."

"Jake doesn't have his neck in a noose," I reminded him. "Besides, he's Jake."

He hesitated for a moment, apparently miffed that I wouldn't let him get away with what Jake could do. But he was in too much trouble for that (also, he doesn't quite have the knack). As if accepting my verdict, he replied, "All I'm saying is that I don't know this Roddy guy."

"Yes, you do, Michael," I countered. "Remember you said that one night at the Pelican, there was another guy flirting with Mandy? An East Asian guy?"

"Yeah, that's right."

"Well, that was Roddy," I said. Michael went silent, no doubt pondering what this might mean for him.

Not Knutsen, though. He had no doubts at all. "The answer to your question is pretty obvious, Ms. Marwick, now that I think about it. Mike killed Ms. Bennett in a rage, then he decided that Roddy Chiang was part of the problem, so he needed to be taught a lesson as well." He seemed well pleased with his off-the-cuff theorizing.

"Why didn't he kill Roddy, then?" I asked.

He shrugged. "He may have felt that the main blame belonged to Ms. Bennett. After all, she was the one who led him on, then rejected him."

"What about Kendrick Page?" I persisted. "He was also interested in her."

"Perhaps Michael didn't know about that."

"Even though Kendrick had rehearsed privately with her and had gone to the Pelican in hopes of seeing her on Sunday, perhaps other times as well?"

"Well, Mike, did you know about Page?"

Michael's blank, confused face gave him all the answer he needed.

"I think it's pretty clear that Mike didn't have a clue about that. That fits in with what Page told us: he hadn't pursued his interest very far."

"Okay," I allowed, "so only Roddy needed to be punished. How did Michael know where to find him?"

Finally a question that struck home; for a brief (but delicious) moment, Knutsen flailed like a fish on a line. "Who knows?" he said. "Maybe Mike gave him a lift . . . ."

He halted abruptly; that avenue wouldn't work. Unlike Mandy or Kendrick, Roddy wasn't connected with the play. Michael knew him only as a guy in a bar flirting with Mandy; he would never have offered him a ride home. That meant there was no plausible way he could have known Roddy's address without having somehow chased it down beforehand. It would be hard to square that with the sudden-act-of-rage scenario Knutson was nurturing.

"Ms. Marwick," Knutsen resumed at last, "none of this matters. We're not thinking of charging Mike with the assault on Roddy Chiang. He may have done it, he may not have done it – it makes no difference to us."

At that moment, Jake burst into the room, startling everyone. "Good morrow, good Lieutenant," he proclaimed jauntily. "I hope I am not too late. I come within an hour of my promise."

Knutsen's mug wobbled in his hand, causing a few drops of coffee to splatter onto his shirt. "Damn it, Benatsky!" he shouted as he slammed the mug down, spilling more of the dark brew.

"I am sorry for your displeasure," Jake replied as the Lieutenant began to dab vainly at his shirt front with a moistened index finger.

"Jake!" I said. "Where have you been all this while? I've been so worried . . . ."

"And where care lodges, sleep will never lie."

"Exactly. I took a sleeping pill but still . . . ."

"Enough of this chit-chat," Knutsen interrupted. "Let's get down to . . . ."

"I crave your pardon." Jake said to me, undeterred. He pulled up a chair and sat down beside me. "A night is but small breath and little pause to answer matters of this consequence."

"It's been a little difficult here, Jake." I was feeling more than ever the weight of the obstacles before us. My nonplussing of Knutsen over the Roddy business now seemed like a minor victory at best; Knutsen was surely right that it wouldn't affect the main outcome. Michael and, by extension, I were still in the frame for murder.

"I told you a thing yesterday," he replied, touching my arm lightly. "Think on't. I have been as good as my word."

"If you two are quite done," Knutsen intervened sarcastically. "It may have escaped your attention that I'm questioning a murder suspect here. Maybe two suspects," he added, glancing severely at me.

"I beseech your honour to hear me one single word," Jake responded. "I have important business, the tide whereof is now."

"Well, it's just going to have to wait."

"Nay, sir, but hear me on."

"Back off," Knutsen bristled, "or I'll charge you with obstructing a police investigation." He clearly needed to regain control, or at least a little of his coffee-blotched dignity.

"And yet, methinks, I could be well content to be mine own attorney in this case."

I couldn't suppress a slight smile at Jake's coy humour. He was right, of course. Since he was here at the police's request, he could hardly be convicted of obstructing them.

"Listen here," Knutsen recoiled, "I don't need you interfering anymore. You've been of some help, I'll give you that, but we've got our man."

"It may be you have mistaken him, and he's indicted falsely," Jake replied. He wasn't joking, I could tell.

"What?!" Knutsen exclaimed. He took a moment

to calm himself. I wondered if he has a blood pressure problem. "So *now* you think he's innocent, do you? That's quite a switch from yesterday. And I suppose you're certain of this?"

"As certain as I know the sun is fire."

Michael was slowly awakening to the realization that something positive might be occurring at long last. "Excuse me, Jake," he said, "but am I understanding you correctly? Are you saying that you think you can . . . ."

"I speak not this in estimation as what I think might be," he replied, "but what at full I know."

"Just a minute!" Knutsen cut in, his patience depleted. "I ask the questions here."

"But Lieutenant," Michael intervened, "if Jake has information . . . ."

"God damn it, shut up!" Knutsen ordered. I was getting seriously concerned about his blood pressure now. Do they have anger management courses for police officers? I wondered.

"Patience awhile, good Cassio," Jake said, placing a hand on Michael's arm to calm him.

Michael stopped speaking, but I could tell that his spirits, too, were rallying; there's something about Jake's self-confidence that induces it. Knutsen was the master of ceremonies, but Jake, it seemed, was going to have all the punch-lines.

The silence that ensued allowed Knutsen some further scope to compose himself. He still wanted our cooperation, however much we irritated him. "Benatsky will get his chance to speak," he said, his tone much more civil, "but in the meantime, I'm going to conduct this interview my way. I don't want to hear a peep out of him – or you – for the time being."

"That truth should be silent I had almost forgot."

"I know the truth, Benatsky, and I can prove it."

"Well, sir, for want of other idleness, I'll bide your proof."

That seemed to mollify the Lieutenant. "Listen, everyone, here's how it went down." He leaned forward and folded his hands on the table. "We know that Michael was involved with Ms. Marwick here. How much is not clear" – he looked first at me, then at Michael; neither of us said a word – "but it must have been fairly serious. Serious enough for you, Ms. Marwick, to get very angry when you saw him give the scarf to Ms. Bennett – the expensive scarf you'd bought him as a birthday present just a few days before."

"So now you believe me about all that," I said. "Yesterday, you claimed I wasn't credible."

"It no longer matters, now that we know Mike went to her apartment. The only thing that matters is that you were pissed off at the party. And that's very credible. After all, she was younger, better looking, and had the leading role in the play – a role that, by rights, should have gone to you. Now she was stealing your man. You had every reason to despise her."

I shook my head, but he raised his hand to forestall any further reaction. "So that gives you motive," he concluded. Before I could protest this blatant nonsense, he added, "But not the opportunity. We know you were at the party till late that evening."

"That doesn't prove you're not involved, however," he continued, looking sternly at me. "How much is uncertain at present; there are two versions that are possible." He paused for effect. "The more benign one is the one you told us yesterday. You confront Michael at the party, demanding to know why he'd given away the scarf. He gives you a totally unbelievable excuse – that it was simply because Ms. Bennett was worried about catching a cold."

He savoured the absurdity of the excuse as if it were a fine wine teasing his delicate palate. "That makes you even angrier. You don't believe him – you sense there's something between them – but even if he's telling the truth, you feel it's unforgiveable that he should have been so free with your precious gift. So you decide to strike back. You tell him it's finished, over. He pleads but you won't listen. You just freeze him out."

"Yes, Lieutenant," I interceded, "what you've said about my behaviour at the party is true, more or less. I'm not proud of what I did that night. But it wouldn't have been enough to make him want to kill her. How do you get from there to Mandy's murder?"

"It's not that difficult. Consider Mike's state of mind. You're furious with him. You refuse to talk to him anymore. He's drunk and frustrated. What you don't know but he does is that, though he'd been hitting on Ms. Bennett, she was actually starting to let him down. 'We need to talk' – isn't that the line she used, Mike?"

Michael nodded dejectedly.

"So, Mike," Knutsen continued, turning to his right to face him directly, "you can't patch it up with Ms. Marwick, but you figure you can try your luck with Ms. Bennett. In fact, you decide you're entitled to an explanation; she owes you that, at least. You know where she lives, so you go there. You tell her how much you care for her, how fantastic she is." He glanced over to me slyly. "But instead of telling you what you so desperately want to hear, she crushes you. Tells you it's over. Some lame excuse about wanting to focus on her career, not looking for a serious relationship, that sort of crap. This makes you even angrier. You spot the scarf lying there – or perhaps you had it all along; it doesn't matter – but either way, you wrap it around her . . . ."

"I didn't, I swear!" Michael exclaimed, leaping to his feet.

"Tell me, Mike, when did you do it? Was it when her back was turned, maybe when she was opening the door to show you out? That's what the forensics guys are suggesting."

"No, of course not! I told you, I didn't kill her. Why

would I? The whole idea's ridiculous."

"Well, it isn't that ridiculous, when you think of it," Knutsen replied, signalling for him to sit down again. "After all, she'd just dumped you. To make matters worse, by pursuing her you'd put your relationship with Ms. Marwick in peril. With Ms. Bennett out of the way, that could presumably be patched up. In fact, Ms. Marwick might be in an entirely different frame of mind if the source of her irritation was eliminated. She might even get the part of Desdemona, which you knew she wanted badly." He glanced quickly at me again and added, "That couldn't fail to work in your favour."

"Lieutenant, I would never . . . ."

He held up his hand to silence me. "Moreover, how could the murder be pinned on you, Mike? No one knew you were going there or, as far as you knew, had seen you arrive or leave. No evidence that you had been in the apartment would be found; you took care of that. And Ms. Bennett's somewhat unsavoury life at the Brown Pelican, her association with two of this city's high rollers, would naturally cause us to look in that direction."

"Unless," I interjected, "those high rollers have enough influence to foreclose that avenue."

"I'll ignore that comment, Ms. Marwick. I don't think this is the moment you should be alienating us with unfounded accusations of corruption. Especially as this is only the more benign version of events," he added ominously.

"I don't really want to ask, but I suppose I must," I responded, taking the bait. "What is your less benign version?" I wasn't going to like this, but at least it would move the spotlight off Michael for a moment.

"The less benign version you probably know, Ms. Marwick. You don't dump Mike because of his infatuation with Mandy; instead, you accept, perhaps even propose, a solution that would work for both of you. He will prove his love for you, and make amends for his sins, by eliminating her permanently. In the unlikely event that anyone traces the scarf to you, you'll admit it was a present for him and claim that you saw him give it to her as she was leaving the party. You'll also claim that you dumped him because of that, just to show you have no reason to be lying for him. Later on when the dust has settled, you'll take him back again – and, of course, take over her part in the play."

"I cannot choose but laugh," Jake interjected, looking up slowly from his lap. "This is mere madness."

"Oh, you think so, do you, Benatsky? We'll see about that."

"Lieutenant," I said, "do you have any proof to back this up?"

"You know, Ms. Marwick, it's funny how often the ones who demand proof rather than protest their innocence turn out to be the guilty ones." He abruptly lurched towards me, stopping so close I could feel his breath on my face. "Ask yourself this: what will the jurors think when they find out that no one else at the party – a party with more than twenty people in attendance – noticed the argument you claim you had with him?"

"That's not quite true. You're forgetting that Jake did."

"So he says, for what it's worth."

"For what it's worth?"

"He didn't mention this argument in his initial statement. I find that odd."

"Of course he didn't. He had no idea it was relevant."

"We don't ask witnesses to tell us only what they think is relevant; you know that. The real reason he didn't mention it is because he's a friend of yours."

"He is a friend, but he wouldn't lie for me."

"Just like you wouldn't lie for Mike?"

I had no answer for that. But Jake did. "I have spoke the truth," he said gravely.

"Oh, have you? Then tell me this: did you hear what the two of them were actually saying to each other? Well, did you, Benatsky?"

"I did not, sir."

He swivelled back to me. "So Mike and you could have been calmly devising your plan, for all anyone knows."

"But that's nothing more than speculation."

He leaned back a little. "I'll be frank with you,

Ms. Marwick: it may not be enough to get you convicted . . . not unless Mike here figures out that he's been played for a sucker and cuts a deal." He looked towards Michael, a sly grin on his face. "He won't now, he's all repentant – and you're in the room. But when he goes back to his cell and has time – lots of time – to think about it, that may change."

"Sir, it cannot come to so much," Jake countered.

"Why do you say that, Benatsky? Mike here is guilty, we all know that. He's the only one with motive, means, and opportunity. The only question is whether he's going to spread the burden a little. I think he will, once he realizes how much he stands to gain from it. Could be years off his sentence."

"You're wasting your time, Lieutenant," I said. "It won't work."

He smirked. "It did with you yesterday. As soon as your attempts to cover things up were exposed, you started talking. Oh, you pretended to be trying to help Mike, all right, but in the end you couldn't have done a better job of throwing him under the bus."

"I wasn't . . . ."

"Relax, Ms. Marwick, you just did what anyone would do. And he'll do it, too. In the final analysis, everyone is looking out for number one, believe me."

Before I could reply, an officer knocked quickly on the door and poked his head in. "Lieutenant," he said, "I'm sorry to interrupt but . . . ."

"What the hell are you doing, Greenfield? You

should know never to interrupt a senior officer when he's doing a formal interview. Now close the door!"

"But sir, it's important."

"Close the fucking door now!" The officer sheepishly did as he was told. "Now, where was I?" He turned back to Jake. "Oh, yes. Sooner or later Mike will start talking because he'll realize that the best he can hope for is a reduction in sentence; any lawyer he gets will tell him so. Or do you still claim he's innocent, Benatsky?"

"O, doubt not that; as I told you before, I speak from certainties."

Knutsen shook his head in disbelief. "The only certainty that matters around here is what comes from evidence, and there's a hell of a lot of it against Mike. More than enough to convict, believe me. If you think you can get him off the hook by finding some way of invalidating his admission that he was at the apartment that night, as Ms. Marwick was trying to do . . ."

"Lieutenant, I was not . . . ."

". . . it's not going to work. You're going to need irrefutable evidence. Do you have it?"

"I have, when you have heard what I can say."

"You're full of it, Benatsky. We've got everything nailed down except Ms. Marwick's role in this, and if Mike's smart, he'll provide that. If not, he'll go down for a longer stretch. But either way, he's going down."

"That he will not," Jake replied calmly. "As I told you, I speak not out of weak surmises, but from proof as strong as my grief. I will tell you, if you'll bestow a small – of what you have little – patience awhile."

Knutsen slammed his fists on the table and shot to his feet, knocking his chair over. "So if Mike's not the murderer," he sneered, "I suppose you know who is?"

"I do, sir."

"Well, who is it? Please tell us so that we can make an arrest." His patronizing tone was bordering on outright contempt.

"Alas, sir, you cannot. It is not possible."

"Oh, no? Well, why not, pray tell?"

"This is the short and the long of it: he's dead."

A stunned silence permeated the room, almost as if a spell had been cast. Michael was the first to break it. He slowly looked up towards Jake. "Jake, who . . . ?"

Knutsen cut him off. "Who are you talking about, Benatsky? I've had no report of any suspicious death."

Jake glanced at the door and raised an eyebrow.

"You mean . . . ?" he asked, puzzlement and frustration sweeping over his face.

Jake nodded resignedly.

"But who is it?"

"Roderigo," Jake answered.

"Roderigo? Who's . . . ?"

"He's dead?" I asked incredulously.

"It is so, I warrant."

"Who the hell is . . . ?" the Lieutenant whined. Finally, his gears engaged. "You mean Roderick Chiang?"

"I can't believe it," I said, mostly to myself.

"I wonder none of you have thought of him," Jake demurely replied. I suppose he was entitled to a little patronizing of his own.

"If you're right about Roddy Chiang being dead," Knutsen declared, his brain suddenly afire, "it only makes it worse for Calthorpe. Now, he's a double murderer. In fact, that answers your question, Ms. Marwick, about why Roddy wasn't killed. It turns out he was!"

"Wait a sec," I interjected. "When did this happen, Jake?"

"Last night."

"In other words, while Michael was being held here." I glanced at Knutsen, who looked absolutely gobsmacked. "So who killed him? Or did he do it himself?"

"So indeed he did." He began to fumble in his jacket pockets. "I have it here about me."

"What is it, Jake?" Michael asked, an unmistakable tremor in his voice.

"A good note that keeps you from the blow of the law," he replied. "Yes, here it is. A letter found in the pocket of the slain Roderigo." He extended it to Knutsen. "This letter will tell you more."

Knutsen reached forward to snatch it just as Greenfield burst in again, accompanied this time by a sergeant. "I'm sorry, sir, but you've got to hear this," the Constable announced. There was more resolve in his voice, now that he had back-up. "Uniform was called out to an address on Marine Drive about an hour ago. We're not sure who phoned – I have the name here somewhere – he had a strange accent. English or something." All eyes turned on Jake, who was gazing distractedly at the wall opposite him. "He reported finding a dead body. He identified the body as belonging to . . . ." He checked his notes.

"Roderick Chiang," Knutsen filled in bitterly.

"You knew, Lieutenant?" the puzzled officer asked.

Jake smirked, which didn't help Knutsen's mood. He turned angrily on him: "You were there, weren't you? At his cottage. And you removed evidence from a crime scene!" he added, shaking the letter in Jake's face. "You're in a whole lot of trouble, buddy."

"To-day, as I came by, I called there," Jake casually admitted. "Pray you, peruse that letter. You shall understand what hath befall'n, which, as I think, you know not." God, this guy is good, I thought to myself.

"Did he write this?" Knutsen asked as he attempted, without much success, to pry open the envelope flap without destroying it entirely.

"It is his hand."

"You sure about that?"

"It will be found so. I beseech you, read it."

Finally managing to liberate the letter, he undertook the task feverishly. After a minute or two, Jake asked, "How goes it now, sir?"

"I don't fucking believe it!" he replied. "It's a confession." He shook his head as if overwhelmed by the folly of life, whether his own or Roddy's I couldn't determine.

"To Mandy's murder?" I asked. I had few doubts; I just wanted to hear it.

"Yes," he admitted. "He says he went to Ms. Bennett's apartment around midnight that night. He saw the man from the nightclub leaving the building and it enraged him. He felt betrayed. He rang her buzzer, but she refused to let him in, which only made things worse. He had a set of keys from the office, so he used it. That in turn made her really angry. She told him to get lost; she was fed up with men pestering her. He pleaded with her, but it was no use. She told him she never wanted to see him or any of the others again. You can imagine his reaction."

"Ay, too well," Jake responded dolefully. "Extremity of griefs would make men mad."

"Well, there's certainly a lot of nonsense here," Knutsen went on, scanning through the pages. "As near as I can make out, her fatal mistake was to turn her back on him, refusing to speak any further, despite all his pleading. Then he spotted the scarf."

"That's enough," I interrupted. "We get the picture. You know, he must have been out of his head, like Jake said. It's hard to believe that poor lovestruck boy could have done such a thing in any other circumstance. And then afterwards . . . well, we saw the kind of torment he was in. How did he kill himself?" (I reflected later that this question makes me no different from everyone else – I had to know how.)

"Greenfield?" Knutsen relayed the request.

"He shot himself, sir," Greenfield replied. "That's what Forensic is saying, based on the crime scene. There'll be a full autopsy this afternoon, but they say there isn't much doubt."

"This did I fear," Jake muttered, "but thought he had no weapon."

"Or the courage to use it," I added. "I find that unimaginable."

"Life, being weary of these worldly bars, never lacks power to dismiss itself. I should have known no less."

He may have been right, but I was still bothered. "Lieutenant, is there anything in the letter that elaborates on why he took his own life?"

Knutsen scanned the letter. "Not much. It's all pretty incoherent. He seems to have been extremely depressed. . . . Uh, let's see . . . . He talks about having killed the one good thing in his life. Says he didn't feel that there was any point in going on. The usual stuff."

What a miserable business, I thought. "You know, Lieutenant, it strikes me that Mandy's murder happened more or less like you said, only it wasn't Michael who did it."

Knutsen nodded, although it must have been small consolation after the mistakes he'd made. Nevertheless, he was willing to admit he'd been bettered. "Okay, Benatsky," he said, "I have to give you credit. You were right again. I picked the wrong man."

"I pray you, see him presently discharged," he replied.

Knutsen nodded again and signalled for Michael to stand up. Jake rose with him. "How now, Cassio?"

Michael threw his arms around him. "Jake, I can't thank you enough. You've saved my neck."

"To-morrow with your earliest let me have speech with you."

Michael smiled back broadly. I'm sure he recognized the line; Othello says it to his character in the play. "You've got it!" he responded enthusiastically. Then he turned to me. "I want to thank you, too, Emma." He spread his arms for an embrace. "I hope you can forgive me."

"Don't count on it," I replied as I reluctantly rose and allowed myself to be hugged. I was more than pleased that Michael had been proved innocent, but rekindling our romance was a different matter entirely.

"Still so cruel?" Jake queried.

"Do you pity him?" I snapped back. "He deserves no pity." Incredibly, Michael looked crestfallen as he was escorted from the room. He must have thought he could have it all, once more.

"I'm going with them," Knutsen said. "I need to sign off on the charges. Then I want to talk to you two. Don't go anywhere; I want a full statement from each of you." He once more shook his head in disbelief. "Christ, I still can't believe it. Roddy Chiang."

"Lieutenant, about that – wasn't he supposed to be watched?" I distinctly remembered Jake making the suggestion after we saw the state Roddy was in on Wednesday.

"Yes, he was," Knutsen acknowledged. "I gave the order. But at most there would have been an officer parked down the block. He couldn't have prevented a suicide, probably didn't even hear the shot." He looked frustrated; there were never enough resources. "I'll be back in a few minutes."

"How many fond fools serve mad jealousy!" Jake observed as the Lieutenant stomped off down the corridor. I couldn't help but wonder if Jake was including Knutsen in that observation.

"It's odd," I mused. "I doubt that Roddy knew the play. He probably never saw the irony of strangling a woman who was playing Desdemona in a fit of jealousy . . . and then killing himself." I looked at Jake. "You're not thinking 'all the world's a stage', are you?"

He just smirked.

* * *

We sat quietly for several minutes. At first, I was immersed in a warm fog of relief – relief that Michael had been exonerated, above all, but also relief that I was off the hook. I'd never truly believed that I was on the hook, despite the carrot that Knutsen had dangled in front of Michael, but I have to admit that even the suggestion had rattled me.

Gradually, the fog lifted and my mind returned to the many things left unexplained by Roddy's letter. The first was, who attacked him? It must have been someone who knew he was guilty, but in that case, why not kill him? And speaking of killing, why did Roddy commit suicide, really? He didn't even know that he was a suspect, much less how much evidence there might be against him. His letter mentioned powerful feelings of remorse, but could that have been enough to provoke such a drastic action? Somehow that seemed doubtful. Finally – and most pressing of all – how did Jake work it out?

"Jake, there are a lot of things you need to explain."

"Do I?" he innocently replied. "Prithee tell me one thing."

"Well, I'd like to know how you figured out it was Roddy."

He shrugged. "I hear, yet say not much, but think the more."

"I was hearing and thinking too, you know – when I wasn't worrying about my neck or Michael's. Obviously, Roddy had to be a suspect, given his interest in Mandy, but he was also the victim of a rather nasty assault. And there were other suspects."

He smiled coyly. "In nature's infinite book of secrecy, a little I can read."

"That's still rather vague." Not to mention gratingly mock-modest, but I felt inclined to cut him some slack. "Jake, I really want to know. We've been partners in this case and, let's face it, you've been holding back."

He surprised me by remaining silent for several moments. Was he insulted by my accusation? He had no right to be, given how angry he'd been yesterday when the secrets I'd been guarding about Michael came out. Finally he said, "If ever I were wilful-negligent, it was my folly. Pardon the fault, I pray."

"Don't worry about that," I replied curtly. "Just tell me how you did it."

But he wouldn't – not in any straightforward fashion. Instead he said: "I am loath to tell you what I would you knew. If it shall please you to make a wholesome answer, I will help you to't. So, let me hear you speak."

It was a challenge. Why had he issued it? Was it to diminish me – to oblige me to try to unravel the puzzle so that my inevitable failure would set the stage for the grand reveal? Or did he really believe that I could do it?

"You really think I can figure this out?" I replied, shaking my head morosely. "I think you may be over-rating my talents."

"You'll find it otherwise, I assure you."

He seemed so sure of it, I decided to give it a try. But where to start? I cast my mind back over the course of the investigation. We began with a suspicion that Mandy's murder must have had something to do with Winfred Gates. He was her lover, but others were circling around her and he knew their affair was coming to an end. It had seemed likely to us that his inflated ego, combined with the ruthlessness and vindictiveness for which he was renown, might have driven him to strike out at her. What caused us to abandon that line of reasoning?

It's true that Gates claimed to be unconcerned about losing her, that didn't deter us: we knew it might have been just show. . . . Of course. It all changed yesterday when the police arrived with the scarf.

"It all comes down to the scarf, doesn't it?"

"That is the true beginning of our end," he affirmed.

"Okay, let's start from there. The police came to the rehearsal yesterday afternoon with the news that the murder weapon was a scarf and that a woman had purchased it. The sales clerk provided a description of the woman, which matched me to a tee. They obviously knew it was me – and so did you."

He nodded obliquely.

"But you also knew I hadn't killed her. For one thing, I was at the party till after one, as were you. Even if you hadn't noticed me there, there were lots of other people who had. So, you must have known, or at least suspected, that I'd given it to Michael."

"Are you sure of that? Why he more than another?"

I paused for a moment. "I think I am sure. I don't think you saw Michael with it – you'd have mentioned it earlier if you had. But you saw me having heated words with him at the party, just after Mandy left. So you knew that something was afoot."

God, I can't believe I said that; now I'm Sherlock Holmes. Jake didn't pick up on it, however, perhaps because 'the game's afoot' line actually originated in

Shakespeare. All he said was, "So indeed I did."

"Oh, my gosh!" I exclaimed. It was a stray thought, but I had to explore it. "During our little heart-to-heart on Tuesday, that's why you wouldn't believe me about giving up on men." I started to chuckle, as did he. "You bastard! You knew that I was reacting not just to being dumped by Bruce, but also to something much newer and more raw. That had to mean that there was another relationship that had gone sour – a more recent relationship. You castigated me in general, but you chose to say nothing about that."

"It were not for your quiet nor your good to let you know my thoughts."

"Well, I suppose there's something to that," I conceded. "That conversation was explosive enough as it was – it probably didn't need more fuel."

He grimaced slightly.

"So you put two and two together and figured that the other man in my life must be Michael. Yet it was really just a supposition at that point – until Helen told us about Michael and Mandy. You saw my reaction."

"And when I ask'd you what the matter was, you stared upon me with ungentle looks."

"Well, 'ungentle' is a generous way of putting it. I was very upset. The investigation had suddenly shifted in absolutely the wrong direction, as far as I was concerned. I had to protect Michael. Whatever sins he'd committed, there was no way he could have killed anyone." I looked hard at Jake. "But you must have suspected him."

"I could not help it," he admitted.

"I understand; you don't know him as I do. What you did know – for sure now – is that there was something between us. Since the scarf had left my possession somehow, I must have given it to him. Of course, it might have been lost or stolen, but that was unlikely. The problem is, Michael denied it – he claimed he'd never seen the scarf – and I was backing him up. So you faced a problem."

"There was the weight that pull'd me down," he acknowledged. "How can these contrarieties agree?"

"Well, you turned to Kendrick for the answer. We hadn't asked him about the scarf when we interviewed him – we weren't supposed to mention it – yet somehow you figured that he must have seen Michael with it. How did you work that out?"

"Ay, there's the question. What might you think?"

As much as my confidence in my deductive skills had grown since we'd begun, I now felt completely stymied. I couldn't see any way he could have reached that conclusion.

"I like your silence, it the more shows off your wonder," he teased, "but yet speak."

Speak what? I asked myself. I was feeling increasingly uneasy. Then I got it. Preposterous though it might seem, it was the only possible answer. "You *guessed,* didn't you?"

His smile broadened into a grin.

"Of course," I said. "You didn't know for certain, but it was a reasonable gamble. I get it now. Since the scarf ended up around Mandy's neck, Michael either strangled her with it, or he gave it to her. Or both, I suppose. Did you know he was infatuated with her?"

"I did not think he had been acquainted with her."

"And you're sure you didn't see him trying to give it to her at the party?"

"No, truly, I did not mark it."

"But you figured that if he had brought it to the party and given it to her, the one person most likely to have seen it was Kendrick. You must have noticed that he, too, was taken with her – probably couldn't keep his eyes off her."

"And what I saw, to my good use I remembered."

"That's right, you even mentioned something of the sort when we interviewed his parents on Monday."

"That I did."

"Still, you were taking a heck of a chance. You might have fallen flat on your face in front of everyone."

"In the reproof of chance lies the true proof of men."

I couldn't help smiling. "I'm not sure about that, but it certainly was a gutsy move. But there's still a problem. If Kendrick were paying such close attention to Mandy, why didn't he see Michael giving her the scarf?"

He shrugged. "In good truth, I do not know."

I reflected further. "Oh, gosh, now I remember! Michael brought it to her just before she left, but she refused it. Kendrick would have seen it in his hand at that point. Then Michael followed her to the front door and it was there he managed to persuade her to take it; that wouldn't have been visible from the living room. I'd seen her take it only because something about the way they were talking together made me suspicious, so I followed them to the door. . . . Unfortunately, I couldn't find anyone else who saw what I saw."

"This was strange chance, but it is no matter."

"Not now, but it certainly was then."

"Or then."

"What? You didn't think it was important even then?"

"I did not," he confirmed.

"Why not? If she left with the scarf, anyone might have shown up later at her apartment and strangled her with it; if Michael had kept the scarf, then the odds are, it was him. How could that not matter?"

"What were I best to say? You forget yourself."

"What do you mean 'I forget myself'?" I shot back. "What have I said to offend . . . ."

"You have mistook, my lady," he quickly cautioned.

"What?" I exclaimed. Then it struck me. Sometimes I really am an imbecile. "Of course, damn it! I am forgetting myself. If Michael had killed her, he wouldn't have used the scarf because he knew I'd seen him with it at the party. He couldn't possibly be sure that I'd be willing to keep that a secret, especially after the blow-up we'd just had."

"Indeed, he could not."

"In fact," I continued, my mind spinning, "even if he had strangled her with it, perhaps in a moment of blind rage, he wouldn't have left it around her neck – for precisely the same reason."

He nodded again.

"But what if Knutsen's other theory were true, that Michael and I had decided that he should go to her apartment and kill her?"

He smirked. "Even so."

"What do you mean? Oh, of course . . . he still wouldn't have used the scarf. He knew how much it meant to me, and besides, it might tie us to the crime." I paused for a moment. "So the fact that the scarf was used to kill her and was left at the scene means that it couldn't have been Michael – even though he's the only person who was seen with it that night. Damn it, Jake!"

"Ay, is't not strange?" he replied, his grin now rivalling that of the Cheshire Cat.

Indeed it was. "Yet we couldn't see that. When the scarf was announced as the murder weapon, the only thing he could think of was to deny he'd had it and hope that I'd back him up. And I did – till you proved otherwise. . . . That makes me wonder, would I have continued to cover for him if Kendrick hadn't seen him with it at the party?"

"Fair one, I think not so," he replied.

I wished I could have agreed, but there was no way I could be sure. Not for the first time that week but certainly more profoundly than before, I had to consider who I really am.

My soul-searching was brought to a premature end by Constable Greenfield, who poked his head in the door just moments later. "You folks doing all right?" he asked. "Would either of you like a cup of coffee? We have some already made."

"No thanks, but would it be possible to take a break while Lieutenant Knutsen is tied up with the paperwork? I need to stretch my legs."

"Yeah, I think that should be okay. There's a coffee shop on the ground floor if you want to get something. Just don't leave the building; he wouldn't like that."

I didn't imagine he would. "Thank you, Constable, I think I'll go there. Jake, can I bring you back something?"

"Nay, I'll come."

I was relieved to find the coffee shop mostly empty. I ordered a tea at the counter and promptly secured one of the few tables. When Jake joined me a few moments later, he was carrying not only a large mug of coffee but a plate with two chocolate-covered doughnuts as well. I don't know how he does it, I thought to myself as I glanced over his rakishly thin body.

He offered me one, but I knew it was pro forma; he was clearly intent on devouring them both. I was happy to let him; in fact, the silence while he indulged himself was entirely welcome. I'd been alternately frustrated and exhilarated by the challenge he'd posed upstairs, but my head was still spinning. The slight hangover I still had from last night didn't help. Unfortunately, I had very little time to enjoy my respite before my phone went off. It was Constable Greenfield, informing us that the Lieutenant would be returning in a few minutes. Wonderful, I thought.

I had to re-focus on the case, but I knew that the most difficult challenge still lay ahead: figuring out how Jake knew Roddy was the murderer. Since Mandy had been strangled in her apartment, he must have gone there that evening. But how did Jake know? There was nothing for it but to plunge in.

"Jake," I said, "it makes sense that you knew it wasn't Michael, but how did you know it was Roddy?"

"What shall I say more than I have inferr'd? Look to't in time."

"No, I want to figure it out right now," I responded. Then I realized I'd mistaken his words again; it was another cryptic clue. "That's not what you mean, is it?"

"The time will bring it out," he elaborated. "Construe the times to their necessities."

"So you want me to work out the timing?"

He nodded.

"Let's see," I began. "The murder took place between eleven p.m. and one a.m. on Sunday night. Most of the cast were at the party during that time. There are lots of witnesses to that, including you and me. So the question is, who didn't have that alibi?"

I decided to go through the possibilities one by one, starting with the easiest. "First, there's Kendrick. He left the party early to look for Mandy. That puts him in the frame, I suppose, but we know he was at the Brown Pelican all evening. Helen testifies to that, and I'm inclined to believe her."

"So do I, too."

"Then there's Brian Chiang, the nightclub owner. He doesn't seem to have any reason for killing her; if he'd been pursuing her, I think Helen would've known about it. Besides, she was Gates's girl, so he lacks a motive. That leaves Gates himself, who also left the party early, and Roddy, who wasn't there at all. . . . Unless there was someone else interested in her – someone we don't know about?"

"That cannot be."

"Why not? Because Helen would have told us?"

"Not only that. There is something else."

"There is? What?"

"The bell."

"The bell?"

"It sounds."

It was like a crossword clue that seems impenetrable at first sight, but yields almost immediately. "Oh, I see what you're getting at. It's unlikely to have been someone who would have had to buzz – not that late at night. So it must have been someone with a set of keys. Gates had one, and Roddy could access one from the office, so it could have been either of them. But she might have . . . no, she would never have given a set to someone else as long as Gates had his; that could have been awkward, to say the least. So it had to be Gates or Roddy."

"One of these two must be necessities," he confirmed.

"But how could you know which one? The timing no longer helps. Both of them are claiming to have been together when the murder occurred, and Brian Chiang was supporting those alibis. How did you decide?"

"It is common for the younger sort to lack discretion."

"Okay, I grant you that Roddy is the younger, more impetuous of the two. And he appears to have wanted Mandy badly, which isn't true of Gates."

"Murder's as near to lust as flame to smoke."

"I suppose," I said, though I wondered how widely the aphorism held. "I imagine it's also likely that if Gates had wanted Mandy disposed of, he wouldn't have done it personally. He probably has contacts who could have arranged it for him."

"No doubt."

"On the other hand, someone thrashed Roddy. Presumably, that person was trying to intimidate him into keeping silent. That would point the finger at Gates. In fact, that's why we went from Roddy's place to his to confront him on Wednesday. So it seems to me that there are factors that point to each man; I still can't see how you could pick one over the other. There must be something else, something I'm overlooking. But what is it? I'm stumped."

"I see the play so lies that I must bear a part," he responded. "If you have writ your annals true, 'tis there. Have you the lion's part written?"

"Yes, the main points," I said. Dammit! How the heck did he know? I'd taken great pains to write up each day's events when I was alone; I hadn't breathed a word to him. Well, water under the bridge now. I bent over and extracted my laptop from my bag. As soon as the file was loaded, I started to flip through it frenetically.

"Can you not read it?" he asked. "Is it not fair writ?"

It wasn't written particularly well at all, but that

wasn't the problem. The problem was that I didn't know what I was looking for. "What am I supposed to find?" I muttered, mostly to myself but also in the faint hope that he would volunteer a clue. He didn't, and nothing popped out at me, either. I decided to go to the interview with Roddy. "Let's see. . . . Roddy's extremely angry when we first talk to him on Wednesday."

"There's matter in't indeed, if he be angry. Who does he accuse?"

"Well, he's probably angry at whoever thrashed him, but he says he doesn't know who it was. But he's also angry at Mandy and, to some extent, Helen as well."

"And then?"

I continued to work my way through the interview notes. "Then, he's in despair over Mandy's death. Eventually, he calms down and we get him to go through his activities on Sunday night."

"Let us from point to point this story know."

"Okay. It begins when he has that conversation with Helen at the Pelican. What she says about Mandy makes him very upset, so he goes for a walk to calm down and eventually returns to the Pelican, where he meets his uncle and Gates, who are having a drink with Kendrick. A little later, Gates and his uncle decide to head back to Gates's house. He goes with them, while Kendrick remains behind. At some point, Roddy realizes that there's something wrong: it doesn't make sense that Gates would be dating

Mandy if she were the tramp that Helen made her out to be. But he has to make sure, so he confronts Gates about it."

"That's true. What was his answer?"

I jumped forward to the interview with Gates at his house. "Gates essentially confirmed Roddy's thinking. He told him that she isn't a bar-girl at all, that he would never have put up with that."

"What is amiss? Do you see nothing there?"

"Yes," I replied, "there *is* an inconsistency." I went back to the interview with Roddy to confirm it. "When we first started to interview Roddy, he was denouncing Mandy vehemently. He said she can rot in hell, for all he cares. But by then he knew that Helen had lied about her; she wasn't any of those things. . . . Well, she was someone who'd been willing to sleep with Gates to advance her career, but he'd always known that. It hadn't stopped him from falling for her."

I checked the conversation again. "He also knew that Gates wasn't that interested in the relationship. Mandy will soon be free, Gates tells him. So that's more great news. He says his spirits shot up on hearing it. . . . Yet he's still bad-mouthing her when we first meet him on Wednesday."

"Ay, but why? What was his reason?"

Why, indeed? I flipped forward to the Gates interview again. "Here's something. After Gates sets him straight about Mandy, he also points out that she might choose someone else once she's free. According to what I have here, he just throws it out as a possibility; he doesn't mention anyone in particular."

"Does he not? Can this be so?"

"No, apparently he doesn't." I went back and forth between the two interviews. "They both agree on that."

Then it hit me. "Oh, Christ!" I exclaimed. "You're absolutely right; it can't be so. He must have named someone!" I walked through the reasoning, just to be sure. "Roddy claimed he left Gates's place upset because Gates had reminded him that there might be a lot of competition for Mandy. That's a reason for him to be discouraged, fair enough – especially given the amount of liquor he'd consumed – but it's no reason to call her a f...ing slut."

"No, indeed."

"There could really only one reason why he'd be bad-mouthing her like that: he must have believed that she was already involved with someone else. So Gates must have told him that. In fact, Gates told us that if she were carrying on with someone else, he'd know about it; Roddy said the same thing. That means that in all probability, Gates knew about Michael and divulged it to Roddy."

"Thus it must be."

"You know, I noticed at the time that Roddy's comments seemed extreme. In fact, I asked you about it before we headed to Gates's house. You put it down to his youth and immaturity."

"Ay, so I thought."

"Well, you were very negative on youth in general that day," I said, recalling his wish that the ages between sixteen and twenty-three be abolished.

"I did in time collect myself."

"Not right away, though. Even after you'd heard both Roddy's and Gates's accounts of that evening, you still exploded at Gates, accusing him of being the murderer."

"My state that way is dangerous; nor reason nor wit can my passion hide."

"No kidding. So when did you work it out? It wasn't when I was haranguing you in the car, was it?"

He smiled coyly. "It may be so perchance."

"You certainly became very calm, almost buoyant – which frustrated me no end. That's probably when you realized that we should have asked Mr. Lapierre if the man he saw could have been Roddy Chiang. But there was no longer any need to ask."

"True, madam, none at all."

"You still didn't know who the other man was, though – not at that point – but you knew that wasn't going to be a problem: you figured Mandy's best friend, Helen, would know."

"I knew she would. It could not be else."

Another thought occurred to me. "You know,

telling Roddy about Michael makes sense from Gates's perspective as well. He tried to appear unconcerned about the approaching end of his relationship with Mandy – both to us and to Roddy. And it may be true; he may have been ready to move on to fresher meat."

Jake winced at the expression, but confirmed its content with a nod.

"But given his ego, there's no way he could just let a kid get away with lusting openly for someone he was still seeing. So when Roddy turns up, salivating at the prospect that Mandy would soon be free, he decides to stick it to him. Hard."

"'Twas so indeed. But more than that?"

"There's more?"

"Ay, that there is."

"More than that . . . ah, yes. It may not have been only Roddy he was intending to punish. There was Michael as well. He may have figured that by naming him to Roddy, he could provoke a confrontation between the two of them, thus meting out a little justice – from his point of view – to both of them. It probably seemed like a clever ploy; I doubt he anticipated that it could end so tragically. The irony is that he was only telling Roddy the truth."

The picture was now beginning to emerge, yet I remained uneasy. "There's still a problem here, Jake. It's all just conjecture. What we have is both men claiming to have agreed that night that the way would soon be open for Roddy to make his move on Mandy, with no other suitor mentioned except as a hypothetical possibility. The only evidence against those statements is that Roddy was bad-mouthing Mandy when we first met him; that could be explained away as a product of his extreme distress over her death. You must have had more."

He smiled again. "I'll give you something else: the rest is silence."

"Silence?"

"You perceive my mind?"

"No, I don't." I recognized the quotation, of course. In my line of work, it would be hard not to: it's what Hamlet utters as he dies. But what was the connection to our mystery? I was stumped – again.

I decided to focus on the word 'silence'. We'd just concluded, tentatively at least, that both Gates and Roddy were being silent about a crucial detail of their conversation Sunday night. If the next hint is silence, there must be another instance of something not being mentioned to us. "So you're saying that something else was omitted or not expressed?"

"Most strangely," he added.

"Most strangely? So it was something that should have been said, but wasn't. Off-hand, I can't think of anything. You think it might be in my notes?"

"Thus it may be," he responded, evidently unwilling to commit fully to their accuracy.

I started to scan through everything I'd written

about the various interviews we'd conducted over the past four days. This threatened to be a lengthy process, but Jake looked content to wait. Fortunately for both of us, it didn't take long at all. In fact, it virtually jumped out at me. When we first interviewed Gates and Chiang senior, Gates had asked us how Mandy had been killed. So had Kendrick, just a little earlier; he was especially concerned about whether she had suffered. Michael had as well, God bless him. It was a theme common to every single interview we conducted – except Roddy's. "It's what Roddy didn't say, isn't it? He didn't ask how she was killed."

"What means this silence?"

"It means that he already knew the answer. You know, I think that also crossed my mind at the time, but I assumed he was simply too distraught about the death itself." I considered the omission some more. "Still, a smart murderer would have asked, just to make it appear as though he didn't know."

"Yes, he would."

"In fact, I bet that's what Gates did. He probably knew how she died, but he asked anyway, just to divert suspicion. But Roddy wasn't that smart. He'd committed a rash act and he was too consumed with feelings of loss and despair to strategize a way out of it. So when he failed to ask, you figured he must be the murderer."

Just then my phone rang again. It was Knutsen with the message: get back here, now.

Surprisingly, the Lieutenant wasn't there when we re-entered the interview room. We took our seats, but I found it impossible to remain quiet; I could see the next step. "Okay, you knew Roddy was the killer, but you still had no proof; nothing put him at the scene of the crime. You also knew that the police were concentrating entirely on Michael, so you decided to pay the kid a visit. Perhaps to put some pressure on him, convince him somehow to confess. Did you call him last night and tell him you were coming?"

"Ay, so I did, indeed. I spake with him."

"But he refused to see you, I'll bet. What did he say?"

"That he dined not at home."

"It was most likely just an excuse. Even if he were out all evening, however, you knew he'd probably be there in the morning. So you decided to drop in on him first thing today. But when you arrived at the cottage . . . ."

"Alas, what shall I say? He was dead."

"Shot through the head," Knutsen interjected as he re-entered the interview room. "Your phone call must have been the final straw, Benatsky."

"I am the sorrier; would 'twere otherwise," Jake responded with more than a tinge of bitterness.

"There's no way you could have anticipated it," the Lieutenant assured him. "Sure, he was depressed

– what guy wouldn't be after having killed the girl of his dreams? – but he had to figure that his chances of getting away with it were pretty good. Your call told him that you suspected him, but he didn't know what evidence you had. That's what I don't get. It would have made more sense for him to find out what you had before taking such a desperate action. Why kill himself at that point?"

"I think I understand," I said. The final pieces were falling into place. "I think the answer lies with what Gates did on the night of the murder."

"What Gates did?" Knutsen asked quizzically.

"Yes. Consider his position. He's had this horny little kid in his face and he's been able to inflict some pay-back by telling him about Michael. But then the kid flies out in a drunken rage."

"Wait a sec. How do you know Gates told him that?"

"Because it's the only thing that would have given him motive. Everything else he heard that night about Mandy was good news for him." I explained how Jake worked that out from Roddy's venomous comments about Mandy when we interviewed him.

"Okay, go on."

"Gates probably gives the kid's outburst no mind at first, just continues his drinking session with Brian Chiang. But later on when he's by himself, he starts to get concerned. Maybe he shouldn't have gone so far – who knows what the kid is capable of?

So he decides to head to Mandy's, just to make sure she's all right."

"He could have phoned."

"Maybe he doesn't want to leave any indication that he's looking for her – just in case. So he goes there, entering with his keys, and finds her body. Maybe he also sees Roddy leaving just as he's arriving. Anyway, he knows who did it."

"Know you what this means?" Jake asked Knutsen. "What follows this?"

"Yes, I think I do," he replied, smiling grimly. "At the very least, it would mean that Roddy would be Gates's bitch for as long as it suited him."

"And just to make sure that Roddy fully understands the situation he's in," I added, "Gates decides to drop by to make it perfectly clear."

"You mean, Gates beat him? How do we know that? There's no evidence that he went to Roddy's cottage that night."

"Have you looked for any?"

"No, we haven't," he admitted. "The assault's been on the back burner. It wouldn't make any difference anyway. If we found fingerprints or DNA evidence to place him at the cottage, he could always say he'd been there some other time. We can't put him at Mandy Bennett's apartment that night, either; we know he'd been there many times. Everything you've said is just supposition."

"Nay, sir, not altogether so," Jake replied. "Look to

th' door."

"What?" Knutsen asked, glancing at the door of the interview room.

"Let the door be locked," Jake added. The Lieutenant remained puzzled.

"Oh, of course!" I exclaimed. I grabbed my laptop and scanned through the file until I found the interview at Gates's house. There it was. "We put it to Gates that he'd gone to Roddy's cottage and assaulted him. He replied that he couldn't have done it because he didn't have a key; he would have had to break in or bang on the door to rouse the drunken kid, either of which would have made too much noise. When we mentioned that Roddy said he'd left the door unlocked, Gates responded that he couldn't possibly have known that. It all seems sensible on the face of it, but it was a giant bluff."

Knutsen still wasn't clued in, so I spelled it out. "Gates is right that it would have been difficult to break in or rouse Roddy in the middle of the night without making a lot of noise. So why would anyone try? No one would. In fact, there were no signs of a break-in at Roddy's cottage. That leaves just one alternative . . . ."

"The perpetrator had to have a key."

"Exactly. So the question is, who has a key, besides Roddy? Not Gates himself; he hardly knew the kid, as he pointed out to us. But Roddy's uncle, who owns the place, would have one."

"So you're saying that Gates knocked on Chiang's door or phoned him to get the key."

"It had to be him. No one else would have any reason to do it, not at that time of night."

"Well, we can check if there was a phone call. But why would Chiang tolerate the beating up of his nephew? That seems strange."

"This is not strange at all," Jake retorted.

"No, it isn't," I concurred. "Not once he finds out that Roddy has just killed Gates's girl. He can see how angry Gates is about it and knows that he wants revenge. The best that he can hope for is that Gates will allow his nephew to live. A beating is a small price to pay for not being killed – or not going to prison for life."

"All right, I can see that. So Roddy was lying about leaving the door unlocked. And also lying about not knowing who attacked him."

"I'm sure it was made very clear to him that he had to take his medicine and keep his mouth shut."

"And Gates is fine with that." He was picking up the thread now. "He wouldn't really want to kill anyone. There's always the risk of forensic evidence being left behind; besides, just being associated with two murder victims might be enough to end his political career."

"So Roddy is trapped," I said. "He takes his beating, keeps his mouth shut, and survives. More than survives – things start to go much better. That's because you are focussing your investigation on Michael."

"Not only that," he replied, "but we're accumulating more and more evidence against him. This information is probably being leaked to Gates through his contacts in the department. From there, it goes to Brian Chiang and then to Roddy."

Jake nodded, but then frowned slightly. "Is there more?" he asked disingenuously.

"Yes, there is," I responded. "Roddy is also aware, or is made aware, that he owes Gates something else. You mentioned, Lieutenant, that Mandy's apartment had been wiped clean. I doubt that in his rage, Roddy had even thought of that."

"No, it doesn't sound likely," he agreed. "And, without it, there would certainly have been some traces of his presence. The inside door handle would have had his fingerprints, for sure – unless he had taken the precaution of wearing gloves or stopped to wipe them off. Neither seems likely, given his state of mind and liquor intake. And who knows what else he touched?"

"That means that Gates must have taken care of it. He probably also gave Roddy his marching orders: don't go to work or see anyone until you heal; if anyone asks about Sunday night, just say you were at my place until one a.m., then went home; if someone sees you before the wounds have healed, say you were assaulted by a man you didn't recognize. What he didn't tell him, apparently, was not to badmouth Mandy."

"It probably never crossed his mind."

"It certainly never occurred to Roddy. He had no idea that by damning Mandy, he'd already pointed the finger at himself. He probably figured he was home free as long as Gates and his uncle stuck to their story that he was with them until one that night. Maybe he thought he wasn't any worse off than before – if you discount the fact that he'd lost Mandy."

"But he never had her. So maybe he figured that the murder wasn't such a bad thing. Not only has he punished her for her betrayal, but he's made sure no one else can have her."

I doubted that was true, considering the anguished state we found him in on Wednesday, but one had to appreciate the Lieutenant's touch for the macabre. "Then you phone, Jake. You want to see him. He resists, so you indicate that it's serious, not something that can be avoided. Did you hint at his guilt?"

"Some such thing I said," he admitted.

"You didn't perhaps go a little over the top?" I prodded. "You've been known to get a little explosive with your accusations."

"I told him what I thought," he replied, "and told no more than what he found himself was apt and true."

"So now he knows the spotlight is going to be thrown on him," Knutsen observed. "Yet we have no real evidence against him. That still bothers me."

"Consider a couple of things, Lieutenant," I replied. "First, he doesn't really know that we have no real evidence, does he? He's been told all traces of his presence at the apartment have been removed, but how could he be sure? Gates isn't exactly a professional in that type of work. At any moment he might find the police at his door with an arrest warrant. If he doesn't act quickly, he may never get a chance."

"Okay, true enough," he admitted, albeit hesitatingly. "In fact, the hairs we found might well turn out to be his. But he could have run for it; his uncle presumably would have helped him."

"Then he'd be a fugitive."

"Not great for him, certainly, but it might have bought him time to find out how much we had against him. I'm sure any good lawyer would have told him there wasn't enough to convict."

"Not yet, but think about what would have happened if your investigation had started to dig seriously into Gates's involvement with the nightclub and with his uncle. Sure, Gates would try to marshal his connections and his political leverage to keep it quiet, but if that failed, he'd certainly be willing to trade Roddy for a little discretion from the police. After all, he owes the kid nothing; in fact, he's extremely annoyed with him for what he's done. And you'd cut that deal, wouldn't you, Lieutenant?"

He pondered the question for no more than a moment. "To be frank," he said, "if Gates had come forward and admitted that Roddy left his house much earlier than one a.m., we probably would have given him a free ride – especially if he also said he'd seen him leaving Mandy's apartment later on. We'd even have turned a blind eye on his attempt to cover for him afterwards; I doubt we could have proved it anyway."

"He could even have spun it to make himself out as an exemplary citizen," I suggested, "a man whose devotion to justice made him willing to turn in even a nephew of a friend. The public would have loved it. Chiang senior probably wouldn't have objected, either. I don't think he's the kind of man to let his cozy relationship with Gates be undercut by the hotheaded actions of an errant nephew."

"Roddy must have known what type of men Gates and his uncle are," Knutsen concluded. "He must have figured that, sooner or later, they'd abandon him. So, for him, there was no way out. Or rather, just the one."

"And why not death," Jake observed, "rather than living torment? Than be so, better to cease to be. Nothing can touch him further."

"You make it sound so rational, so logical," I said. "Be honest with me, Jake: are you sure you didn't see this coming?"

"I did not," he replied. "It is something of my negligence, nothing of my purpose."

I believed him, but his tone concerned me; it had become almost morose. "You sound like you feel responsible, nonetheless."

He shrugged wearily. "Ay, I do. To be honest, this is my fault."

"I don't think you're being fair to yourself. You had to do something."

"And yet I bear a burden. 'Tis a cruelty to load a falling man."

"Far from it," Knutsen objected. "I don't think this guy would have fallen at all if it wasn't for you; we were too focussed on Mike Calthorpe. On behalf of the department, I want to thank you."

"For what, Lieutenant? I did some service, it is true, but I am much to blame. I have done ill, of which I do accuse myself so sorely that I will joy no more."

"Meaning what?" I asked.

"Meaning henceforth to trouble you no more." Once again, he was out the door in a flash.

"What about your statement?" Knutsen exclaimed. In the suddenness of it all, he'd managed to spill his coffee again.

❊ ❊ ❊

Jake's sudden escape left me not only perplexed but also trapped. However much I pleaded, Knutsen wouldn't let me go before I'd spent another couple of hours honing my statement to his testy requirements. Once I'd finally escaped his clutches, I dashed to my car and drove to the theatre as fast as I could. It was after two o'clock when I arrived. I hurried through the entrance and onto the main stage, only to find Eddie with an unwelcome message for me: the play had been suspended.

I phoned Walt immediately. Jake hadn't been in contact with him, so I gave him the news that Michael and I were exonerated and ready to go. He was pleased for us, of course, but unfortunately a cloud still hung over the play. The fact that three prominent cast members had been taken in for questioning in connection with the murder of a fourth – the play's leading lady, no less – had provoked a media free-for-all. The story was going national – even international. In consequence, everything was on hold pending the outcome of an emergency meeting of the Board of Directors, to be held later that afternoon. Their decision would be announced at a six-thirty production meeting, which we were all expected to attend.

He promised to let the Board know the news, but he doubted it would make any difference: the play would be cancelled. That the woman who was to be the murder victim in a play had actually been murdered might sound like a publicist's dream, but in reality no one else wanted to be connected with it. Not the commercial sponsors, not the Parks Board which provided the site, and certainly not the City Council – including Gates himself, who was the culture kingpin at City Hall. I decided to go home, take a long bath and reflect.

The first item in my inventory of ponderables was Michael. The morning had begun with him accused of murder and me implicated as an accessory. My fear that one or both of us would be in jail by day's end had been totally dispelled, which was great news. I'd been wrong about a lot of things in this investigation – clearly wrong to have sheltered him for so long – but my instinct about his innocence had been spot on. Whatever else he is, he's no murderer and I was glad to have played some role in vindicating him.

My reflections then shifted inward. The situation with Michael had caused me to question what kind of person I am, and I needed to face that issue now. Earlier, my concern had been with my willingness to cover up for him, even to Jake; now, my mind turned to my unwillingness to forgive him for his 'dalliance' with Mandy. I knew the one was influencing the other: my anger at myself for covering up was amplifying my anger at him for creating the need for it. Irrational though it was, I was blaming him for my failings as well as his own.

Did this mean I should forgive and forget? Jake thought so; he seemed to see the dalliance as a 'mere distraction' that should not be allowed to cloud the long-term prospect. He had a point: every relationship must have its moments when one party or the other wavers, when the future of the entire enterprise seems – if only briefly – to hang in the balance. Why couldn't I step back a little and see it that way?

I knew that my attitude reflected a degree of shallowness on my part; an ego too fragile to forgive even a passing distraction, if that's all it was, is nothing to be proud of. But, I decided, there is a fundamental truth underlying my attitude, however shallow it may seem in the cold light of reason. That truth is that relationships need to be founded on something inviolate. For some couples, the occasional dalliance may not be that critical; the foundation lies elsewhere. But that kind of relationship would never work for me. Perhaps if I were the type of woman who draws men like flies, as Mandy had been, I'd be more relaxed about such things, but the men I've cared about seriously have been too few and the betrayals too many. To form a lasting relationship, I need a higher degree of fidelity than Michael had been willing – or perhaps able – to offer.

Besides, I thought, how much have I really lost with Michael? We'd been seeing each other for only a few weeks. Because there seemed to be so much promise, we'd instinctively proceeded slowly and cautiously. Now, I've found out the truth about him – that he's not someone I could count on where it matters – and I haven't wasted years doing so, unlike with Bruce. So I'm not really any further behind, am I? Perhaps I should be more optimistic about the future, as Jake urged. Better choices may follow.

This thought brought Jake to mind. He, too, faced

a reckoning of sorts – over the way he'd handled Roddy. If he'd revealed his suspicions to Knutsen earlier, perhaps he could have persuaded him to bring the kid in, thereby foreclosing the possibility of a suicide. Instead, he'd chosen to keep his cards close to his chest and contact him directly. Why had he done that?

Although Jake's motivations often seem obscure and open to multiple interpretations, I felt inclined to believe that he genuinely hadn't anticipated what Roddy's reaction would be. He probably thought the kid too weak and spineless – the kind of person who might muse about suicide in moments of despair but lacked the intestinal fortitude to follow through. I suspected he was also driven by an awareness of how meagre the evidence was against the boy. Confronting him was a bluff, let's face it, and he probably figured that Knutsen wouldn't be able to deliver on the bluff by extracting the confession they needed. In fact, it's doubtful Knutsen would even have tried, given how fixated he was on his prime suspect, Michael. So Jake concluded he had to do it himself. The reasoning was hard to fault, but unfortunately, it proved wanting. He got the confession, all right, but not the way he wanted. I was worried about him.

Deciding that there was only so much one could deal with in a single soaking, I rinsed myself off in the shower, got dressed, and made myself a pot of camomile tea. I was now ready to deal with practicalities, foremost of which was phoning Henry Bennett to let him know the news. On Jake's behalf, I'd promised him an early resolution of the case and I looked forward to being able to deliver it. It would provide both of us some needed solace.

I was to be denied that comfort, however. Henry informed me that Jake had already dropped by, fulfilling the commitment I'd made on his behalf. Henry seemed very pleased with the outcome of our investigation, though I couldn't help feeling that 'closure', that modern El Dorado, would not be as forthcoming as he believed. He again offered money, but I declined – as I'm sure Jake had also done.

I then turned to the other practicality – downloading the recordings and bringing my notes up to date. It was no easy task to get down all that had transpired, and it took me almost till six to produce a reasonably coherent version. By then, it was time to head to the theatre. I wasn't looking forward to hearing that the professional highlight of my year was going to be extinguished, but I hoped at least to find Jake. I didn't want to spend this evening alone.

*F*RIDAY, JUNE 19. EVENING.

The less said about the meeting the better. The message was as blunt as it was expected: the production was cancelled. Several cast members urged the Board to re-consider in view of this morning's developments, but it was quickly apparent that their efforts were pointless. The decision was irrevocable.

By seven, everyone was filing back to the dressing rooms to begin the tedious task of collecting belongings and making farewells. No one was in good enough spirits to toss out even the tersest of quotations, not even Ollie or Stan. Jake stood off to one side, his usual position – physical as well as psychological – in this setting, but he now looked more bewildered than self-absorbed.

"Jake," I said as I sidled up to him.

"Madam, I am here. What is your will?"

"You don't seem your usual self," I replied with as much levity as I could muster.

He smiled grimly. "Life is as tedious as a twice-told tale vexing the dull ear of a drowsy man," he muttered.

I burst out laughing, and with only a moment's hesitation, he joined me heartily. "What shall we do about it?" I asked.

"Shall we rest us here, and by relating tales of others' griefs, see if 'twill teach us to forget our own?"

"I think it'd work better somewhere else, preferably with a bottle of wine in front of us."

His smile this time was softer. "How wise you are! Come, let us go, and we two will rail against our mistress the world and all our misery."

"Hmm. I've got an even better idea: let's make it dinner at Chez Panisse – to make up for last night."

For a moment I feared he might refuse, but then he seemed to relax. "Madam, I am most apt to embrace your offer. Let's to supper, come, and drown consideration."

We took a table in the garden patio at the back of the restaurant, where we could avoid the boisterous crowd that was beginning to take over the main dining room. The choice proved to be inspired; the waning sunset had turned the sky a lustrous crimson, while a gentle breeze flowed sensuously over us, as if we were being fanned by servants. If this setting couldn't lighten our moods, nothing could.

Jake selected a bottle of that very fine *Veuve du Pape* to complete the task of 'drowning consideration'. The bottle arrived promptly and was immediately subjected to scrutiny. "I pray, come and crush a cup of wine," he declared after giving it his approval. We lifted our glasses to toast . . . neither of us knew what. We crushed fulsomely, nonetheless.

"You still seem a little down," I said. I was in the mood to tackle things head on; besides, I reckoned, he usually appreciates the direct approach. At least, he uses it often enough.

"It is true, indeed," he admitted. "I am wrapp'd in dismal thinkings." He swallowed another mouthful with less than his usual gusto.

"You're still bothered about Roddy's suicide, aren't you? I understand why it would be on your mind, but like I said this morning, you shouldn't be blaming yourself."

"Whether I have been to blame or no, I know not, for nought I did in hate, but all in honour. I thought all for the best."

"Jake, I'm sure that's true." I wasn't lying; I was more convinced than ever that there was no other way it could have been handled. "I think you should cut yourself some slack."

"Should I do so, I should belie my thoughts."

"What are those thoughts?"

He went silent while our food was delivered, then began to eat in a slow, methodical manner. I gave him a few minutes, then repeated the question. Finally, he looked up and said, "I had a thing to say, but I will fit it with some better time."

"Well, I have a few things to say." If he wasn't going to give himself a break, then I was going to do it for him – or at least give it a good try. "You know as well as I do that Knutsen wouldn't have bothered to take on Roddy; he was far too obsessed with Michael. Even if he had been willing, you figured he'd never have been able to extract a confession with so little evidence to threaten him with. You're right about that as well. You bring a unique combination of rage, provocation, guile and charm that's almost impossible to resist."

A slight smile eased his features.

"Besides, it wasn't a fear of your voodoo that drove Roddy to suicide. Not really."

He looked curious. "Why think you so?"

"What you saw was a young man who was following a script he'd been given, a story-line that would keep him out of prison. You had to break that, if only to save Michael. What you couldn't have known was how conflicted Roddy was feeling. Though he was trying to get away with it, he was also racked with guilt over what he'd done. Having to endure that burden in prison – it was never going to be an option for him."

"In that there's comfort," he conceded after a moment's reflection.

I could tell he wasn't entirely satisfied. "What is it?"

"I know not how, but I do find it cowardly and vile,

for fear of what might fall, so to prevent the time of life."

"You didn't earlier. You said . . . ."

"I pray you choose another subject," he cut in, raising his hand to halt me.

It didn't make sense to press him further. Like many people, he was torn between seeing the rationality of ending a living torment, as he'd called it, and his basic revulsion at the idea of suicide. He needed time to work it through for himself. "Okay, what else would you like to talk about?"

"Your heart is full of something that does take your mind from feasting," he observed. It was true; my cassoulet had been sitting in front of me untouched for several minutes.

"Well, you know what it is," I answered as I picked up my fork. "It's Michael. I know you don't want to hear this stuff again, but I can't get it out of my mind. He claims he still loves me, wants to spend his life with me . . . ."

"May be he tells you true."

"Yeah well, maybe he does. But still, it just doesn't make sense that he could actually mean it, given what happened between him and her."

"And yet, to say the truth, reason and love keep little company together nowadays."

"Jake, maybe that's just male-speak, but you still don't seem to get it: building an enduring relationship implies a willingness to 'forego all others' . . . ."

"But to my mind," he countered, "it is a custom more honour'd in the breach than the observance."

I knew he was poking fun at me. It was partly the coy look on his face, partly the fact that he'd just used a well-known quotation, which he almost never does. It was his way of saying, 'lighten up'.

"So what do you suggest I do?" I was warming to the mood.

"Live a little; comfort a little; cheer thyself a little. Let's to-night be bounteous at our meal."

"Well, I definitely intend to be bounteous with this wine." I refilled my glass to prove my commitment. "Have you any other advice, while we're at it?"

"Come, give me your hand." His tone was more serious now. His eyes were beginning to take on an intense, melting glow as he started to stroke my hand gently. "All other doubts, by time let them be cleared. What wound did ever heal but by degrees?"

I smiled. "So time will do the trick, is that what you're saying? I could say the same to you."

"You may, indeed, say so," he accorded. "This wide and universal theatre presents more woeful pageants than the scene wherein we play in."

I had to laugh. "Isn't that essentially what Humphrey Bogart says to Ingrid Bergman at the end of *Casablanca*? That the problems of three small people don't amount to a hill of beans in this crazy world, or something like that?"

He laughed with me. "I do beseech you, madam,

be content. Think not on him till to-morrow."

"Well, if you can put Roddy out of your mind," I replied, "I reckon I can manage that." In fact, it would be a relief.

"Good, very good, it is so then."

I took another forkful. "So's this cassoulet, by the way. Very good, I mean. How's your risotto?"

"I like it well." He picked up his fork again. It seemed like a cue, for we both began to tackle our meals with single-minded intensity.

"Well, that was scrumptious," I said when I'd finished mopping up the last of my sauce with a remaining butt-end of baguette. "What now? More wine?"

"Yes, by all means." He signalled to a passing waiter and, before long, a second bottle appeared. Without further ado, he took it and refilled our glasses.

"Aren't you forgetting something?"

"What, I prithee?"

"You didn't test the wine."

"Pardon me: it is a matter of small consequence."

"Really? That surprises me."

"You must not think, then, that I am drunk."

I smirked. "The thought never crossed my mind."

His eyes responded with a coy sparkle as he leaned back in his chair a little awkwardly and gazed starward. "Dear lady, tell me one thing that I shall ask you."

"What's that?"

"What sport shall we devise here in this garden, to drive away the heavy thought of care?"

"Well, I'm not sure . . . ."

"Emilia, come," he prodded. "Be as your fancies teach you; whate'er you be, I am obedient."

"Hmm. That's a most interesting proposition." I slowly savoured another sip of wine. "You wouldn't happen to have any suggestions, would you?"

"Only this, if I may be bold." He sat forward.

"Go for it."

"May I, sweet lady, beg a kiss of you?"

"A kiss?"

"If it not be too much."

I couldn't help smiling. "Well, given all that's happened, I suppose 'you might take occasion to kiss'."

He leaned across the table and brushed my lips with his. Then he kissed me for real – softly, sensuously, almost sinuously, and square on my lips.

"That was some kiss," I said, once I'd recovered my breath.

"So it was. More than so, in good truth. Tell me this, I pray." He searched my eyes for a moment. "Would you desire more?"

"Be as your fancies teach you," I replied.

SATURDAY, JUNE 20. MORNING.

The morning brought more glorious sunshine. I wasn't bothered in the least. Everything that mattered had dissipated. The murder was solved, the play was cancelled, and I had no idea what I was going to do with my summer. Or my life. It was as if everything were floating, suspended in a warm, viscous gloop in which only slow-motion action was possible, if action were possible at all.

My reverie was broken around eight-thirty by a phone call from Helen. She'd heard the news, of course. She expressed disbelief that sweet little Roddy had done such a thing, but I didn't get the impression that her incredulity was total. Anyway, she wanted to meet. I did, too; I'd missed her over the last couple of days. She suggested Ingrid's for coffee. Then she mentioned that Jake would be joining us. I felt a strange buzz, a current of I-don't-know-what coursing through my body. I wondered how it had been arranged.

❀ ❀ ❀

I entered Ingrid's from the side entrance just before the appointed time. I quickly spotted Jake and Helen sitting at an outside table next to the front door, their backs towards me. They were evidently deep in conversation. Using the hustle and bustle of the weekend crowd as my cover, I weaved my way forward, stopping just before the entrance. Sometimes, there's nothing so delicious as a conversation overheard.

As I came within earshot, I heard her say, "You know, so much of this business revolved around love: finding it or not finding it. I can't help wondering if I'll ever find it. The real thing, I mean. To tell you the truth, I can't imagine it." I wondered how someone so different from me could sound so similar.

"I doubt it not," he replied as he took a sip of his *café au lait.* "You are a great deal abused in too bold a persuasion. The lustre in your eye, heaven in your cheek, pleads your fair usage."

"Actually, my looks plead anything but. I'm not treated with fair usage; I'm treated as fair game. Even you think I'm a slut." She didn't seem bitter as she said this, just resigned and perhaps a little wistful.

"Come, you are deceived," he hastily replied. "I think of no such thing."

"You did last Monday at the Pelican. You called me worse."

"When I was green in judgment, cold in blood," he explained.

Cold in blood certainly, I thought, perhaps not so green in judgment. I was almost certain that the abuse he'd dished out that night had been nothing more than a ploy to get her talking.

"But it forced me to think," she went on. "A lot of what you said about me, the life I'm leading . . . well, it's true."

"I cry you gentle pardon; you are as virtuous as fair," he responded. "To report otherwise were a malice."

"Say what you will, but I know what I know. Let's face it, whatever I really am, who's going to have me after the life I've led? Some slimeball I meet in here?"

"You must not be so quick," he objected. "'Tis true: you are not for all markets . . . ."

"Ouch."

"Pardon me, madam, for I meant not so. I know your worthiness. Give me leave to speak my mind."

"There's no need," she cut in. "Meeting you and Emma has made me reckon with my life. It's something I'd been avoiding for a long time."

"It is a common thing," he replied, apparently content to let her proceed.

"Yeah, exactly, and it's what I'd been doing. Look at you two. You both have your acting careers. Emma has her teaching career as well, and you have . . . well, I don't know what, but I'm sure it's something. And what am I doing with my life? Slinging drinks to a bunch of drunken, horny old men."

"Do you amend it then; it lies in you. There is still time to change the road you're on."

"Do you really think so? I hope so. I've got to try anyway, before it's too late."

"What will you do? How will you live?"

"I don't know, exactly. Not yet. But I'll tell you this: it's not going to be because of some sugar daddy I meet at the club. Or even some poor sap I finagle into marrying me. I want to stand on my own two feet and be proud of it. Maybe I should try college, see if I can get some kind of qualification."

"In what?"

"I'm not sure. But it's got to lead to a job that doesn't depend on my looks." She smiled as if that would be an extraordinary novelty, which it probably would.

"I am glad of it," he replied, smiling as well. "The want is but to put those powers in motion that long to move. It is the purpose that makes strong the vow."

"And who knows?" she added. "Maybe if I can remake my life, even get a career – God! I can't believe I'm saying this – some sort of love life will also emerge." She chuckled at the idea.

"There's a time for all things," he concurred. Then his tone became much more solemn. "Think on this: in the end, the love you take is equal to the love you make. Remember what I have said."

They both fell silent for a moment, perhaps contemplating the possibilities of life revealed in that quotation. It felt like a good time to make my entrance, but then she said something that froze me to my spot.

"Do you think he was faithful to her, after all? Michael, I mean."

"So he says."

"Yeah, well, I'm not convinced. The way Mandy and he looked at each other. You didn't see it, but believe me, it was something." She paused for a moment, then asked, "Tell me this, could he actually be in love with Emma, despite everything?"

"That Cassio loves her, I do well believe it."

"Really?" She seemed surprised. "After his fling with Mandy?"

"This was sometime a paradox, I grant you, but now the time gives it proof."

"Why do you say that?"

"What sign is it when a man of great spirit grows melancholy?" he replied. "How hard it is to hide the sparks of nature!"

"I suppose . . . but what about her? She was really upset when I saw her last."

"I find her milder than she was."

"She may have calmed down, but can she truly forgive him after what he's done? Personally, I can't imagine it."

"And yet a dispensation may be had," he suggested. "What's gone and what's past help should be past grief."

"That's very noble, but I'm not sure it's very realistic. I guess the real question is, does she love him?"

"I am sure she does. She looked yesternight fairer than ever I saw her look, or any woman else. Heavens rain grace on that which breeds between 'em."

These words stunned me. I felt both flattered and flattened. Is there anyone else who could combine admiration and rejection so adroitly in the same breath? Yet, I scarcely had a moment to assimilate what I'd just heard when it became so very much worse.

"You must be pleased, too, now that you've finished your investigation."

"'Tis very true. I am glad at heart to be so rid o' the business."

"But you're leaving, aren't you?" It was more a statement than a question.

"What must be shall be," he replied, "for I can stay no longer."

"How shall I explain it to Emma?"

I couldn't hear his reply clearly, but I could almost swear he said, "Say that I did all this for love of her."

I had to join them. Yet I couldn't. Tears were welling in my eyes; I feared my voice would break if I tried to speak. I took several deep breaths, which helped but didn't bring the degree of composure I needed. I slithered back to the side door and left.

Once outside the café, I collapsed against the wall, holding a hand to my chest in an attempt to calm my pounding heart. Thank goodness the lane was empty; I must have looked a fright. I forced myself to take slow, deep breaths. It may have been the fresh air outside, but more likely it was simply escaping the atmosphere inside that helped to settle my nerves. In any case, it worked, and within a few minutes, I was ready to attempt a new entrance – from the front this time.

"I am very glad to see you," Jake declared as I approached their table.

I smiled cautiously, not sure of what to say.

"So am I," Helen chimed in.

"Me, too. I should have called you earlier, Helen; it's just that the last couple of days have been a bit of a nightmare."

"Jake's been filling me in," she replied. "It sounds like it's been a real roller-coaster ride. Here, grab a seat."

I did so and immediately pretended to absorb myself in the roster of coffee and coffee-tinged beverages posted on a sandwich-board by the door. In truth, I was just buying time before facing him. Finally, I decided upon a regular coffee and a neutral approach.

"Jake, I understand you've been to see Mandy's father. I forgot to ask you about it last night – how's he holding up?"

"Her father is but grim," he replied. "Grief and sorrow still embrace his heart. That old common arbitrator, time, will one day end it."

"I hope that day isn't too far off," I said, "though I fear it will be. His burden is almost unimaginable. I'll go see him, too, as soon as I can."

I thought I was doing pretty well so far, but I was deluding myself. I should have known that he would see through it. He acknowledged my offer to visit Henry with an approving nod, then said: "Give me your hand and let me feel your pulse. How is it that the clouds still hang on you?"

My pulse, needless to say, was hammering away. Before I knew it, my composure evaporated. I blurted out, "Oh Jake, I have been in such a pickle since I saw you last."

It was a line straight out of *The Tempest*. Damn! I thought; I'm still doing that. Am I cursed forever to quote Shakespeare in moments of extreme agitation? Or will it be just when he's around? That thought jolted me instantly: it reminded me of what I'd just heard.

Jake, of course, is never diverted by a Shakespearean quotation. He went straight to the point. "Pardon me, 'twas not my purpose, thus to beg a kiss."

"A kiss?" Helen asked, puzzled but intrigued.

"What kiss?"

We both ignored her. "It's not that," I responded. In fact, if I weren't working so hard at dissembling, I might have confessed how welcome that kiss had been. More than welcome – and more than a kiss; much more, if the truth be told. Instead, I simply said, "It's about Michael."

He appeared eager to embrace the issue. "What say you? Can you love the gentleman?"

"I have more cause to hate him than to love him." Fuck, another quotation! God, help me.

"How can that be?" he asked. "It is a great price – for a small vice."

Perhaps he was just trying to lower the emotional temperature, but his comment struck me as flippant. "How do you know it's small?" I challenged him. "Maybe it'd gone much further. I don't even know if he's been faithful . . . ."

"You have heard him swear downright he was."

"But he would say that, wouldn't he?" I countered. "Doesn't mean it's true."

"What should I say? Whether this be or be not, I'll not swear."

"Exactly!" I exclaimed. Then it hit me how ridiculous I was being: no one can ever know for certain that someone else has been faithful. I throttled back and said, "I don't think I can forgive him. I mean it."

Jake wasn't inclined to desist, despite my obduracy. "This is not the way," he admonished. "Let me persuade you to forbear awhile."

"Forbear?" I replied sarcastically.

"Take time to pause. Time is the nurse and breeder of all good."

"Time seems to be your solution for everything, but it can't change what's happened. We'd only been dating a few weeks and already he's been tempted away by another woman. You've got to understand I'm looking for a heck of a lot more commitment than that."

He took my hand. "Come, you are too severe a moraller. I could heartily wish this had not befallen, but since it is as it is, mend it for your own good. Do you not see you move him? Go, girl, seek happy nights to happy days."

"Just like that?" I was incredulous.

"I see you what you are, you are too proud. Pride can hurt you, too."

"What?"

He expired heavily. "Good lady, hear me with patience. The web of our life is of a mingled yarn, good and ill together. Our virtues would be proud, if our faults whipped them not, and our crimes would despair, if they were not cherished by our virtues."

"Jake, I understand what you're saying: no one is perfect; we all have our faults; we all make mistakes. I get it, I do." I hesitated, searching for a way to capture the essence of what divided us. "Maybe you're just too much of a male to understand. There are a lot of things a woman can forgive, but there's one line that – for me, anyway – can't be crossed. He crossed that line. He's a . . . ."

He placed a finger over my lips to silence me. "I have but this to say: look in a glass, and call thy image so."

I was stunned. He must have read the shocked look in my face because he hastily added, "I say no more than truth, so help me God."

There are certain lies we tell ourselves – lies so central to our self-conceptions that we expect those who know us well never to challenge. He has just violated that expectation; by urging me to compare myself with Michael, he'd called a core bluff, a big lie that I'd been nursing throughout this mad adventure. That he did it seems very sensible, very justified in retrospect, but at the time I felt absolutely shattered. I'm sure I blushed profusely. Helen, so savvy when it comes to men and women, knew immediately what was going on, I could tell. Sagely, she said nothing.

After an interminable few moments, I asked him, "What would you have me do?"

He replied simply, "Pray you, let Cassio be received again."

"Don't ask me to contact him; I couldn't."

"Nay, it is in a manner done already. I have sent to bid Cassio come speak with you. He's gone to seek you at your house."

"Why?" I asked. "So that he can explain again how he's always loved me, despite everything?"

"It would do you good to hear it."

"Then what?"

He expired deeply. "You, that have so fair parts of woman on you, have too a woman's heart. Cry the man mercy, love him, take his offer. There stays a husband to make you a wife."

"A husband! Don't you think you're going a little fast?"

"Go and meet him; that's all I seek. Prithee now, say you will, and go about it."

Dammit, another 'prithee'. It made my back bristle. "I don't know. I really don't want to get trapped . . . ."

"Come, come, I know 'tis good for you," he chided. "Do as I bid you do."

"What are you trying to do here, Jake? Push me into his arms so that you don't have to deal with me any longer?"

"You mistake me much. I would not for the world."

"Then what?" I retorted. "I cannot love him."

"I do not fear it; I have seen you both."

"So that's it?" I countered. "You can just peer into our souls and know we're in love?"

"Fear not my truth: the moral of my wit is 'plain and true'; there's all the reach of it."

"But how do you know what's plain and true?"

He shrugged apologetically. "I learnt it out of women's faces."

Two women's faces stared at him incredulously.

Sometimes the right line from Shakespeare just shuts you up. That's how I felt at that moment and I'm sure Helen felt pretty much the same. We averted our stares towards the street, each choosing a slightly different direction, lost in her own thought-bubble. Helen, who had much less at stake in this conversation, was the first to re-emerge.

"I can't help thinking about Mandy," she said. "She was such a good friend. And so much fun. You know, although she was really ambitious, she always had time for me. And she was genuine, despite all the stuff going on around her, around us. I haven't been able to warm up to any of the other girls at the club the way I warmed to her."

"I would I could have spoken with the woman herself," Jake lamented.

"Why?" I responded. "To learn from her face?"

The facetiousness in my question totally passed him by, or so it appeared. All he said was, "She was beloved."

Was that comment for me? I wondered. If so, it was too facile, it wouldn't wash. "Perhaps too much beloved," I suggested. "She had Gates, the big wheel, squiring her about; she had Kendrick and Roddy hanging around, puppy-eyed; and she had Michael, who seems to have affected her the most." I pained me greatly to say that last part, but I had to.

"Yeah," Helen interjected, "but, you know, I don't think she wanted any of them – really." Was this another comment meant for me? "What she really wanted was her freedom, and for her, that meant her career. Gates was entertaining, but really just a means to an end. Michael . . . I'm not sure. When I talked to her those last few days, she was much more worked up about the play than about him, to be blunt."

"You mean, the play really was the thing?" I couldn't resist suggesting.

She smiled at that. I doubt she knew the reference, but she'd been hanging around us long enough to deduce that it must be from Shakespeare. "Yeah, pretty much," she answered. "I know she was excited. Truly excited. She didn't talk about it much, but her life had been hard – with her mother's death and all. This play was going to be the turning point in her life. She really believed that." She looked as if her composure might go as she spoke these last words.

"So much the more must pity drop upon her," Jake commented, looking somewhat wistful himself. We'd boxed ourselves in again.

It felt like my turn to break out of the funk. "What's going on with Gates and Chiang, I wonder. I haven't heard anything about them."

"What's become of the wenching rogues?" he mused. "I know not how it stands."

"It's funny," Helen observed. "They were both in here Thursday night and last night as well. They're acting as if nothing's changed." She paused. "Do you think anything'll ever be proven against them?"

"It's unlikely," I responded. "We know that Gates beat up Roddy and that he wiped Mandy's place clean after her murder. Both are serious crimes. But Roddy said he didn't recognize his assailant, and Gates can always claim that it was Roddy himself who removed his traces; there's no way to prove otherwise. All that can be proved is that Gates and Chiang misled the police about the time that Roddy left Gates's house on the night of the murder. And they can probably dodge that by saying they were so drunk that evening that they didn't realize what time it actually was. I hate to say it, but I think they're both going to get off scot-free. I don't mind so much about Roddy's uncle – he's paying a price – but it annoys me that Gates will get away unscathed."

"No, 'tis impossible he should escape," Jake objected. "You shortly shall hear more. Time shall unfold what plighted cunning hides."

"What do you mean?" I said.

"Why, 'tis this naming of him does him harm," he explained. "The people are incensed against him. Return he cannot, nor continue where he is."

"You don't think he can spin this in his favour?"

"It doesn't seem to be working so far," Helen replied. "You probably haven't had time to notice, but the media are really coming down hard on him."

I wasn't convinced. "But don't these kinds of accusation just die away fairly quickly? A few months from now, won't he be back to business as normal?"

"They are burs, I can tell you," Jake demurred. "They'll stick where they are thrown. The man's undone forever."

"Well, I certainly hope so," Helen added. "It'd be a blessing for the waitresses if he can't go back to business as normal."

"I believe you. Were't not madness," he mused, smiling wryly, "to make the fox surveyor of the fold?"

Madness indeed. I think we could all agree with that.

Jake's amusing analogy had raised our spirits, and we were ready to move on to new territory, conversationally speaking. Helen led the way. "You know, Jake," she began, "we've talked about what Emma and I should be doing with our lives, but what about you? What lies in your future?"

"I like this place, and willingly could waste my time in it," he replied, "but travellers must be content."

There it was again. I'd been hoping all along that

I'd misheard his earlier comment, but in the back of my mind I knew otherwise. There was no avoiding it now. "Jake, what are you saying?"

"I look on you as one that takes his leave," he replied.

"But why?"

"Have you not heard men say that time comes stealing on by night and day? There is a world elsewhere; my spirit is crying for leaving."

Well," Helen observed, "you are somewhat odd, but we were just getting used to you."

"And in such a case as mine, a man may strain courtesy," he replied, still smiling. "We are time's subjects, and time bids be gone. I take my leave with many thousand thanks," he added, performing a little bow to us both.

Charming though this was, I couldn't be assuaged so easily. Far from it. To me, it felt like another blow to my soul. "Oh God, don't say that," I implored.

"Can I not say, I thank you?" he responded, still light and jocular. "Accept my thankfulness, I prithee."

He reached across and took my hand again, those intense eyes of his boring into me as he did so. The one undid the other and I felt flustered; I could sense panic coming on.

Helen noticed my mounting distress. "We'll see you again, though, won't we?"

"Whether we shall meet again I know not," he

replied. "If we do meet again, why, we shall smile; if not, why, then, this parting was well made."

"I don't think so," I countered. I hated to spoil his breezily eloquent departure line, but nothing about this parting seemed well-made to me. My mind scrambled feverously to find some remedy, some means to make it all right again. "Is it something I've said? I know I've been a little impatient sometimes."

"Not at all, good lady; things are often spoke and seldom meant."

"I'm really sorry, honest, if I . . . ."

"I never wish'd to see you sorry, and I forgive and quite forget old faults," he replied. "Pardon me all the faults I have committed."

I would have pardoned him anything at that point. "Jake, please!" I pleaded. "I don't like this news. Please don't do this, not now. We've had such an extraordinary time."

"These few days' wonder will be quickly worn," he responded. "Give me leave to go, dear lady." He was looking more serious now.

"But what about us?" I could see Helen's eyes widen at this, but I didn't care. "Can you not stay a while?"

He grasped my other hand as I started to sob. "You have bereft me of all words, lady."

Rendering him speechless, even for a brief moment, was no small thing, but I took no comfort from it. Amid my tears, my mind was still scanning frantically for some solution. In my desperation, I hit upon Michael as a bargaining chip. "Please, Jake. I'll see Michael, if you think I should. Maybe you're right; maybe there's a future there."

"Then weep no more," he replied. "Be strong and prosperous in this resolve."

"I will be."

"And let your mind be coupled with your words."

"Okay," I said. It flashed through my consciousness that I was almost beginning to believe it. This thought should have given me some relief, but it didn't. I'd mentioned Michael only as a way to dissuade Jake from leaving; that stratagem had failed and that's all I could think about. I was totally at sea.

Helen saw in my perplexed state another chance to soften the blow. "Jake," she asked, "are you really sure this is necessary – so soon? It's only been a few days since we met. Can't you stay just a little longer?"

"I know my hour is come; 'tis time that I were gone." He looked from her face to mine and back again. "I must lose two of the sweet'st companions in the world."

"Then why go?" I cried, my emotions flaring up once more. "I just don't understand."

"Though it be great pity, yet it is necessary," he responded. "I am sorry for't."

He did look genuinely sorry, though it seemed to have no effect on his determination. Despite my best efforts to forestall it, my sobbing resumed.

"I beseech you, punish me not with your hard thoughts," he added, "wherein I confess me much guilty, to deny so fair and excellent ladies any thing."

These words brought home to me the force of inevitability that was driving this conversation. I sensed it, I recognized it, but still wasn't prepared to yield to it; I had to fight. "But wait!" I said. "I thought we were friends. It's not like you have a lot of them." It was a desperate gambit, a low blow that shamed me even as I launched it.

"There's few or none do know me," he acknowledged.

"But . . . what?"

"Your being by me cannot amend me. Society is no comfort to one not sociable."

"Don't you need some kind of foundation – people you know and can depend upon? Everyone does."

"But 'tis not so with me. I am a feather for each wind that blows."

"More like a hammer sometimes," I said.

Helen smirked, despite herself. "Where will you go?"

"To unpath'd waters, undream'd shores, most certain to miseries enough."

"It doesn't sound entirely appealing," I interjected.

"It is a life that I have desired: I will thrive." He turned back to Helen, who still had a trace of a smile on her face. "Helena, adieu! I rest much bounden to you: fare you well."

"I'm going to miss you. You really have been my tall cool drink with a kick. A kick I badly needed." She was trying to keep it light, I could tell, but I could also tell that she was distressed. Slowly, her eyes began to well up.

"I thank you for that good comfort," he said. He rose to his feet and opened his arms towards her. I averted my eyes as they embraced. When it ended, I could feel between them that strange calm that signifies a physical release of strong emotion.

Then he turned to me and gently pulled me to my feet. "It is no little thing to make mine eyes to sweat compassion," he admitted.

I noticed that his eyes were indeed moistening, ever so slightly. I rummaged desperately for some way to use this to my advantage, but my mind was numb to all entreaties. "I don't know what to say."

"Come, no more words of it," he replied as he drew me toward him. "What needs more words? 'Twixt such friends as we, few words suffice."

"But . . . ."

"Come, leave your tears: a brief farewell. There is no more to say." He wrapped his arms around me.

"I don't want to forget you," I said as we slowly disengaged. "These last few days have been . . . incredible."

"Forget me when I am gone?" he chided. Then,

gesturing toward my bag, he added, "Let this be copied out, and when it's writ, for my sake read it over, and keep it safe for our remembrance."

I resolved then that I would take this advice. I would write the story out, in as much detail as I could muster. It seemed to me that this might be the only thing that would get me through the next few days. I wasn't wrong in this, as it turned out.

"Will you miss me?" I asked.

"Ay, that I will." Then he smiled. "Loose now and then a scatter'd smile, and that I'll live upon."

"But our friendship . . . ."

"We lose it not, so long as we can smile."

It still seemed so light, so insubstantial. I was feeling better now, more resigned to what must be, but I needed more to hang on to. "Will you really remember me, or are you just saying it?"

"For ever and a day, I'll well remember you."

His eyes were again burning holes in my mind as he uttered these words. Suddenly, it all felt so unbearable; I couldn't let it go. "Must you really leave?" I pleaded.

"I must perforce." The look on his face told me that he meant it. "Farewell! God knows when we shall meet again."

"I'm not sure I can manage."

"Believe me, I beseech you: when possibly I can, I will return."

"Do you promise?"

"You may take my word."

I felt reassured, but only a little. "I still don't see why you have to leave."

"O gentle lady," he interceded. "Muse not that I thus suddenly proceed; for what I will, I will, and there an end."

"But what about me? I don't want this."

"Pardon me, my dear one," he replied, "for I must tell you friendly in your ear: you can't always get what you want."

"What?!" I exclaimed.

But it was too late. He'd disappeared into the bustling sidewalk traffic, leaving nothing behind but a twenty dollar bill. I thought I saw a coy smile on his face as he vanished, but I couldn't be sure.

E *PILOGUE*

S o ended this 'strange eventful history'. If you
were thinking that Jake's final comment is not
from Shakespeare, you'd be absolutely right; it's
from the Rolling Stones. A number of his earlier
comments on that last day also quoted rock-and-
roll lyrics, as I realized later when I was transcribing the recording. I happened to mention this to
Stan shortly after that, and before I knew it, the
news swept through the acting company like wild-
fire, leading to a great deal of speculation. Was it a
sign that he had been putting everyone on all along?
Or was it an indication that his 'issues' went much
deeper than anyone suspected?

Neither interpretation was totally persuasive. If
it had all been merely a put-on, there was the obvious problem of why he had persisted with such
a perverse mode of behaviour when he was dealing
with what was, after all, a serious crime. Those who
favoured a deeper interpretation – some mental dis-
order perhaps – found themselves in an even greater
miasma. They could comfort themselves on their

capacity to entertain a much more profound reality, but it remained an intractable one for them. Efforts to unravel it inevitably flirted with the absurd, as even they appreciated.

What do I think? I really have no idea why he threw in some rock lyrics at the end, nor indeed why he spoke as he did beforehand. There's a story there, I'm sure, but not one any of us could ever figure out. I do, however, have some definite thoughts concerning the more fundamental question – is he insane? My definition of an insane person is someone you'd want to change to make more whole, better functioning in some fundamental way. It's true that Jake could be exasperating, bewildering and obtuse; he could also be fascinating, exhilarating, empathetic, insightful and, of course, extremely effective. In the week I knew him, he not only had more impact on the case than even the professionals could muster, he also had more impact on my life that any man I can remember. Given this, why would I want to change him? Wherever he is and however he's expressing himself, I'd like him to remain the same extraordinary person I'd known and, yes, even loved during those few amazing days. I can't see why anyone would want it otherwise.

I can't deny, though, that I've wondered a lot about why he left. I would have liked to have him remain in my life in some capacity, not just in my memories or in these pages. Indeed, I still wish it. But it was not to be, and for a time, trying to figure out why became quite an obsession. The problem is that, as with so much of his behaviour, more than one interpretation is possible.

The first interpretation I had to consider seriously is that it was because of Roddy's suicide. I don't think he was terribly upset over the suicide itself; though he would have preferred that Roddy face the music over what he'd done, he also saw it from the boy's perspective as a rational solution to a rather bleak prospect. What did trouble him was his failure to anticipate it. It clearly weighed on him a lot in the last couple of days, and when things troubled him, I'd noticed, he tended to withdraw in order to work them through. Yet he's also a man who likes to face up to things; slinking away for a while to contemplate a problem is imaginable, but slinking away permanently merely to lick a wound to his ego doesn't sound like him at all.

The other interpretation is that it had to do with me. That sounds like vanity, I know, but it need not be. It could be that the closeness that had developed between us, especially towards the end, was just an illusion; he'd merely wanted to show me that I, too, could be tempted. He might have thought the lesson necessary to induce me to repair my relationship with Michael, and mustered his considerable charm (or Shakespeare's), not to mention those riveting eyes, to make the point. That done, he had to disappear so that we'd get on with it.

His parting comment fits in with this scenario. I

knew from the get-go that its significance lay not in his switch to rock lyrics, but in the content of those lyrics. 'You Can't Always Get What You Want' is the title of a Rolling Stones song. It forms the first line of the refrain, whose remaining lines are: 'But if you try sometimes/ You just might find/ You get what you need'. And that's what he'd wanted for me. Yes, Michael had been tempted by Mandy. As I had, by Jake. Indeed, who hasn't been tempted at one point or another? But as he'd realized all along, Michael was the one for me in the long run.

I like to think that there was more than this, that he genuinely cared for me, even loved me in his own peculiar way. I certainly hope so. Although I always knew we weren't really suited to each other – he's too much a 'feather in the wind' – I don't think I've ever felt the electricity flow as I had that week. Especially that night. I like to think he disappeared because he felt its power, too. The power of something that cannot be. It's a thought that comforts me greatly, but I don't suppose I'll ever know for sure.

In any case, things did unfold as he wished. Michael and I followed the normal pattern of our times – we settled down together, a baby came along, and we married. Do we honour each other? Certainly. Do we love each other? Yes, but in a quiet way. Do we cherish each other? That will come with time and age. As Desdemona tells Othello, "Our loves and comforts should increase, even as our days do grow!" It didn't happen for them, but I'm convinced it's happening for us.

Another change is that I abandoned my journal. It wasn't the added responsibilities of caring for an infant, nor those of coping with a live-in partner that put an end to it. In fact, I returned to full-time teaching after missing just one school year. No, I stopped writing because I knew that nothing in my future life could be as intense or absorbing as what had transpired that week, and that the contentedness I've found since then is neither easy to write about, nor interesting to read. My darling baby boy, and any other children that come along, will just have to get to know me in the flesh. I must also confess that I'm tired of Shakespearean phrases leaping into my mind every time I set fingers to a keyboard; it's become as tedious as a twice-told tale. . . . Well, you can see what I mean.

As for the case itself, the public's attention waned quickly after Roddy's body was discovered. One might have supposed that the murder of a rising actress might have produced a more sustained – if prurient – interest on the part of the public, but she was not well-known enough, even on the local scene, for that. It became just a case of a jealous young man murdering a woman he couldn't have, a murder like so many others – back-page fodder. With time, ample evidence emerged to support that interpretation. The hair recovered from the crime scene did turn out to be Roddy's, proving he had been at her apartment, after all. In addition, his computer was found to contain a huge file of photos of Mandy, taken surreptitiously at numerous locations. He'd apparently been stalking her for several weeks. There were also love poems written to her, rather pathetic ones, though no indication that they were ever sent.

Sure, there've been the occasional internet crazies – conspiracy theorists, publicity hounds, crackpots of all favours – who've tried to stoke the flames of public awareness, but they've remained on the fringes. Even Simon, for all his enthusiasm, quickly abandoned interest. Perhaps he concluded that there was nothing further that could be extracted from the story – or more probably he, or his editor, had a little chat with someone of influence. In any case, he moved on to a different job in a rather distant place, and I haven't heard anything further of or about him. Not the great crusading journalist, after all. Jake had been right about that, too.

There were consequences, however. Gates's involvement in the whole business quickly put paid to his public career. True, he wasn't convicted of any crime, but it was all enough to mobilize political forces against him. Within a month, he had resigned: the price, it was rumoured, for burying any further attempts to investigate his conduct in office. His exit also brought an abrupt end to Chiang's influence at City Hall; nobody in local government wanted to be linked to him in any way. He's still around, but without any chance of involvement in major development projects. Some justice, after all, though not much.

Finally, what of Jake? The only communication I ever received from him was one postcard. It was posted somewhere in the UK (illegible) a couple of months after he left. It consisted of the following poem:

> Lady, you are the cruell'st she alive,
> If you will lead these graces to the grave
> And leave the world no copy.
> For beauty starved with her severity
> Cuts beauty off from all posterity.
> Why then, rejoice therefore; sigh no more.
> Who seeks, and will not take
>   when once 'tis offer'd,
> Shall never find it more.

As with much of what he said, it's a pastiche of quotations. There's no doubt about its meaning, though; the other side shows a photo of an ancient fertility goddess with an extremely rotund belly. To underscore the point, he'd also added a postscript: 'P.S. The world must be peopled!'

He needn't have worried on that score; Michael was over the moon when I told him the news, and so, with a few misgivings, was I. But I can't help wondering: how did Jake know? Had he read my future in my eyes once more?

That isn't the only thing I wonder about. That last postscript is from *Much Ado About Nothing*, a play in which two people who bicker constantly are manipulated into acknowledging their mutual love. Is that what had happened to Michael and me? If so, there'd be a 'double meaning' to the quotation, which itself is a quotation from that play. Surely even he couldn't be as convoluted as that. But, of course, I can't be sure.

There's just one other thing I can report about him. He's not Jake. Or at least, that was never his name. I suspected as much early on in our adventure and, with more time to search the internet thoroughly after it was over, I eventually found the answer. It's so simple really. Jake or Jacob is an English version of Iago and Benatsky is Czech for 'Venetian'. So he was Iago the Venetian, the character he was to play in our production of *Othello*. Who is he now, I wonder?

A CKNOWLEDGEMENT

J ake's not around to acknowledge it, but he obviously owes a tremendous debt of gratitude to William Shakespeare; I don't know what he would have done without those plays to draw upon. In total, the utterances I've recorded here consist of more than 1340 distinct quotations from the bard, ranging in length from the briefest of phrases to entire sentences and more. These utterances frequently combined quotations from different scenes and/or plays. He was quite ruthless in this regard, as he was in severing a quotation from its original meaning whenever it suited his purpose. What he never did, as far as I've been able to tell, was to use only part of a phrase or clause – it was all or nothing, as far as he was concerned. Nor – with one exception – did he alter a quotation to make it fit better with the conversation. That exception, as you've probably guessed, is the substitution of the word 'scarf' for 'handkerchief' in several of the quotations from Othello. The reason is simple: no one gets murdered with a scarf in Shakespeare.

Others who figure in the story occasionally used Shakespearean quotations as well. This occurred some sixty-four times by my count. Most of these instances were intentional – contributions to the quotation game – but there are sixteen instances where someone used a phrase or sentence from Shakespeare without being aware of it. Naturally, these usages didn't follow Jake's rules to the letter; they tended to be adapted slightly to sound more natural to contemporary ears. For those of you with a compulsive turn of mind or simply too much time on your hands, I offer the following challenge: can you find those sixteen unknowing quotations?

I can also propose another challenge for the truly obsessive. Jake never used a phrase or line that is not from Shakespeare, except when he began to quote from rock and roll lyrics at the end. The final rock lyric, 'You can't always get what you want', has already been identified, but can you find the other four?

These, of course, are trivial pursuits. Some of you may prefer to turn your minds to larger things, such as the challenge of figuring out why Jake spoke exclusively in quotations. Feel free to indulge your wildest imaginings; just keep in mind how well that worked out for various members of the acting troupe.

THE JAKE BENATSKY TRILOGY
Modern Mysteries with a Shakespearean Twist

A Piece Of Malice

Emma Marwick and Jake Benatsky go on a bizarre Shakespeare-filled quest to solve the murder of classical actress Mandy Bennett. As the investigation drags them from the cocooned world of classical theatre through the seedy netherworld of sexual exploitation to the upper reaches of political power, Emma must face some very tough questions. Questions such as: Who is she, really? Who is Jake? And can they really take on the powerful forces that lie behind this barbarous crime?

The Thief Of Occasion

Six years have passed in the tranquil and contented life of Emma Marwick, high school teacher and part-time Shakespearean actress, when violence strikes once more – this time much closer to home. Far too close, in fact. If only that strange Shakespeare-spouting man from her past, Jake Benatsky, would re-appear to help her get to the bottom of this vicious crime.

The End Of Reckoning

Jake Benatsky's past catches up with him at long last as he finds himself on the run from a murder charge. To save him, Emma Marwick must at long last unravel his past, and in so doing, transform both their lives forever.

Manufactured by Amazon.ca
Bolton, ON